WICKED INTENTIONS

A KY LANG ADVENTURE

Written by:

L.J. Diaz

Copyright 2025 @ L.J. Diaz

ISBN: 978-1-968069-52-0 (Paperback)
        978-1-968069-53-7 (Ebook)

The views expressed in this book are solely those of the author and do not necessarily reflect the views of the publisher, and the publisher hereby disclaims any responsibility of them.

Olympus Story House

Contents

This book is dedicated to my extraordinary friends, Diana Lynn Hecker and Stephen Lang, both of whom are better writers than I am.

Thank you for challenging me, encouraging me, and not letting me quit. I learned a lot from you both.

I thank my husband David, a true artist, for his support and understanding.

And a special thanks to the hardest critics to satisfy—my sisters, Geri Breaux and Cheryl Ferguson.

I hope you enjoy my next book as much as this one. I love you all.

Chapter 1

The sun was just coming up over the horizon as Detective Philip Jameson leaned against his unmarked car at the entrance of the park. Watching the two FBI agents' approach, he noticed one seemed rather young, and he smiled. He had that rookie look about him—the kind that walked with an I'm-a-tough-professional-asshole attitude. The other man, a little taller and older, had more experience written all over his face.

This is going to be fun, he thought as he stood up to greet them. "Detective Phil Jameson. I'm leading the investigation. You can call me Phil," he said, putting his hand out.

"I'm Special Agent Jax Monahan," the older one said as they shook hands. "This is my partner, Agent Justin Riley. What can you tell us?"

"We got a 911 call about three hours ago from a cell phone. Before the caller could say anything, we heard screaming, then nothing. With the line still open, we traced the call to this area. It was pinged off the tower just over the hill by the lake residents. From there, we spread out and let the dogs do the rest. We called you when we discovered the body—male, Caucasian, midtwenties near as we can tell. Past that, not much. Once you get there, you'll see why. If you gentlemen care to follow me, we can drive up fairly close to the clearing where he was found."

"Lead the way, Officer," stated Riley, promptly turning to return to the car.

Monahan, seeing the amused look on Jameson's face, just shook his head. "Don't mind him. He's only been in the field a few months."

Jameson snickered. "Can't wait to see his reaction. This will be priceless."

"That bad, huh?"

"Never seen anything like it. Damned near lost it myself."

"Let's go then. By the way, call me Jax," he said, smiling.

Both men returned to their cars driving further into the park. It was well maintained with a lake big enough for boating surrounded by thick groves of trees. Side roads shot off, here and there, leading to cabins that lined one side of the lake. They drove to a fair-sized parking lot with a small picnic area and boat dock. A controlled beach area on the opposite side was too far away to identify those enjoying the sand and water. All looked peaceful and serene like a picture in a magazine if it weren't for the squad cars, ambulance, and onlookers.

Parking off to the side, Jameson led the agents down a path through the woods. They walked in silence enjoying the surroundings for its peaceful beauty. It wasn't long before Jameson turned into the trees carefully watching where he stepped. Wildflowers of blue and white carpeted the ground everywhere between patches of long blades of grass. About fifty yards in, they came to a clearing where he stopped. Turning, he spoke to Monahan. "We've contained the area where there were footprints, for all the good it will do. Lots of traffic this time of year. We're coming in from another direction," Jameson explained stepping back to let them through.

The entire grove was roped off and reeked of vomit. Forensics and officers were scattered collecting evidence. In the center, both state and local law enforcement, along with park rangers, stood in a circle around the crime scene talking among themselves. As they approached, two men nodded, acknowledging their authority, and parted, allowing them access.

Agent Riley, entering first, looked down, turned his head hurling his breakfast and then some.

Monahan turned to Jameson with wide eyes. "You weren't kidding."

There lay a naked torso torn open like a piñata; blood splattered everywhere. Arms, legs, and head ripped apart lay a few feet away. It reminded Monahan of a scene in an old Western movie where a man was tied to four horses before being torn apart. As he got closer, he saw the chest had been torn open like how kids tear through the wrapping paper of a present on Christmas morning. Shredded mayhem. The heart, kidneys, and liver were gone. Brains and tongue were missing from the cracked open head with eyes scooped out like the yolk of a hard-boiled egg. He pulled out his cell phone and began dialing. Jameson looked at him curiously before noticing Riley had gone back to the car.

"Hey, Kurt"—Monahan spoke into his phone—"remember that flooded field we worked ten years ago? Yeah, that one. Would you pull the files up for me? We got a fresh one." Putting his phone back in his pocket, he turned to Jameson. "Do you remember the big flood along the river back then?"

"Man, do I? It caused all kinds of havoc two states wide."

"This guy in Iowa was clearing off some unused land on his family's property when that happened. After the water went down, it washed away a portion of where he was working. Several bones surfaced, and an excavation team was brought in. We didn't follow up on it because forensics reported they were at least a hundred years old."

"Why would this make you think of that?"

"See the way the body parts are laid out? It kind of makes a star shape with the head at the top point, all within a circled clearing, all similar to the layout and bone damage we found back then. We didn't think much of it at the time. Just figured the water had spread them out, and the guy's equipment cut into the bones like a shredder."

Jameson studied the layout more closely. "So what do you think all this means?"

"Don't know yet. When I get the files, we'll talk. In the meantime, let's get what info we can here. Did you find his clothes anywhere? We have a name, keys, anything?"

"Clothes were with his phone about twenty feet from the shore. No wallet or ID. We figured he was planning on taking a dip in the lake or already had. Couldn't tell with all the blood. Got to wait for the coroner's report. One of the guys took his phone back to the office to start going through his contacts. There doesn't seem to be a car anywhere either, so he must be staying close or rode with someone. No one has reported a missing person. Probably too early yet."

"Let me know when you do. I'm taking the kid back to town and get a hotel room." Monahan turned to leave when another officer came running up to them.

"Detective, Agent"—he nodded at them, slightly out of breath—"we found something you need to see."

Chapter 2

Ivy Meadows woke startled hearing a female voice call her name. She turned to look at the clock, which read 1:37 a.m. Her heart began to beat a little faster. She shivered as a chill crept up her spine. Throwing the covers off, she climbed out of bed to check on her dogs trying not to wake her boyfriend, Wolfe. Continuing down the hall and then the stairs, she heard nothing from her two rat terriers. Finding them both sound asleep in their kennels, Ivy looked for her cat. Snickers was a caramel-colored Manx, named for her looks and the sound she gave when flipping an attitude. Finding nothing wrong, she wandered the house to her office. The door was open. Ivy always closed that door to keep the dogs out. There, she found the cat sitting in front of the computer, cleaning herself. Snickers stopped long enough to give her that it's-about-time look! After a low grumble and a whip of her tail, the hairless feline went back to grooming.

"I'm not going back to sleep yet, am I?" she said, glaring at her smug cat.

Snickers stood stretching her legs. One paw lightly tapping the keyboard brought the computer to life. Crossing to the other side of the desk, she laid on Ivy's notebook, curled into a ball, and ignored her.

"Fine, I'm getting a cup of coffee first," she stated out loud. Still feeling chilled, she went back to grab her robe and proceeded down the stairs once again. Ivy stepped on the bottom stair, for-getting it squeaked when the dogs went wild barking. "It's just me. Settle down!" she yelled as they both ran for the back door. "Really? You want out now?"

They stood there wagging their tails still excited, waiting. As they scurried outside, Ivy decided not to brew a fresh pot and heated a cup of old coffee in the microwave instead. She had no intention of staying awake too long and was going back to bed.

The dogs barked just as the microwave dinged. Grabbing her cup, she let them in and headed for her computer. Still not sure what woke her, she sat down and clicked on her social media page. She'd only been asleep a couple of hours, so there hadn't been much posted. As she scrolled, a private message popped up from Ky.

Ky Lang and Ivy had been friends in college. They connected as if they had known each other their entire lives and since formed an unbreakable bond. Ky was there during Ivy's divorce and protected her when her husband became violently abusive. Ivy was the maid of honor at Ky's wedding and helped her through the hard times after her husband died in a plane crash a year later.

> Ky: You up too? *(Ky's message reads.)* I've been up since 1:30 a.m. Thought I heard my name. You know me, once I'm up, it takes hours for me to get back to sleep. Can't remember what I was dreaming though.
>
> Ivy: Well, isn't that special? I'll blame you. I was up shortly after that. I heard my name too. Now that you mention it, I can't remember what I was dreaming either. Are you cold? It seems a little chilly here. I didn't think the temperature was going to drop that much. *(Ivy typed back.)*
>
> Ky: It didn't, and yes, I'm cold too. Ah, shit. You know what that means. Trouble.

Both women immediately went to split screens to pull up their personal site they fondly referred to as their "Who You Gonna Call" page. Each read the same message:

> Need help! Rockford, IL. Please find me before they do. Reese.

Time-stamped at 12:03 a.m. Reese Michaels was a paranormal investigator Ivy met when she was called in to cleanse a friend's house he had been looking into. They hit it off well and became close friends over the years. He was a lovable man with a big heart and easy on the eyes. He was an exceptional investigator with a military background but not so good at protecting himself from paranormal entities.

> Ky: Didn't he go there to check out some band or
>   something? *(Ky messaged.)*
> Ivy: Yep, a band called Road Rats, I think.
>   Something about everywhere they go seems
>   to have an underground cultlike following,
>   but no one knows much about them. No
>   pictures or where they come from, no back-
>   ground. No videos online, and he likes their
>   music. *(Ivy replied.)*
> Ky: Well, I guess we know what the topic over
>   coffee will be today then, huh?
> Ivy: I guess so. Right now, I'm going back to bed,
>   and you should too.
> Ky: Good luck with that. I'm going to try. See
>   you at 10?
> Ivy: Of course. Love you, bye for now.
> Ky: Sweet dreams if you can. Lol. Love you too.

Ivy signed off her computer and took a sip of coffee. It was cold again. She looked up to see it was now 2:00 a.m. As she headed for the door, she turned to see Snickers sleeping soundly on the window-sill. The dogs were quiet in their beds, so she left the door open and the cat undisturbed. Climbing back into bed, she was already making the list of what would be needed if they had to travel. Ivy never went anywhere without being prepared when it came to Reese. His investigations tended to find more trouble than ghosts. She closed her eyes and was out like a light.

*****

Ky knew it was going to be hours before she went back to sleep, if at all. She leaned back closing her laptop deciding to use her time to feel the energies. Both her dogs came and sat beside her, wagging their tails. If she was up, they were going out. Ky no sooner opened the kitchen door when Charlie headbutted the storm door. Charlie was the bigger of the two, being a chocolate Lab weighing in at over 125 pounds. Bear, a chow shepherd mix, was a 90-pound ball of long fur. They both took off in a dead run like they were after something. She knew they only wanted out so they could get a treat when they came in. It had become a game to them. Ky decided to put on a pot of coffee while she waited and contemplated the current situation.

Reese sent, "Find me before they do." *They who?* He hadn't given them much information to go on. Usually, he was very explicit in details. Still feeling chilled, she grabbed a small blanket from the pile of laundry she hadn't put away. Wrapping herself up, she looked at the sink full of three days' worth of dishes. "You need a wife," her late husband used to tease. A small giggle escaped as she remembered how he always made her laugh. It's what made her fall in love with him. Her warm, fuzzy memory broke when Bear let out a low bark to let her know they were done. Once inside, they went straight to the treat box and waited.

"Only one," she said. "You're not getting anything else till breakfast."

Ky poured herself a cup of coffee before the maker finished brewing and took a sip. The stronger, the better—sometimes it helped her sleep. She headed for the couch with the dogs beating her there. They lay on each side leaving her in the middle, knowing what she was about to do. Ky curled up into a ball with her knees to her chest. Picturing herself in a bubble of swirling grays, she could feel the energy grow allowing her essence to travel the astral plane. When her protection barrier hit full strength, she focused on Reese, slowly letting her subconscious take over.

Ky felt the fear from the negative force of what seemed to surround everything. It felt odd. Something wasn't right, but she couldn't put her finger on it. Images began to take form. A lone, dark cloud hovered over a small town. Lightning flashed down on a dumpster near a building. A small army of red ants poured out of one of the cracks swarming an unsuspecting small animal so fast she couldn't tell what kind it was as it let out a bloodcurdling scream. Dark-yellowish eyes peered through tall grass some distance away, watching. Then nothing. She opened her eyes finding her dogs each with a paw on one of her shoulders, growling low. Looking at the clock, she saw it read 3:33 a.m.

"I guess that's it for now. You two can relax. Our witching hour is over. I'm fine. Try to get some sleep," she said.

Both dogs headed to the bedroom with Ky following. As she lay down, surrounded by her furry protectors, she tried to analyze the visions. That didn't last long; she fell into a deep sleep. While Ky didn't sleepwalk, she was known to physically lash out as if fighting demons in her sleep. In the past, her husband wrapping her in his arms would bring her peace. Now both dogs laid full length to her body pinning under the blanket like a tightly wrapped burrito. They were making sure she couldn't move or hurt herself. Ky slept peacefully for a couple of hours before waking again to the sound of Charlie snoring. Bear lifted his head, licked her hand, and went back to sleep.

"You can let me up. Now move please," she said softly.

Bear let out a moaning grunt and rolled off the side of the bed. Charlie opened his eyes long enough to let out a huff without moving. Ky was always up before the sun, and the dogs knew they wouldn't get breakfast until the morning light peeked through the window no matter how much they begged. Charlie stretched out across the bed going back to sleep while Bear followed her. He curled up on the couch next to her as she drank her coffee. No matter the time or the place, one of them was always at her side. She was never alone.

*****

Ivy's boyfriend, Wolfe, was an early riser. He slept through her getting up and coming back to bed in the middle of the night. She was so dead to the world that when he climbed out of bed, he felt the need to check and see if she was still breathing. Satisfied she was okay, he began to walk away when she yelled, "Oh, hell no!" Ivy got out of bed with eyes half closed and headed for the kitchen. He knew she walked in her sleep at times of stress and followed her. Ivy went straight to the counter and grabbed one of the big knives. Wolfe, being taller and a lot stronger, took a side step before locking her in a bear hug.

"Whoa, baby girl," he whispered in her ear, "I got you."

Ivy took a deep breath and relaxed in his arms, closing her eyes. He threw the knife in the sink and carried her back to bed. It had been years since she had an episode such as this, making him wonder if he should stay home and talk with her or let it go and see how she was when she was truly awake. An hour later, he was ready for work. He checked on her again.

She woke up enough to say, "Kiss?"

As he leaned down to kiss her on the forehead, she smiled and went back to sleep. Wolfe shut the alarm clock off allowing Ivy to sleep as long as she needed. He would talk to her after work.

Chapter 3

Reese Michaels just finished setting up his equipment when he heard the screams. Now he was on the run with a frightened woman on the verge of panic. He could hear something coming and had to think quickly. They got lucky when he saw a mass of tree roots sticking out of a ravine where a small creek ran. Entering the water, they went upstream to hide in the mud bank beneath the roots. The woman went quietly into shock. Reese couldn't help her; he was watching the woods on the other side. He could see two silhouettes of what looked like large dogs through the trees moving fast and low, stopping where they entered the water. One paced in a circle while the other jumped the width of the creek, checking the area.

Reese caught his breath midstream. What looked to be a large dangerous animal suddenly stood up on two legs looking more human than animal. All he could do was stare. After a brief moment, it jumped back to the other side and down on four legs again. Sounds of snapping teeth and snarling at each other were heard before they headed back in the direction they had originally come.

Reese finally released his breath remembering he wasn't alone. As the woman sat shaking and staring into the night, he realized she had seen everything he had. With both of them covered in mud and wet from the creek, he put his jacket around her and began to rub her arms to warm her against the cool night air

"Hang in there. We'll be okay," he whispered in her ear. She looked into his eyes and began to cry, burying her face in his chest. "What…what were they?" she stammered through tears.

"I have no idea," he replied, pulling her closer to comfort her as much as himself. "I'm staying in a house down by the lake. We'll head there as soon as I'm sure we're safe. My name is Reese. What's yours?"

"Katiya. Katiya Cortez," she replied. Breathing a little easier, she sat up. "Do you have a cell phone?"

"It's at the house. I don't get reception out here. What about you?"

"I think I lost it when I saw…" She buried her head in his chest again. "I'm not sure what I saw." She sobbed, trembling again.

"Don't think about it right now. Just concentrate on being safe and getting to my place. We'll figure it out there," he said as they sat watching and listening to the too-quiet night.

It seemed like hours before they headed for the house. Trying not to make any noise, they hurried through the brush. Reaching the shoreline, Reese pointed to a cabin-looking structure with a car parked on the side. Taking another look around, they ran the rest of the way.

Once inside, Reese sat Katiya at the kitchen table and closed the curtains, but not before he peeked out to see if anything was lurking around. Lighting a couple of candles, he looked at Katiya sitting silently at the table with her head in her hands trying not to cry.

"How are you holding up?" he asked.

"Okay, I guess. Still trying to wrap my head around it all. What about you?"

"I've seen a lot of weird shit in my business, but this? I'm not sure what to think yet. Do you want something to drink? Water, coffee, juice maybe?"

"How about a shot? Or two? Hell, the whole bottle would do right now."

"Sorry, I don't drink much anymore, especially when I think I found something."

"What is it you do?"

"Paranormal investigations."

"This is all too crazy. You chase ghosts, and I'm living in a nightmare that I can't seem to wake up from."

"What do you do?"

"I'm a personal trainer here on vacation."

"Well, that explains the great shape you're in," Riley said, smiling.

Katiya looked him in the eye, with one eyebrow raised, more confused and angrier than afraid.

"Strictly a compliment, not a come-on," he said quickly. Katiya was tall, with dishwater-blond hair cut short, and attrac-tive in an athletic kind of way. Dressed in a tank top, shorts, and ten-nis shoes, and being covered in mud from head to toe dramatically outlined her features.

"Either way," she said, smirking a bit more calmly but still sus-picious, "thank you. I take pride in keeping in shape. You have to lead by example in my work. If you don't look the part, you can't teach it. Thank you for saving my life."

Reese smiled back, starting a pot of coffee before sitting across from her. They sat in silence again, going over in their minds what they just went through. Reese spoke first. "I don't know what you saw. I came running when I heard you scream. I heard a bunch of commotion and voices, but you were so scared I just grabbed you and ran. Are you up to talking about it?"

"I'm not sure I believe what I saw." Katiya hesitated a moment in thought. "It looked like someone was being torn apart, literally, by four, maybe five others, I think. I'm not sure. It all seems like a bad blur of a dream now."

"I'm surprised you could see anything through all the trees with the moon only half full. What were you doing out there so late?"

"I couldn't sleep. It was so peaceful and quiet that I thought I'd go down for a late-night swim. I thought I heard something and wanted to make sure I wasn't going to have an audience. That's when I saw…" She fell into silence, staring at her hands.

"The sun will be up soon. We'll contact the authorities then. No point in taking a chance in the dark of running into whatever or whoever they are. I'm not even sure how to explain it without sound-ing like a nutcase."

When the coffee was done, Katiya got up to pour them each a cup. Reese got out the cream and sugar. He could see she was still shaking. Though he was handling things better, he too was unsettled.

Reese had been investigating the unexplainable for many years, debunking the majority of reports, but now and then, he would find evidence that made him a believer in the paranormal. This, however, he couldn't explain with any form of a logical conclusion. He always had his gear with him. He'd set everything up because something about that part of the woods gave him chills. Reese began to worry about his equipment. Was it safe? Was it found? More importantly, did it pick up anything?

"So why were you out there?" Katiya asked as she sipped on her cream-colored sugar fix.

"The best time to get any recording is around what they call the witching hour, about three a.m. I came into town to check out some-thing else and was drawn to the park. Every time I walked through the area you found me in, the hair on my arms would rise. So I thought I'd set up my gear to see why."

"Which brings us back to the big question, What do we tell the police, without sounding crazy?"

"Once they find the body, assuming there is one, they might see things a little differently."

"What do you mean, if there is one? Don't you believe me?" Her voice quivered with fear rising again.

"I do, but we didn't exactly stick around to see what happened, did we?" he said in a soothing tone. "They could have moved the body to somewhere else. For all we know, it's some college kid stunt that only looks like a bizarre murder. Some hazing tends to get way out there. I watch a lot of news, and you wouldn't believe how many think it's cool to reenact satanic crap just to get their kicks or get attention on the Internet."

"I don't know if I can do this. I just want to go home," she said, fighting back her tears.

"I'll be there. I won't let you go through this alone, but you have to tell what you know. It could be more important than you think. You might even remember important details you didn't know you had or haven't thought about yet."

Reese looked at the clock. The sun would be up in under an hour. He walked across the room and turned the TV on low. Access to the only three local networks showed each one reporting *breaking news* just in. Multiple law enforcement agencies closed off a small section of the park. As to why, no one knew yet. They were all waiting, each in their own way, building anticipation for the viewers.

"They must have found the body. That's a plus for us," said Reese as he looked back at a very nervous Katiya. "I think we should get cleaned up." He realized they were both still covered in mud. "I'll get you some towels and let you get cleaned up first. Then we should head for town. All this attention on something at the lake, we should be safe."

Katiya never looked up. She just stared at her empty cup while Reese went to the bedroom to get things ready. He grabbed a pocket-size recorder. Making sure the batteries were fresh, he slipped it into his pocket. If Katiya decided to talk, he would have it on tape. He knew this was going to be like a three-ring circus and wasn't sure how Katiya would handle an interrogation. Reese walked back into the main room to find it empty and the front door open. Running to the porch, looking around in the dim light of dawn, he saw nothing. Katiya was gone. Cussing under his breath, he headed for the shower.

*****

Katiya wanted to go home and forget the nightmare. She grew up in the worst part of Chicago where witnesses either kept their mouths shut or took the risk of getting killed. She ran the half mile to her rented lake house. After making sure doors, windows, and curtains were all shut and locked, she felt safe. Showering was quick; she didn't want to stay long enough for anyone to approach her. Once her bags were packed and at the door, she looked around one last time to make sure she didn't leave any trace of her stay. Her phone was missing but could be replaced easily. If asked, she would say she lost it jogging. As she picked up the first bag, there was a knock on the door. She froze. The second knock was louder.

"Miss? I'm Officer Sanders. I know you're in there. I saw you go in. I just have a few questions. Please open the door," came a low male voice.

Taking a deep breath, she replied, "Please make it quick. I've got other places to be and short on time." She opened the door to see a uniformed middle-aged officer built like a Chicago Bear linebacker.

"I understand. This will only take a minute," he said, smiling. Before she could think, his hand was around her throat. Pushing her back, he closed the door behind him.

Chapter 4

Monahan and Jameson followed the young officer deeper into the woods, about a hundred yards, where they found wires, cameras, and other equipment.

"Well, what do we have here?" Jameson asked.

"Your park haunted?" Monahan snickered.

"Not that I'm aware of." He laughed. "I take it you recognize this stuff."

"Yeah, you got ghost hunters around somewhere. We need to find them. Hopefully not be involved or as another victim and, with any luck, a recording of anything that might give us something to go on. Have your men widen the search. Call me if you find anything. I've got to get the kid in a hotel room and my hands on the report I requested."

After exchanging contact information, Jameson turned to the closest group of officers and gave new orders. Monahan headed back to his partner. As he cleared the woods to the parking area, he noticed some of the officers were trying to hold back a small group of media and curious onlookers.

Monahan approached a park ranger, keeping an eye on the crowd from a distance, and asked, "Is there a campground around here?"

"Yes, sir, as well as lake houses and cabins for rent," she replied.

"I need a list of residences and guests."

"Yes, sir. Have an officer already on it."

"We need to get those people's names and numbers," he said, pointing to the growing audience. "We're going to want to interview everyone we can. Make sure you don't tell them anything. We don't need a panic."

"Yes, sir. Detective Jameson already sent out those orders by radio a moment ago."

Jameson impressed him as a good, thorough cop. He was going to enjoy working with him. After taking a quick survey of his surroundings, he crossed the picnic area. More media showed up as the crowd of people kept growing bigger by the minute. The officers kept them far enough back for him not to have to talk to anyone. Nor would they be able to see anything when the body parts were brought out. He was sure Jameson had the paramedics put all the pieces in one body bag. That's what he would have done.

Monahan turned toward the company car to see his partner sit-ting inside writing in his pocket notebook with the door open. When he pulled out his keys, the local news reporters began yelling ques-tions. He ignored them. Monahan didn't like being in front of the camera. He'd leave that to his partner. Justin Riley was a good-look-ing, charismatic young man, well-trained in briefing the public with-out having to say much.

Justin looked up, embarrassed. "Sorry, Jax."

"It's okay, kid. I did the same thing during my first autopsy. Go through a few of those, and you'll get over it if you can get past the smell. We're going into town to get a room so you can get cleaned up. I'll get us some food."

*****

Justin Riley stood under the hot water beating himself up over the rookie move he made. Jax Monahan was his mentor. He admired and respected the man. Riley was well-versed in combat, weapons, research, public relations, and protocol. Jax Monahan was teaching him the intricacies of investigation, and the one thing that came to Monahan naturally was instinct. "Something only time and expe-rience could teach," Monahan said to him. "Observation is the key element."

*****

Monahan was waiting for the burgers and fries he ordered when his phone went off. Pulling it from his pocket, he answered like he always did. "Monahan."

"Hey, Jax. How do you want this sent to you?" asked Kurt.

"Just email me. I'll make a hard copy at the sheriff's office. Hang on a minute." He paid for his order and went to the car before continuing his conversation in private.

They discussed the two cases comparing what little detail was available. There wasn't much to go on. Both men came to the same conclusion. The coroner at the time wasn't equipped to get the information they needed. Kurt would get a forensic pathologist to study the old bones and then send the results ahead to the examiner.

Monahan entered the hotel room finding Riley on his laptop. He looked better and fully focused. Setting the food on the table, he waited quietly. It was a couple of minutes before Riley looked at him, slid his laptop toward Monahan, and showed what he'd found. The screen was split. The first frame was on sacrificial rituals, and the other was a list of professors in ancient philosophy and religion. Highlighted was the name Professor Martin Delaney, currently teaching at a small college not far from where they were. Monahan noticed his credentials and wondered why he was teaching at such a small university.

"I was still within earshot when you told Jameson about how the body was laid out. It made me think. I was going through the many pages of rituals and noticed this guy's name appeared as a reference more than once. That's when I looked him up," stated Riley.

You're starting to show some instincts," Monahan said with a grin.

"It's just research."

"Looking up the rituals was your instinct. You finding the common denominator, so to speak. Sometimes it's the little things that are important."

They ate as they devised a plan for meeting Delaney. Having finished their conversation and meal, Riley turned the TV on. Being the public-relations man meant needing to know where the local news thoughts on the situation were coming from so he knew wha he would have to deal with. Monahan flipped the laptop around to check his email. He wanted to study the report before making a hard copy for Jameson and himself. It was a coroner's report from a small town. It simply read as follows:

> Adult female; five feet, seven inches in height. Bones appear to be approximately a hundred years old. Teeth marks on the victim's bones were shallow and could not be identified. Position of the bones was probably created from flood waters. No cause of death or age group. Other than the pictures taken there was nothing more to see.

Riley, on the other hand, was getting an earful of people creating stories and wanting attention. To Riley, it was no surprise with the amount of law enforcement and medical teams. News of the brutal killing spread fast. There still had been no briefing from law enforcement's involvement. Witnesses claimed the usual—satanic rituals, bears, wolves, gangs, serial killers, even Bigfoot. Some lunatics went so far as to claim to have seen a werewolf in the area. Riley had to shake his head and snicker. *Piece of cake*, he thought. He couldn't tell them anything as much as he could to calm their fears. He began forming a speech as he opened the phone book. Time to call the college and make the appointment with Delaney.

"I'm going to the station to make a hard copy and talk to Jameson. What are you going to do?" Monahan asked as he closed the laptop.

"I'm making the call to set up a meeting with Delaney. I'll get my briefing for the press done and meet you there."

"I'll send a car to pick you up."

"No need. While you were getting food, I figured out it's just a few blocks away. I could use the walk, clear my head, you know. I'll call you when I leave so we don't pass each other."

Monahan nodded, then phoned Jameson to let him know he was on his way, and the file he asked for had come. Phil was already there waiting for more information. He ordered all the evidence be brought to his office for them to examine including a second cell phone. Body parts were on ice, awaiting the coroner, with orders that nothing was to be touched without the two of them being present. Monahan headed out the door.

Chapter 5

Ky, staring down at her cup of coffee, was lost in thought about the message from Reese when she was interrupted by wet tongues and soft barking. The dogs wanted breakfast. "Okay, okay, I get it. You're hungry. Let's go," she said to them as they followed her to the kitchen.

Once the morning routine was complete, Ky looked at the clock. "Got to go," she said as she bent down to kiss them on their noses.

Charlie nibbled her chin before retiring to the couch. Bear pressed his nose to hers and snorted. It was his way of saying he was going with her.

"Not today, baby. I'm just going to coffee. You'll see Aunt Jess soon enough."

Bear dropped to the floor head down and pouted. Dressed in comfortable black jeans and a red T-shirt with the saying, "I love big Mutts, and I cannot lie," and decided to grab her jacket. It was beautiful outside, perfect for a ride. She was a short, petite woman with a motorcycle much larger than one would expect for her stature. Ky looked like a child on a Clydesdale, but it made her feel strong and confident controlling that much power between her legs. Laughing to herself, she thought, *I understand why guys like driving big trucks.* Her late husband lived life to its fullest. He always said, "Enjoy the little things. It's what makes up the whole picture." That statement stuck with her, so she went out and bought the Harley and a Camaro on the same day two months after he passed. To her, it all started with how you ride the road of life with a bit of flare. As she climbed on her bike, she looked up to the warm sun and whispered, "Thank you," then sped off.

*****

Ivy was the first to arrive at their favorite hangout. A quaint little coffee shop called Java Junkies was a nice-size café close to where they all lived. Melody Fine, the owner they all called Mel, already had their usual table set up for two. Busy instructing a new waitress, she looked over and smiled. Ivy sat and poured herself a cup of coffee from the carafe. Startled by a tap on the window next to her, she looked up to see Ky standing there laughing at her.

"Bitch," she mouthed back, smiling.

Ky always got a kick out of Ivy's expressions and stuck her tongue out.

"Giving you a hard time already?" Mel asked as Ivy jumped again. "Jumpy today, are we?"

"You both seem to be getting a kick out of sneaking up on me," she said with a pouting face.

"You'll get over it." Mel smiled at Ky and went about her work.

"Get any sleep?" Ky asked as she sat and poured herself a cup.

"Not enough, and you?"

"Same. You know me." Ky began to fill her in about the vision when they both looked up at the window.

To their surprise, Jessie Carlisle showed up. Jess introduced Ivy to Ky one night during a girls' night out. Ivy met Jess when she took a dancing job for some fast cash. Ivy, a tall, slender redhead, was a natural. Dancing came easy to her. It was like Ivy could see and feel the music, dancing with it instead of to it. Jess was almost as tall as Ivy. She was a well-built, voluptuous woman with shoulder-length auburn hair. Her dream was to open her restaurant. She bartended during the day, waited tables at night, and danced on the weekend to raise the money she needed to fulfill her dream. That's where she met her husband, a reputable mechanic who built a small chain of repair shops he'd started from his home garage. He turned Jess's life completely around. Lance Carlisle convinced her that her cooking was too good for the headache of running a restaurant and should market her talent and creativity. Now she grew her herbs and vegetables making a living from publishing her cookbooks. Jess found sharing her knowledge rewarding with its own freedom. Creating new dishes was her art, and Ky's helpful talent in photography brought them to life.

Ky dated Jess's brother in high school. They bonded and made each other a promise to stay close like sisters would. Though they didn't see each other as much, with the lives they led, they were still close and stayed in touch as often as they could. Then when Ivy came along, the three of them became as close as the Three Musketeers, always there for one another, and together, a force no one would want to mess with.

Mel had a cup on the table before Jess got to the door. Ky poured coffee as Jess greeted them and sat. Being the girls they were, they spent the next hour just catching up. Mel only had to tell them to settle down and stop having so much fun once. Their giggles and laughter were getting a little loud. Mel was always telling them she'd throw them out for disturbing the other guests, even when they were the only ones in the room.

Ivy explained to Jess about being awakened and the message Reese left. Ky filled them in regarding her visions, which started the discussion forming a plan of action. By the time Mel brought the third carafe of coffee, the only thing they knew for sure was that someone had to go to Illinois. Both Jess and Ivy looked at Ky.

Ky rolled her eyes. "Yeah, okay. Guess I'm going on a road trip. But that means, Jess, you get the dogs, and I'll need some of your special tea as well as anything else you think will help. Ivy, you're doing the research. I'm sure you know more about where Reese was going and why than I do. How much time do you need?"

"I know exactly what you'll need and can have it ready by this afternoon. You know, I never miss a chance to have your dogs. They love me." Jess smiled ear to ear. "We love them. Mine miss playing with them, and yours probably could use the exercise. You spoil them, and they're getting fat again. I'll bet."

Ky laughed. "Yes, I do. They're all I've got and all I need. I want them to be happy now that they're getting old. I want them to enjoy the time they have left. I know Bear is ready. He got huffy with me this morning before I left because he couldn't come. It's as if he knew you'd be here."

"I should have something for you by tonight. That way, you can start in the morning, after you get some sleep. Don't need a headache worrying about you getting tired on the road," Ivy stressed. "I'll follow after I talk to Wolfe."

"Who said anything about you going? You hate that state, and I don't need a babysitter."

"You think I'm going to trust you to not overreact? People get hurt when you're off your leash, woman," spouted Ivy.

"That's an understatement," chimed Jess as the three of them laughed.

News on the TV caught Jess's eye as she placed her hand on Ivy's arm, getting both her and Ky's attention. A bizarre murder had taken place outside a small town in the middle of Illinois. Rumors were going wild from animal attacks to satanic rituals. The girls looked at one another. They were all thinking the same thing—Reese.

Chapter 6

Ky had everything packed in her car when she leashed her dogs. They were excited and knew where they were going, to see their playmates. Being a freelance photographer, whenever Ky was out on assignment, they would stay at Jessie's house. They loved her as much as they did Ky, but Tucker and Nala were their buddies. Tucker was a little shih tzu, and Nala was a pit bull. Nala and Charlie were older and would watch the other two play, only getting involved once in a while. Mostly they stayed close to Jess, both being the alpha in their respective gender, always on guard and protective. They climbed in the back seat of her Camaro and sat patiently while Ky locked them in the seat belts she had installed just for them. After dropping them off and picking up her care package from Jess, she headed for Ivy, the reference queen, as they liked to call her. There, she would have a quick cup of coffee and go over the plan once more before hitting the road.

*****

Jess was up since the crack of dawn. Known as the group's kitchen witch, she began pulling herbs and oil extracts from her cabinet by pure instinct to prepare three thermoses. One was what she called gotta-go tea, to keep Ky awake and alert. The second would help Ky try to sleep. Everyone knew Ky rarely slept well or for very long. And the third was her special blend potion, designed to enhance Ky's natural abilities for protection and sensing danger. All the other herbs Ky would need were bagged up the night before. Jess called to confirm what crystals Ivy was going to put in the mojo bag so she could match up the proper ingredients to activate their power and purpose.

Her two fur babies jumped and went running to the door, telling her Ky was close. They could recognize the sound of her car a block away. As she packed everything in a small carry-on cooler, the shiny black-and-gold car pulled into the driveway. Jess stood at the door, telling her dogs to get back, waiting for Ky to open her car door. Ky released the seat belts before getting out. Turning to Jess, she nodded, and both women opened their doors. Charlie and Bear bolted on a dead run for the house. Coming to a stop after sliding across the kitchen floor and colliding with the cabinets, they turned to face their friends. Once Ky was inside, both girls yelled hey at the same time to calm the playful chaos. Bear and Charlie ran to Jess, and Tucker and Nala ran to Ky, all full of wet kisses, wagging their tails and butts.

"Yes, I missed you too," said Jess. "Now, everybody, out."

They all ran out the back through a door made just for them into a huge yard full of toys and a medium-sized dog pool.

"And you say I spoil them." Ky laughed. "They couldn't wait to get here. They whined and yelped the whole way. I thought they were going to break their seat belts when I turned the corner."

"We love having them," stated Jess, reaching for the phone before the first ring. She was like that sometimes, very intuitive.

Ky waited as she watched Jess start to cry. Jess hung up, looked at Ky, and cried harder, slightly smiling. Ky jumped up, throwing her arms around her, letting her get it out.

"Are you okay?" Ky asked concerned.

After a short pause and a deep breath, she said, "Yes, I'm pregnant."

Both girls screamed with joy as they hugged. Jess and Lance had been trying for a couple of years to have a child. Their dream was finally coming true. All four dogs, hearing them scream, came running inside to see what the commotion was about. Ky looked at Charlie as they bounced around the women sniffing and whining and told him to go play. Deciding the girls were okay, he let out a short low bark and ran out the door with the others on his heels.

"Please, don't tell Ivy. I want to tell Lance before anyone else knows," Jess asked.

"You know, I won't. Just don't tell her I knew first." She chuckled.

The phone rang again. "Now what?" Jess said. "My phone never rings this much." She picked up the phone, but before she could say hello, a loud female voice could be heard. It was Ivy, yelling.

"Tell Ky to get her ass in gear. I'm not liking what I'm finding. And by the way, have you been to the doctor lately? You need to. I'm not saying anything is wrong, just that you need to go," Ivy rattled fast.

Overwhelmed with joy and unable to keep the secret any longer, Jess spilled the news. "I already went. I'm pregnant. But you can't tell anyone! I just found out a few minutes ago."

"I told you to stop worrying and just let it happen. I was doing a reading on the trip for Ky when you showed up in the cards, between the moon and the two of cups."

"What's the rest of the reading say?" asked Jess, changing the subject.

"I'm not done. When you came up, I had to call. This means when Ky leaves, you are to be out of this altogether until it's over, understand?"

"Got it. I'll get her going now and catch up with you later." Jess was very familiar with Ivy's gifts. She didn't mess around. Turning to Ky, she said, "You have to get going. Ivy will fill you in."

With a hug and a kiss, Jess sent Ky on her way without saying goodbye to the dogs. Bear and Charlie had never let Ky leave them behind, except at home, after she rescued them from the local animal shelter. Jess could settle down the chaos of barking and whining when Ky snuck out, but Lance was the only one strong enough to hold them back when they fought to go with her.

*****

Ky pulled into Ivy's driveway ten minutes later. Jumping out of her car, she saw Ivy waiting at the window. Ky walked swiftly to the door, then stopped dead in her tracks, and froze looking down at the grass.

"Are you kidding me?" yelled Ivy. "It's just a garden snake. Get over it! Jeez, you fight worse things than that on a regular basis."

"Sure, coming from a woman afraid of mice," Ky replied with a glare.

"Mice are rodents. Rodents are dirty, disgusting little creatures. I have two rat terriers and a cat to keep them away," said Ivy, cackling like a witch.

Once the snake slithered further into the grass, Ky made a mad dash for the door. "You can stop laughing anytime now," she said with a grin. She knew her fear of snakes was silly, though it was something she couldn't get over. "They're sneaky, and you never know when they'll bite."

"Oh, you mean like you? Only you're more deadly than sneaky," Ivy stated as Ky hugged her.

Ky sat on the couch as Snicker jumped in her lap, then head-butted her chest. "Hello, little one." Looking up at Ivy, she asked, "So what's the big emergency?"

Ivy handed Ky some papers. "Here's a copy of my notes. I don't know what kind of trouble he got into, but it appears it might have something to do with the news report we saw. Oh, and that band he went to see has got to be involved somehow, I think. After doing a lot of digging, I found the band is playing in a bar and restaurant called Redemptions just outside city limits but near the park. There's also been two other deaths in the surrounding counties, over the last week and a half. One was a farmer in his field. The other one was found a short distance from his car on the highway with a flat tire. Both reports are claiming animal attacks, which in itself is unusual, but no one is making a connection or an issue of it. Probably because of the distance between the locations. If they have, no one is saying."

"Where's the connection to the band?"

"In my head for now. I found articles about missing persons, unknown cause of deaths, and claims of demons after people. Each published in the local papers the day after they've played there."

"So what else are you making me take besides reading material?" Ky teased.

Ivy gave her an evil look handing Ky a small mojo bag, a necklace, and a small sack. "You know what to do with the mojo bag. Wear the amulet at all times, even in the shower. It's so no one can sneak up on you," she stressed. "The other bag has the usual stuff—holy water, white sage, and a few other things. You'll know what to do with when you need them. You're taking your sword, right?"

"I never leave home without it. Even if I'm just coming to see you," she said, trying to sound wicked.

"Now be off with you, woman. The game is afoot. The clock is ticking, and all that stuff. And for God's sake, be careful!" Ivy said, scowling again.

"What? I don't get my coffee? And don't yell at me. I don't do this for God. I do it for you," Ky said, blowing Ivy a kiss.

"Save it. We'll debate that when you get back. No time for coffee. You can get it on the road. You've got a long drive ahead of you, and I still have work to do. Now go."

With a quick hug and a giggle, Ky was out the door. Ivy stood at the door, watching the shiny black-and-gold Camaro head down the street. Snickers rubbed her body around Ivy's ankle with a purr, letting her know everything was going to be okay.

"I hope you're right," Ivy said, looking down. She picked up the cat and returned to her table where cards and crystals lay spread out. Standing above the low table, she studied the layout and found a message hidden within the reading. Placing Snickers on the couch, Ivy went down on her knees pulling four more cards from the deck—the king of wands, an older male close to the heart; then the tower, turmoil; ten of swords, battle; and the last card, death. Ivy closed her eyes and took a slow, deep breath. "Shit."

*****

Ivy was right. Ky was deadly, familiar with both death and evil. Her mother died before she reached the age of four. The last time she saw her father was the day of the funeral. She looked so much like her mother he couldn't handle it. With a bottle in his pocket, he walked out of her life, never looking back. She was raised by her maternal grandmother, a humble Gypsy immigrant from the old country, who woke the gifts she was born with. Ky was taught the ways of magic and how they could be manipulated for good or evil so she could walk freely in either world. Ash she had seen firsthand what most could only imagine in movies and nightmares, her short little grandmother had one rule. "You can't take the devil down if you can't look him in the eye." Growing up, she studied fencing and martial arts where she learned the art of sword fighting and knife throwing. It gave her confidence knowing even a small stature could take down the big bad. Her grandmother believed the fascination with swords had something to do with a past life. Her talent in photography was discovered while working for her high school newspaper. Ky could capture the very essence of her subject, from the pure innocence of a child to the eerie essence of a haunted forest. Being a freelance photographer gave her freedom others didn't have, and her skills in fighting kept her safe.

It was a six-hour drive from Omaha, Nebraska, where they lived. Ky loved the peacefulness of the open road and especially the excitement of an adventure. Hitting the highway with the radio blasting, she began to form a plan in her mind as she spoke to herself.

"Get to Rockford. Find an out-of-the-way motel with easy in-and-out access where anyone can go unnoticed. Check for any updated info on the killing. Locate the bar Reese was going to."

Ky knew Ivy was looking into what was so special about the band that would make him travel so far. Reese never did anything without reason and research first. Why his message was short of info had both of them puzzled and worried.

Halfway there, she stopped for gas and snacks in a quiet little Iowa town a few miles from the Illinois state line. No one seemed to be talking about what happened in the next state over. Either the news hadn't gotten this far yet, or they were being hush-hush about it. As she had a full tank of gas and a bag of junk food, she started the car. The radio went to static. *Odd.* She hadn't noticed that when she pulled in. Flipping through stations, she found one that made her giggle. The song playing was "Highway to Hell" by AC/DC. Ky never left anything to chance and didn't believe in coincidence, but Ivy always saw a connection with everything. Picking up her cell phone, she called to check in.

Talking as she drove, Ivy gave her the rundown. The band was relatively unknown other than in small towns. She didn't have much other than what she had already told Ky. Party the last night they played and gone the next day, to where no one knew. They seemed to show up in various places throughout the Midwest, always a sell-out show, even with little prior notice of the booking. However, it seemed to always be where someone died of unknown causes or mysteriously disappeared by the time they left. Hearing that, Ky chose to tell Ivy about the radio and song. Ivy believed in omens.

"Damn it, Ky, I knew I should have come with you!" Ivy yelled.

"Chill out. You'll get your chance. Let me lay the groundwork first. I'll call you when I get there and have a chance to check into a motel."

"Are you driving and on the phone?"

"Yes, don't freak. I bought a Bluetooth last night. Modern tech nology and all, you know. I should be there in about two hours. I'm making good time." After saying bye and hanging up, Ky smiled again. The radio station was just starting "I Can't Drive 55." It was starting to look more like a real adventure.

Chapter 7

Monahan and Riley walked into the main building of the college. They met Delaney in his office on the fourth floor where he was preparing for his first class. After brief introductions, they all sat at his large desk cluttered with books and papers. The man looked to be in his late forties, a little young for his status but a well-dressed, intellectual type.

"So, gentlemen, how can I help you? Our phone conversation was a little vague," he said politely without getting up.

"I understand you are the local expert on ancient religious rituals," Monahan stated.

"Yes, yes, we established that on the phone with your colleague. Come now, get to the point. I have classes I must prepare for," said the professor with a touch of arrogance.

"Can you tell us anything about rituals that involve body dismemberment?" Manahan replied with the authority to match, not taking his eyes off the professor.

Riley sat quietly suppressing the urge to laugh as he thought if Delaney didn't take a step down from his pedestal, Monahan would knock him off it altogether.

"That can be found anywhere on the net. Please don't waste my time. If you want some sort of particular information, you'll have to be more specific."

Monahan didn't flinch. He simply laid the pictures of the crime scene on the desk and stated, "Not this kind."

Delaney looked down and smiled. "Humph, looks like a pack of wild animals fighting over food to me," he said, shuffling more papers around.

"Look again," Monahan said firmly.

With a look of disgust, Delaney picked up the photos. "So the torso is torn apart." He dropped the photos back on the desk. "The torso is the warmest body part. Some animals like their food warm." He looked at Monahan and could see the man's cold serious eyes looking back at him. "Body parts mean different things in different cultures. Tribes defile the bones for disgrace or revenge against their enemies. Others display the body in honor of the dead for their sacrifice keeping their memories alive within the tribe. Some think if they consume certain body parts, the brain for instance, they will absorb any knowledge their enemies may have. There are medicine men who think the heart gives them some sort of magical power. Of course, some are just cannibals and psychopaths. You know, the kind that society puts in prison. And there's those that harvest organs for the black market."

"What's your opinion based on these photos?"

"That depends on how they were removed. The body is ripped as if torn apart by an animal, not surgical. Internal organs wouldn't be worth anything on the black market. Still looks like an animal attack to me." He hesitated, hoping for Monahan to say something. When he didn't, Delaney continued. "Anything else I can help you with?"

"One last question. Are you aware of any cults in the area that would practice these rituals you referred to?"

"Can't say I do without more information."

"You're a renowned expert in this field, Professor Delaney." Riley smiled. "We would appreciate any help or insight you can give us. Please call us if you hear anything. I'll try to keep you updated if we learn anything new."

"You're probably making this out to be more than it is. Now if you gentlemen don't mind, I really do need to get ready before my first class arrives."

The men thanked him for his time. As they were leaving, a well-dressed middle-aged woman entered with a small cooler and a big smile. She appeared very professional-looking and seemed out of Delaney's league. Driving in silence, Riley stared at the photos with a puzzled look on his face. Monahan grinned to himself.

"What's on your mind?' he asked Riley.

"Well, besides the fact Delaney is a dick, I can't figure out why he brought up body parts. All I see is a mass of blood and guts. These are the general scene shots, not the close-ups."

"Your intuition is kicking in. Well done, grasshopper," Monahan stated, changing his voice slightly.

"Grasshopper?" Riley asked, now looking more confused.

"Old reference. Never mind. I forget how young you are and how old I am." He laughed. "I caught that too. I think he likes you. We can use that. I, too, believe he knows more than he's saying. In the meantime, we need to see if Jameson has anything new. The pathologist is due today. I was a little surprised that he could make it so soon, but apparently, something piqued his interest. Kurt said the doc had the entire team working through the night after hearing what we found."

"Do you know who this doctor is?"

"Karl said it's Sam Coletrain. Not one I'm familiar with, but he's supposed to be an expert in this field. Guess we'll know soon enough. He should be here around two this afternoon."

Pulling into the station proved difficult. Town residents gathered along with reporters, all demanding answers. Monahan chose to park in the back lot avoiding the crowd with all their demanding questions—questions even they had and were unable to answer with the investigation just starting and no leads to follow.

Jameson hung up his phone as the two agents entered the small corner office. "Just in time," Jameson said with a grim look on his face. "We think we have identified the victim. His fingerprints match a missing-person report out of Chicago."

"If the prints match, why did you say think?" Riley asked.

"Too many discrepancies that don't make sense. The report is eight years old," Jameson said as he handed them copies of the papers on his desk. "Andrew Thomas would be twenty-seven now. He was a junior at the University of Illinois at the time he disappeared. He studied computer science. According to his mother, he was a good kid. Went to a Halloween party that year at some fraternity and came home acting strange. She thought he got hooked up with drugs, started hanging out with some shady characters as she put it, and started skipping school. Then a month later, before the holiday break, he never came home or was heard from since."

"Okay, so what's not adding up?" Monahan asked.

"The blood report. There's no sign of drugs, but there is an anomaly that the lab can't identify, and the blood type doesn't match. According to records, Mr. Thomas had A positive. Our victim has AB negative, and the coroner said the body is that of a late teen to early twenties."

"The lab is sure about this?

"Yes. I told them to hold everything till your pathologist gets here."

"Excuse me, Gentlemen," came a female voice. "I'm Dr. Samantha Coletrain, and I will need to quarantine your morgue until I confirm my theory."

To their surprise, in the doorway stood a tall woman of African descent with golden-brown skin, dressed in a lavender three-piece pantsuit looking elegant and exotic, standing confident in her authority. She appeared to be early to midtwenties, too young for her credentials.

The men were stunned. Jameson was the first to stand up. "Please come in. I'm Detective Jameson. These men are with the FBI—Special Agents Monahan and Riley."

She nodded in acknowledgment. "I don't mean to sound rude, Gentlemen, but can we save the conversation? It's imperative I get the morgue locked down. Oh, and I'll need at least two armed guards at the door at all times. Please if you can assign an officer to help me"—she waited only a moment—"I'll be glad to explain later," she said impatiently.

Jameson looked at the other two. "If you'll excuse me for a minute?" He left the room.

Monahan and Riley sat, looking a little bewildered at each other. Now they had more questions than before. Why the lockdown and guards being first?

Chapter 8

Reese was cleaned up and ready. He decided to check his equipment first. Knowing that without Katiya, there wasn't much he could give the police. He had nothing to back his story unless one of his cameras caught something. A park ranger stopped him as he got closer to where he was set up.

"Sorry, sir, this area is closed off."

"My apologies, may I ask what's going on?" Reese asked.

"I'm not at liberty to say. Frankly, even I don't know. I was just told to secure the area," the ranger said with a half smile.

Reese smiled back as he turned around, thinking, *Shit, now what do I do?* Walking back gave him time to think. He'd begin by going into town for breakfast and figure it out from there. He was tired, hungry, and needed a lot more caffeine. Starting the car, his eye caught the sight of something in the left side mirror. It looked like a wolf's head peeking out between the trees where he and Katiya came from earlier that morning. A shiver went up his spine with the flashback. Shaking off the thought, he pulled away. Taking another look in his mirror made him hit the brakes. Where the wolf had been now stood a man. He turned for a better look but found nothing there. No man, no wolf. Shaking his head, thinking his mind was playing tricks on him, he wondered if wolves were common in the area as he drove off.

*****

A man crouched in the bushes watching Reese leave. Once the car was out of sight, he walked toward the back of the cabin. The door was locked, but a window was slightly open. He made a small cut in the screen along the frame. Slipping a clawlike nail through to unlatch its lock, he lifted it enough to get his hands underneath. Raising the window, he entered the kitchen and wandered through the three-room cabin. Entering the bedroom, he stopped at the end of the king-size bed. Lifting the spread, he made note of the legs and thickness of the mattress. Sniffing in a deep breath in each room gave him the scent of both occupants. Having another quick look around and finding two cups in the sink told him all he needed to know.

Confident everything would go off without a hitch, he left out the back door making sure it locked behind him. Fingerprints and slits in the screen were of no concern; neither would be found once the plan was put in motion. Disappearing into the woods without a trace, he made sure not even footprints could be seen.

*****

Reese pulled into a busy truck stop on the outskirts of the city. Being in a crowd seemed safe for the moment. He sat himself, choosing a corner table and giving him an advantage to see the entire room including entrances and windows. TVs hung in every corner. Two carried the news, while the others were on sports channels. After ordering coffee and a light breakfast, Reese pulled out his phone only to find it blinking low battery. *Damn it*, he thought. He'd not only forgotten it was on vibrate mode, but he failed to charge it. Just before it died, he noticed it had reception and cussed again.

"Need to charge your phone?" the waitress asked as she poured his coffee.

"Yeah, is there somewhere close I can plug in?"

"Under your table," she replied with a smile.

"Thanks, I'll be right back. My charger's in the car."

"No worries, you won't need it. Everything's there under the table. You'll find your connection should be there at the end of the table."

"That's different," Reese replied as he plugged in.

"The owner thought it would be a good customer-service move, and it stopped people from skipping out on the bill saying they needed their charger." She smiled. "A lot of people use their phones instead of carrying credit cards nowadays."

Reese sipped his coffee while staring out the window when a white pickup truck slowly pulled up behind his car and stopped. The windows were tinted, too dark to see who was driving. He waited, thinking maybe the driver was dropping someone off. No one got out when the truck pulled away. Moments later, his food arrived, and he began to eat when he noticed the truck came back again, stopping like it had done before. This time, he could see the driver's door open next to his car. The driver got out and, seconds later, was back inside driving away. With sunlight coming through the open door, he could see the passenger side appeared empty. Observing details, skepticism, and suspicion were three of the things that he relied on when investigating. License plates in the dark rear window and a broken taillight on a large older truck were all he could see. This day was getting more suspicious at every turn.

Finishing his meal, he signaled the waitress to bring his bill. First, he would go to the police station and try to get his equipment. Second, he wouldn't say anything about what happened earlier that morning. If asked, he would limit any information he gave until he knew more and had to. Sometimes it was best to keep quiet and play dumb. You could learn a lot that way and stay out of trouble.

"Is there anything else I can get you?" the waitress asked."Yes, you can tell me how to find the police station."

She wrote the directions on her pad, laying the paper next to his bill. "Have a good day, Mr. Michaels."

With his cup halfway to his lips, he hesitated and looked up. He hadn't really paid any attention to her till now. She looked to be in her midthirties, short with mousy-brown hair. Her name tag read the name, Dee. Dee was easy on the eyes, but no one he recognized.

"Do I know you?" he asked, perplexed.

"I'm sorry. I recognize you from your website," she replied quickly. "I've followed your work for a long time now. May I ask what brings you here? This is a small town. I usually know all the gossip, and I haven't heard anything about a haunting. So I got real excited when I saw you walk in," she rattled, suddenly becoming a giddy schoolgirl full of curiosity.

"Actually, I came here to see a band called Road Rats." "Oh," she said with a tone of disappointment and concern. "They're a very good band. My friends and I try to see them every chance we get since they don't come here very often. And," she said with a slight hesitation, "Redemptions is the only place I know of that you can catch them within a hundred miles."

"You make that sound like it's a bad thing?"

"Well, it is the only time we'll go there. It's sort of a rough bar and not just biker gangs. Not that it's violent, it's just—I don't know how to explain it. The people there are…different in a way that gives you the creeps, if you know what I mean. And I was hoping for more of a ghostly reason for you being here." She grinned shyly.

"Well, you never know what you'll come across in my business. Maybe I'll see you there, and I can buy you a drink. You can tell me more about this area. Right now, I really must be going." Reese paid, thanking her again for everything. Paying close attention to his surroundings, Reese circled his car looking for any hints as to what the driver may have been doing but found nothing. As dusty as the car was, there were no handprints. Even the gravel he was parked on gave no clues to the actions he witnessed. Tire tracks were there, but no footprints showed that he'd gotten out. That alone was puzzling. Taking a deep breath to subside the anxiety attack coming, he reminded himself that "paranoia only fogs a person's mind." Hoping to get his equipment back without much trouble, he studied the directions Dee wrote. Surprisingly, they were very clear with a detailed map. Following her instructions made it easy to find the police station. It only took a few minutes to get there from the restaurant. Anxiety began to raise its ugly head again when he arrived.

Outside the entrance, a small crowd gathered on the steps— mostly reporters with their cameramen, talking and drinking their gourmet lattes, from the looks of the cups. Next to them, a half a dozen women looking like they could be the local PTA cackled like a bunch of hens and made comments on the safety of kids in the park. Further away sat three older men on a bench in the shade of trees pointing at some in the crowd and talking among themselves. The station was a nice ground-level brick, almost elementary school style, surrounded by well-kept grass, bushes, and a couple of maple trees. No one paid any attention to him as he approached the doors, but he could hear them talking. The women didn't want their kids near the lake till they got answers. Men on the benches were going on about kids being too coddled these days instead of being taught that life is tough. Reporters were speculating on what would be said compared to the rumors being spread through town. One comment caught his attention when a female reporter mentioned the cops were looking for some ghost hunter, and another asked if they were a witness or suspect. She heard both, but nothing had been confirmed either way. A few were laughing about ghosts and werewolves being a thing now and how they must have gotten bored in Hollywood.

Reese entered the station. Two officers at the desk were discussing the video they found near the crime scene, showing a man grabbing a young woman and running. Also, the video picture wasn't clear enough, and the ghost hunter was now looking more like a suspect. Reese stopped dead in his tracks. Accused of being a possible suspect scared him; he had to think fast. Three men dressed in hunting gear came barreling through the main doors, each armed with shotguns and rifles.

John Dunn, owner of the local gun range, spoke first. "Okay, Sanders, what are we after? Man or beast?" he demanded.

"Hold on there, JD. We ain't after nothing yet," said the older officer.

"You guys have had all morning to figure it out. Me and my boys are here and ready to help. Don't be playing city cop on us, letting whoever or whatever get a head start."

"Jameson and the FBI are running this show. You'll be notified when we get orders."

"Then we want to talk to them!" the man demanded. Reese slipped out the doors while the two men proceeded to argue. Now the street was lined with pickups and heavily armed men with a variety of guns. Reporters were talking with a few. Making his way around the crowd, Reese quickened his pace to his car.

"Sir!" a male voice yelled behind him.

His heart skipped a beat as panic tried to rise its ugly head once more. He turned to see an officer getting out of a beat-up old car, making his heart race. Panic was trying to win. He took a deep breath.

"You can't park here. This is for employees only."

"I just figured that out. I'm moving it now. Thank you," he said, sighing in relief.

The officer nodded and walked toward a side door to the station. Reese climbed into his car to leave. In a hurry to get out of there, he didn't see the dark spot pooling under his car. Pulling out of the parking lot, he noticed the dirty-white pickup truck parked on the street. He was sure it was the same one he saw that morning. After writing down the plate number, he drove off. His mind went whirling with confusion and fear wondering how a pleasant weekend getaway of music could turn into such a nightmare. At that moment, it dawned on him why he was here at all. He'd almost forgotten the mysterious band that was rarely seen but well-known for its unique rock sound. The plan had been to come early, enjoy the peace and quiet of the lake, maybe get some swim time in, and relax away from the big-city hustle.

That was before walking through the trees sent shivers up his back and pulled his curiosity into a web of murder and mayhem. A woman he thought he was saving was now gone without a trace. Reese could prove who he was and why his equipment was found, but could he prove his innocence of any wrongdoing? What is on the tape that makes me a suspect? And with no way to find Katiya to verify my story, how will I? Is she still around? Is she even alive? he wondered knowing she fled in fear of her own life.

Needing to clear his head, he hit the road taking the first highway he came to. All he could think of at the moment was getting away from the city, the problem, the people, everything. Driving always cleared his mind; it was peaceful and mundane. It took about an hour for him to convince himself to just go back. Confronting the issue was the right thing to do. Tell the cops he was the one they were looking for and why he was here. Seeing an exit for a country road, he pulled off the highway to turn back. When he slowed down to stop at the turn, his brake pedal went to the floor. He pumped them twice; no response. Dropping the engine into low gear slowed the car with a jerk, but not enough. Grabbing the emergency brake sent him sliding through a T-intersection sideways into a ditch bordering a freshly plowed field. Hitting his head hard on the steering wheel over the seat belt caused the airbag to inflate. For just a split second, all he saw was a brilliant white flash, then everything went black.

Chapter 9

Ky was tired. After checking into a roadside motel, she decided to take a quick nap. Since it was going to be a long night, she reached into the cooler grabbing the thermos labeled "Sleep," pouring two ounces into her cup. Jess was an expert at creating strong, fast-acting elixirs. Ky took pride in knowing how much her body could handle and believed in moderation. Its bitter sweetness across her tongue felt warm and soothing as it flowed down her throat. Hidden in the potent liquid was the taste of chamomile, valerian root, and honey. Falling into deep sleep for two hours, she woke feeling she'd gotten a full night of rest. Drinking half a glass of Jess's energy tea, enough to get her through the night, she called Ivy.

"Thought I'd better check in before heading out," she said when Ivy answered.

"It's about time I heard from you," Ivy scolded.

"Sorry, I took a nap. So you have anything new for me?"

"Other than Wolfe won't let me come there alone? No. They still haven't released much information about the investigation. Just the usual. They're urging everyone who may have seen or heard anything to come in, and they will be doing door-to-door inquiries."

"Wolfe loves you very much. I don't blame him."

"I don't need a babysitter."

"Chill, woman. At least till I see if there's a connection to Reese. I figure I'll get something to eat at one of those little places around the lake. You know how gossip gets around fast in a small community. Then maybe wander around the park, take a stroll on the beach, find a place to meditate, and see what I can pick up. Then I'll check out the bar where that band is supposed to play."

"From what I can tell, the body was found on the opposite side of the lake from the beach."

"Perfect. They probably still have that roped off. I can sneak in after dark. I just wish we knew where Reese was staying."

"Let me check with a couple of his friends. Make sure you keep your phone on, please! I know how you get."

"Fine. I'll do you one better. You know I'm going to mute it. Download my location app. I'll send you the link. That way, you'll know exactly where I'm at all the time."

"That's not like you, little miss. I can handle anything. What's going on that you're not telling me?"

"I feel too comfortable in my own skin? I mean, I got a good nap in, but I almost feel too good. Know what I mean? And that was before I drank my tea. As you always say, better to be safe than sorry. I just can't tell if it revolves around Reese or just the area. Besides, the app helps me find my phone, and it's programmed to my dogs so no one can ever steal them. I had them chipped last year when the city had that issue of dogs being stolen by those fighting-ring assholes."

"I'll leave first thing in the morning. Text me with where you're staying. I'll let you know when I get close."

"Didn't I say chill? I'll call you in the morning. Then you can decide. You hate Illinois, remember? You never did say why though."

"I'll tell you when I get there," Ivy said, "maybe."

"You can be such a wench," Ky teased as she hung up. Ky headed to the closest diner near the lake. Burger, fries, and a chocolate shake sounded great but would be too heavy. Sitting at the counter, with her back to the only two tables that were occupied, placed her in hearing range of their conversation. Not knowing what to expect, she wanted to eat light and ordered just a burger and a Coke.

Most of the talk was about them being scared. One boy mentioned his father said they found ghost-hunting stuff. Another said he heard the guy who died wasn't much older than any of them. Ky took a breath of relief. That was enough to tell her Reese was still alive but not where he was. As Ky finished her meal, the conversation turned to plans for the weekend party to be at someone's house instead of the lake. Paying her bill so she could leave, the waitress looked at her saying, "Stay safe out there," and walked away. Ky climbed into her car and sent Ivy a text, letting her know the body found was not Reese, but his equipment were found. Ivy sent back that the news had just reported that the victim was a male, in his late teens, or early twenties. No other information was available with an ongoing investigation. She also found out Reese was staying somewhere at the lake, not a hotel.

Ky headed for the lake rental office. After explaining to the young male clerk that she was looking for her brother Reese and had popped down for a surprise visit from Chicago, he gladly gave up which cabin Reese was staying in. Ky had a way of getting the information she wanted easily. She didn't have to flirt every time, but sometimes, it was fun. Giving her his name and cell number, he let her know if she needed anything, he'd be glad to help. He looked barely over twenty-one while giving off an air of being the bad boy, and smelled of a cheap wood-scented cologne. His personality, age, and job told her he knew the gossip and people she would want to talk to if needed. Finding the cabin was easy with the directions he gave. Approaching the cabin, she noticed a dirty-white pickup truck. It wasn't Reese's. Two burly-looking men were lurking around, peering through the windows. Ky drove a little further before parking off the side of the road. With the sun going down, light had become dim. Dressed in her usual black, she could blend in the brush easily. With her sword strapped to her side and a six-inch knife inside her boot, she made her way through the underbrush toward the cabin. Stopping close enough to hear but not be seen, Ky watched, listening as the two men circled the cabin one more time. Her senses indicated they weren't entirely human. *Interesting*, she thought. One was slightly bigger and dressed in a local law enforcement uniform; the other dressed like a local farmhand.

"He should have been back by now. What do we do?" said the smaller one, heading for their truck.

"We go as planned. If he's here when we get back, great. If not, it won't matter. The master said either way gets the same results."

Ky waited as they got in the truck and left. Thankful she was downwind and that they went in the opposite direction, she relaxed a bit. Most paranormal creatures have senses that are acutely heightened, being very observant and having a unique sense of smell. She'd have to be more careful knowing at least part of what she was now dealing with. Ky turned to leave coming face-to-face with a tall slightly overweight blond man dressed in jeans and a dark-green T-shirt.

With a grin on his face, he said, "Well, what do we have here? Aren't you a pretty little thing?" He raised his hand forming a fist aimed for her face. Ky ducked his swing, dropped to her knees, and rammed her fist into his groin. Rolling to the side, she stood with her sword in hand. The man doubled over screaming, "Bitch!"

"And then some," she replied, wondering how he got so close. "What are you?"

He looked up seeing the sword first. "Whoa! I'm a guy taking a walk. Isn't that obvious?"

Ky studied him closer. No scent of a werewolf, no enchantments of a vampire, not the slightest sensation of a demon, just the stinking body odor of a man needing a bath. That only left one thing—human. She was going to have to talk to Ivy about that damned amulet.

"How about a predator, pervert, asshole maybe?" Ky spouted.

"A what?" he snickered. "You have a hell of a punch for a little girl.

"From the way you look, you need more than just a walk. I tend to react when I see a fist aimed at me. Want to explain that?"

"You put that blade down. I can."

Ky wondered if he was that stupid when she heard a twig break behind her. Stepping forward and to the left, flipping her blade flat side out like a bat, she spun around in a circle. The sword made contact with the face of a woman, slightly cutting her cheek and ear, knocking her to the ground, and taking the man with her. She was a few inches taller than Ky with auburn, shoulder-length hair, and built like a hefty farm girl. In her hand, she held a pistol by its barrel, ready to knock Ky out.

"That's enough!" Ky yelled. "Someone better start talking now!"

The couple crawled backward a few steps, their eyes full of fear. Ky was used to having that effect on some, but not usually this intense, unless they knew they were facing death.

"Arbitra!" a male voice shouted behind her.

Ky froze in her tracks. She hadn't heard anyone call her that since her grandmother passed. The hair on her arms and the back of her neck stood on end as she turned slowly. Before her, stood a man just an inch or two taller than herself. Well-built with shoulder-length gray hair and a nicely trimmed beard, he appeared to be in his late fifties. She was drawn to his colorful hazel-green eyes. Something about them seemed familiar. Behind him stood four men, similar in stature, were younger, and looked like burly bouncers found in rough bars. The men circled Ky, keeping their distance as they made their way to the couple on the ground. One lifted them each by the collar while another pinned their hands behind their back.

"Who are you? Why did you call me that?" Ky demanded.

"That's of no importance right now. We'll take these two. Your destiny lies elsewhere. As far as the name, I will tell you when the time is right. I recognize your sword. We will meet again, then we can talk. Right now, you must go. What brought you here is only the beginning," the older one said.

Ky stood there, staring in disbelief, as they disappeared into the trees from which they came. Totally confused, Ky began to panic and ran back to her car to call Ivy.

"Ivy!" she stressed her name before she could say hello. "Pack your bags and get your ass up here. I don't know what Reese got into, but I need you. This is getting weird even in my books."

"On my way, see you in eight" was Ivy's only response and hung up.

Ky was shaken and drove back to her motel to regroup. The night seemed to be coming fast with the setting sun. Pulling out onto the highway again, she noticed the white pickup truck ahead. Keeping her distance with a couple of cars between them, she followed. It wasn't long before the truck pulled off on a gravel road. Ky slowed to get a good look at where now that it was dark. A sign on the side was partially blocked by brush. All she could read was

"Redem——ons." Not ready to follow without knowing more, she made a mental note of the area. Driving back to the motel, she chose a fast-food drive-through on the way. Food could settle her nerves but not her mind.

In her room, Ky sat in the middle of the bed and opened her bag of tacos and chips. She couldn't get what the old man said out of her head. Her grandmother was the only one who had ever called her Arbitra and never fully explained why other than it meant "fair and just," which is how she saw Ky. Picking up her phone, she dialed Jess.

"Hey, Ky. I wondered how long it would take before you called. How's it going?" Jess answered.

"It's going," Ky replied, trying not to sound shaken. "How's my babies?"

"Doing fine. Having fun. They played in the pool most of the day. Got a little restless about an hour ago but settled down when the phone rang. Now they're sitting here looking at me like they know I'm talking to you. I'll put you on speaker. Say hi to Momma," she said to the dogs.

Both barked excitedly, loud for about a minute before letting Ky say anything. "I miss you guys too, now be good for Aunt Jess. I'll be home soon."

"Now tell me what you've learned so far," Jess said, taking back the conversation. "I can tell something's up by your voice and the fact that these two don't get antsy without reason," Jess said sternly.

Ky gave her a brief version of the two men, what she heard at the cabin, as well as the truck. She lied saying Ivy was coming in the morning to help, not that she was already on her way, leaving out the incident in the woods with the old man. Jess knew Ky's grandmother and the name. It was not something she wanted to discuss with her yet. Not until she knew more herself, especially in Jess's condition. Ky wasn't going to take any chances of upsetting her. Jess and Lance had tried too long to have a baby. Jess was level-headed with a big heart but definitely an emotional one. Ivy was the rational visionary who could sense things others could not.

"I don't want you going back there tonight, Ky. Something doesn't feel right."

"I'm not. I'm too tired from the drive anyway. I just wanted to say good night to my boys before going to bed and then deal with everything else tomorrow. Sweet dreams, Jess, and give my babies a kiss for me," Ky assured her, and they hung up. Ky didn't like lying to Jess. On top of everything else, now she was feeling guilty.

Laying back on the bed, she stared at the ceiling needing a plan before Ivy arrived in the morning. Ky thought about shutting her phone off, but that would only get her in trouble with both Jess and Ivy. Sitting up, she took a bite and pulled up Google Maps on her phone to find Redemptions. When she found the web page, an advertisement for Road Rats filled the screen. They were playing on Friday and Saturday night. Now she had something to work with. If Reese was okay, they should be able to find him before then. The problem was the if. After her encounter at the cabin and in the woods, she wasn't too sure about anything at the moment. Ky pulled up a map of the bar to see where it was located compared to the lake. After telling Ivy she wouldn't go back to the cabin, Ky couldn't help feeling the need to go to the crime scene.

"Maybe I could take a moonlit walk on the beach first," she said out loud, looking toward the edge of the bed expecting to see her furry companions. "And I'm missing my buddies." She sighed, remembering she was alone. Ky bit into the taco, as her throat tightened, trying not to cry. She wasn't used to leaving them behind for more than a night. Her dogs were more than protection to her. They were a comfort that kept loneliness at bay. That was enough for her to wrap the half-eaten taco and put it back in the bag. Ky needed to get her head back on the situation at hand for the sooner it was over, the sooner she'd be home. Gathering the proper herbs and crystals for protection, she headed for the car.

On the way to the beach, she noticed how easy it was to see the stars. The sky was only lit by the half-moon with no city lights hindering its beauty. It looked like a black mirror clear enough for stars to appear as glistening diamonds scattered across a reflective surface. Something you don't see in the city. Trees, however, were a different story. Being in full bloom, during the day, the trees were like a canopy in varying shades of green. At night, it was almost ghostly and a bit creepier more than anything. As dark as it was, she almost missed the sign indicating her turn to the beach even with the speed posted being twenty miles per hour. Here, the trees were much thicker in density. After slowing for several curves, the woods began to thin out, giving the moon more light. Ky was startled when something large darted across the road so fast that she couldn't tell what it was other than big and furry. Too big to be a dog, too much tail to be a deer, and with the hair on her arms standing on end telling her it was more than just an animal just made things worse.

The beach seemed like a bad idea now, but she wasn't going to let fear get the best of her, even when it tended to warn her common sense. Grandma always said, "You learn from mistakes. Just make sure you don't make one that gets you dead. Know your enemy well and use what you learn." Ky studied intensely to understand and use the philosophy and beliefs of religion, science, and magic and the way they worked and its effects. That and her skill with a blade made her both feared and revered. There were only two people who knew her completely, Jess and Ivy. Ivy, most of all, even if she spent more years with Jess.

Ky pulled over to park at the edge of the beach area. She walked to the middle of the beach and sat just beyond the shoreline. At the far end, a small group had gathered around a firepit with the smell of hot dogs, marshmallows, and laughter filling the air. The crime scene could barely be seen at this distance and light. Police cars in the dock parking lot were the only indication of their presence. Gathering her thoughts, she prepared to send out her senses, focusing on the woods on the other side of the lake. Ky dug her hands into the soft sand for grounding, making her want to take her boots off and bury her toes in the wet sand under the water. A swim under the moon sounded nice, but sadly, it wouldn't be tonight.

Ky began missing her dogs again, always relying on them if she went in too deep or if they sensed danger. She pulled her knees to her chest. Forming a bubble of smoky darkness around herself to blend with the night was the easy part. Venturing out without her bodyguards was not. Ky steadied her breathing, focused on the woods across the lake, and began drifting to the other side. Trees and under brush were thick, letting little moonlight penetrate. This time, she could see the area for what it was, beautiful and serene. Ky whisked her essence around the taped-off perimeter, finding three uniformed officers guarding in a triangular pattern. Each, keeping in contact by radio, was talking about how eerie things seemed since the body was found. Hovering among the tree branches, she moved in for a closer look. Where the body was found, it reeked from the remains of blood and vomit. The area felt like a vast pocket of void. No life other than natural vegetation, no birds, nor insects could be heard. A tiny blinking light caught her attention. Descending for a closer look, she was delighted to find one of Reese's cameras hidden in a tree branch.

As she searched for more, the awareness of wolf crept through her. Knowing their keen senses, she rose higher, spreading herself thin through the leaves. Low to the ground approached a medium-sized female wolf, red with spots of brown blended in. Wolves were not common in the area, and there was something different about this one. The wolf seemed more like an illusion. She sniffed the ground, pawing at spots as if searching for something. A high-pitched howl pierced the silence, filling the night sky from all directions and grabbing both of their attention. Looking down, Ky found the translucent female looking up as if she could see her before dissolving into a vapor, disappearing in a breeze that wasn't there.

Ky snapped back into her body at a pace that almost knocked her over. She shook her head out of a fog and opened her eyes. About ten feet ahead stood a man and the biggest German shepherd she had ever seen. The man of Latin descent was about her height with shoulder-length black hair. Alarms in her head went off along with Ivy's amulet getting hot against her skin screaming he was part demon and part something she wasn't familiar with. His broad shoulders and chest went well with his fit physique. The dog was a beautiful mix with wolf markings of silver and strains of black tips scattered throughout the fur. They stared at each other for a moment; the dog cocked its head to the side before letting out a yip.

"Are you okay?" the man asked.

"Yes," Ky replied, not taking her eyes off her visitors.

"Pardon our intrusion. My name is Damon Artesta. This is my friend, JJ. He picked up on your scent just before the howling. He was afraid you might be in danger. I have no doubt you already know what we are. Not many have your type of ability. May I ask what you were searching for?"

"How do you know I was doing anything but meditating?"

"I could see the smoky aura swirling around you like a storm was building. I must say it was impressive. Don't worry. You were virtually invisible to everyone else. JJ followed his nose." He smiled, reaching to scratch behind the dog's ear.

"I'm sorry. I didn't mean to be rude. I'm Ky Lang, and I wasn't searching for anything. What happened over there had my curiosity working overtime," she stated with a smile.

"I see," replied Damon, hiding his doubt. "Well, as long as you are all right, we'll leave you be." Bowing his head to Ky, he and his canine friend headed toward the beach bonfire party.

Ky watched till they were a good distance before getting up. Grandma taught her to trust her instincts over people and only sometimes to not trust what she could see. Things weren't always what they appeared to be. This was just one more thing to talk to Ivy about. Ky was almost in her car when a second howl filled the air. This one was longer and mournful. Taking a quick look around, she quickened her pace. Once in the car and feeling safe, she went straight back to her motel. Insecurity was not a thing she was used to and began to wonder how powerful the amulet Ivy gave her was. Taking off the necklace, Ky climbed into the shower. It felt warm and soothing. With the shower raining over her head, she didn't hear her phone ringing.

*****

"Talk to me," Damon said, squatting near the firepit.

JJ stood next to him in human form, gazing across the lake. Built like a Celtic warrior, he stood at six foot two. With shoulder-length silver hair and a beard, he could intimidate anyone with his appearance alone. He looked no more than 50 years old instead of the 106 that he was.

"There's something over there she wants," JJ replied.

"That's what I said, remember?" a husky female red werewolf said as she finished turning back to human form. "We both saw something blinking in the tree. I didn't stay to find out what."

"So she lied. We figured she would," Damon said.

"Actually, no she didn't," JJ said, looking down at Damon with a smile. "She stretched a half-truth. Her self-control is off the charts. I like her."

Damon looked up smiling. "She's cute too, but right now, we have other things to take care of. What else did you pick up?"

Athena said, "She's looking for a friend who seems to be missing. Past that, I've got nothing. Like I said, I didn't stick around to see what the blinking thing was when I heard the howl."

"What do you suppose she's after?"

"I have no idea, but logic says it has to do with that ghost hunter. The men make their rounds about every fifteen minutes. I heard them mention someone was coming with food and coffee in a couple of hours. I can sniff around then. Maybe I can find something she missed."

JJ sat in the sand crossing his legs and raised his nose to the air. "Damon."

"Yeah?" He turned to look at him.

"I smell death, and it's fresh."

"So do I," Athena whispered. "It's human."

Chapter 10

Ivy sat at the kitchen table with hands wrapped around her coffee cup, waiting, contemplating. Wolfe walked up behind her laying a kiss on the top of her head.

"You packed and ready?" he asked.

"Yes," she said, sighing.

"Then let's hit the road. We should be there in time for breakfast."

Ivy looked at Wolfe, agitated. "I told you I'm capable of going by myself."

"You heard me. I know how you feel about that state even if you won't say why. Don't think I'm letting you go alone. Any time you and Ky are on to something, it's always trouble and usually dangerous."

"What about work?"

"It'll be there when I get back, darlin'. Now how about you get that pretty little ass of yours moving"—he looked into her deep emerald-green eyes and smiled—"before I get other ideas?"

Suddenly the dogs went wild, barking and running to the front door, then came the knocking. Wolfe walked back to the bedroom, while Ivy went to the living room. To her surprise, there was Carrie, Wolfe's little sister. *Of course, he would have thought ahead*, she thought.

"Hi! I hear you need a dog sitter cuz you're going on a trip," Carrie said with a smile that beamed. "I think it's wonderful you two are finally getting away for a few days. It's about time. You going to let me in or just make me stand out here?" She looked at the dogs. "Hi, guys. You want to go for a ride?"

As Carrie bent down to their level, the dogs ran past Ivy and jumped into Carrie's arms to be cuddled. After smothering her with two wet kisses, they ran to their leashes, jumping with excitement even more with Carrie following them. Ivy stood for a moment appreciating Carrie and Wolfe being in her life before closing the door. She had never planned on getting him involved, but Wolfe made arrangements while she had been busy packing and worrying. Wolfe came out of the hallway with two bags—one small with clothes, but the other was his hunting bag. He looked up smiling and shrugged his shoulders.

"It's Ky. How often does she call freaked? Got my guns, your crossbow, and our knives. We're all good, darlin'." He blew her a kiss and headed to the back door to the garage.

Carrie came back with the dogs in one hand and a bag of treats in the other. "We're ready to go. You two have fun. I'll see you in a couple of days," she said, with a big grin, leaving the door open behind her.

Ivy closed the door again; this time, she locked it and headed for the kitchen. Wolfe poured coffee into a large thermos, then opened the fridge pulling out a bag of sandwiches. Ivy just stood there looking at him in wonder.

"Sandwiches?" Ivy asked bewildered.

"Yep. Made 'em while you were frettin' and packin'. Figure you want to get straight there only stopping for gas or coffee. So I got us covered."

"You know me pretty well." She smiled, sheepishly.

Wolfe placed everything on the table and stood in front of Ivy. Slipping his hands around her waist, he pulled her close. "I love you, baby girl. You give my world meaning it didn't have before." He kissed the top of her forehead. "Now let's get rollin'." He smacked her butt, pushing her toward the door.

Ivy headed for her car, but Wolfe gently nudged her toward his truck. As she turned to argue, Wolfe put his finger to her lips.

"My truck can go where your car can't, and its engine puts yours to shame. Besides the fact, with that flat topper across the bed… better than hiding a body in your trunk." He smiled.

Ivy gave him an evil eye look. "Are you sure you aren't related to Ky somehow?"

"Nah, sweetheart, I watch, listen, and learn. I've seen what the two of you have done and are capable of. You've shown me a world I never knew existed."

"I never meant to get you involved in what we do," she said sincerely.

"You didn't. I did that all on my own. You stole my heart with a kiss. After that, I knew I was willing to follow you anywhere. I'm a better man for that now, and I thank you."

"How does that make you a better man? I know a few that would call that whipped." She laughed.

"Maybe a little"—he smiled—"but I call it committed to a woman like no other."

"That's nice to hear, but just because I walk the path of ancient Druidic mystics and know how to hunt and handle myself in a fight does not make me any different or special. I have the same needs and wants as any other woman. I just can't cook," she stated.

"You are intelligent, vicious when protecting the innocent, as wild as any animal in bed, and you are right. Your cooking sucks, which is another reason why you need me. Now stop frettin' and get in the truck. Time's a wastin'. You and I both know Ky won't sit still for long."

*****

The dogs had been outside for a couple of hours after talking to Ky. They were quiet, almost too quiet. Jess got up from the table and turned down the stove to keep dinner warm. Lance and his men always worked later than most during the week so they could start their weekend by noon on Friday. Family meant everything, and his men liked the arrangement.

The dogs were barking wildly before she could reach the door, running past her so fast they almost knocked her down to meet Lance, demanding his attention. Still barking and jumping, they went to the cookie jar. Jess laughed reaching for the treats she made the night before. Giving each of them a cookie, she noticed Charlie wasn't there. Knowing he was an escape artist, she ran to the backyard telling Lance he was missing. Lance hit all the yard lights following her. Both called for Bear. The other dogs ran, surrounding the couple and trying to get their attention.

"You know where he is, don't you?" Jess looked down at Bear. All three sat, wagging their tails. Nala with her head down slightly while Bear whined softly. Lance went to the far edge of the property and back, looking worried.

"Well, I'm not finding a body."

Jess looked at him disgusted. "He's not dead. He's gone. Dinner's on the stove. I've got to call Ivy."

Back inside, Jess grabbed her phone and dialed, pacing with worry. Ivy lived closer to Ky, and if Charlie went home, she could get there faster. The moment Ivy said hello, Jess rattled off what happened.

"Slow down and breathe, Jess. Ky has GPS chips in both of them, and I have access to the locator app. I'll call you when I find him."

Ivy hung up telling Wolfe what happened. She gasped when the map showed his location. "He's just past Walnut, Iowa," she said, looking at Wolfe fearfully.

"For an old dog, he moves pretty good," he replied.

"Yeah, but that means we've got to get there quick. He's heading for Ky. At that pace, he'll kill himself."

Wolfe reached over her, turned on the police scanner, and sped up.

"Don't worry. We're about thirty minutes from there. We'll have him in less than that."

Ivy never took her eyes off the map. Expanding it, she could tell where he was by the mile markers. As they got closer, she noticed Charlie hadn't moved for the last ten minutes.

"He's not moving," she said with a quiver in her voice. Ivy knew what that dog meant to Ky as well as Jess. "Slow down, we're right on top of him."

Pulling off to the shoulder, turning on the high beams and blinkers, they got out and started yelling for Charlie, searching in opposite directions. It was dark, even with the half-moon over head.

They could see enough to make out the terrain, but finding a dark-chocolate-brown dog was a whole different story. The locator map showed he still hadn't moved. This made Ivy anxious, but inside, she felt he was still alive. Ivy stood still for a moment, took a deep breath, and concentrated on her hearing and other senses. She called Charlie in a low, calm voice. A yelp came from further down where a small group of young trees were growing in the ditch.

"Wolfe!" she yelled. "I think I found him."

He already started running toward her, having heard it himself. Ivy called again. Charlie responded a little louder, giving away his location. Wolfe disappeared down in the ditch. Ivy ran to the edge and waited. It was too dark to see through the growth, and the ditch looked deep. Traffic going by made it difficult to hear anything below. She began to pace impatiently on the verge of a panic attack. Coming to a stop, she took a breath and was about to yell for both of them when Wolfe appeared with Charlie in his arms. Wet, muddy, and frothing at the mouth, he still managed to smile and wag his tail.

"You guys were scaring me. How is he?"

"He's hurt and needs your attention. I'll put him in the back seat. You grab the first aid kit."

Ivy was suddenly glad Wolfe was there with a truck and muscles. Running to the truck, she grabbed the first aid kit holding the door open. He laid the dog on the seat, patted him down, checked for other injuries, then went to the back of the truck. Ivy examined a small but deep gash on his leg and began to clean the wound. Wolfe opened the lid on the bed of the truck, reaching in for a crowbar, rags, and a gallon of water. Using the crowbar, he popped off a hubcap, cleaning the inside with a wet rag. He laid it in front of Charlie, filling it with water. Ivy glanced at Wolfe who mumbled something about it being the only bowl he could think of and took another rag to wipe the slobbering dog's mouth.

"Slow down, big guy. Don't want you getting sick too," Wolfe said in a comforting voice. He had a way with animals, especially dogs. It's one of the things Ivy first noticed about him when they met and loved him for it.

"He was caught in some roots. I think he cut himself trying to get free. He'll be fine once he gets some sleep, but taking him home is going to delay us."

"No, it won't. He's coming with us," Wolfe said as his eyes met Ivy's. "If we don't, he'll just try it again. We'll give him a bath when we get there before we tell Ky."

Ivy's green eyes were now an emerald glare.

"Okay, *I'll* give him a bath," he said, smiling.

"I'm taking one first," Ivy said, assessing the mud all over her. "You two are going to destroy the bathroom. Did you forget how Ky fights with him in the tub?"

Charlie lifted his head and licked Wolfe's hand, then Ivy's. Pulling his leg from Ivy as she finished securing the bandage, he tried to get up. Wolfe put his hand on Charlie's shoulder, telling him to stay. With a short huff, he closed his eyes, showing just how exhausted he was.

"Charlie, you are getting too old to be doing this," Ivy said softly.

Charlie just lay there with a smile on his face, still panting. Wagging his tail splattered mud on Ivy's face. Wolfe laughed, moving away fast. Knowing she was about to hit him, he climbed into the driver's seat, put the truck in gear, and pulled back on the road. Ivy called Jess to give her an update, making it a point that she was not to call Ky. They would take him along to surprise her and keep him from running again.

The motel was easy to find. Ky's Camaro was parked in front of one of the rooms, so they took a room next to hers. Charlie woke up barking. A stern look from Wolfe quieted him down. The drive had only taken four and a half hours the way Wolfe drove, only stopping for gas once. Among the three of them, all but two sandwiches had been eaten. Charlie hobbled into the bathroom and laid on the cool floor, staying close to Ivy as she showered while Wolfe went for supplies and real dog food.

Wolfe came back with plenty of everything they needed, including more bandages. Picking up all the bags, he heard a female voice behind him.

"Need a hand?" He turned to see Ky standing there with a smile on her face.

"I could, yes, but I don't want you dropping anything when you get inside," he said.

"What's that supposed to mean? You two weren't supposed to be here until morning. What happened?"

"Just come with me." As he closed the door of the truck, the barking began.

Ky recognized the bark and ran to the room just as Ivy opened the door. Charlie sat on the bed, barked loudly, and bounced on his front paws.

Wolfe yelled, "Quiet!' The barking stopped but the bouncing didn't.

He sat there wagging his tail, trying not to fall off the bed waiting for Ky.

Fighting back the tears, she threw her arms around him, rolling them both into a bed filled with as much-dried mud as the floor. Ivy looked at her, then Wolfe, and just shook her head.

"It's all good, darlin'. Easy to clean," he said, grinning. Wolfe placed the bags on the table, kissed Ivy on her forehead, and then out the door to his truck for the mini vac he kept stashed when hunting. Wolfe cleaned the room with the girls' help, and having bathed Charlie, he now sat in a chair with a beer, listening.

Ky relayed her experience, including the man in the woods, but omitting he knew her, and recognizing her sword. That would be research she would handle personally when this was over. The girls spent the next two hours talking about the situation they were in and planning their next move. Ky sat on the floor with Charlie half curled in her lap, his head under her chin, pinning her to the side of the bed. Her arms were around him like she was afraid to let go. Ivy lay on the other bed with her head on her hands, taking in the scene. It was a good moment for all.

Chapter 11

Monahan stood at the window sipping coffee listening to Riley snore softly. Their hotel room was on the top floor with a beautiful view overlooking the park and lake. Sunrise wouldn't come for another hour or so. Gazing out over the scenery, he could see flickering lights in the distance coming up over the trees. Something was on fire. Sirens could be heard from the highway, followed by the flashing emergency lights, breaking the serene silence and view. He swallowed the last of his coffee and headed for the shower.

Sunlight began peeking over the horizon when Riley woke to Monahan's phone ringing. He called out for Monahan but got no answer. The caller ID read "Jameson," so Riley figured he'd better answer it.

"Hello, Detective, this is Riley. Monahan's not here at the moment. What can I do for you?"

"I need you two down here as soon as you can. We have another body. I'll explain when you get here."

Riley confirmed they would. As he hung up the phone, Monahan came through the door with a fast-food breakfast; Riley relayed the message.

"You need to shower? Jax asked.

"Nah, I'm good. Just need to brush my teeth and shave."

"Then we'll eat on the way."

*****

Detective Jameson looked at the reports scattered across his desk feeling a bit overwhelmed. He'd never had a case so bizarre. None of the interrogations panned out with facts, just nonsense. Between werewolves and Bigfoot, he wondered if the whole town had gone crazy. Dr. Samantha Coletrain wasn't being much help. Still locked in the mortuary, she hadn't given them any reason why there was a need for guards and quarantine.

Along with quite a bit of equipment, she brought a team of people with her. Jameson assigned a young rookie officer to help with whatever they needed and had been locked in the morgue all night with them. Officer Danny Williams had been the only one to come in and out. He'd been seen with coffee and food but mostly on his phone, using the computer and printer, never saying a word. Jameson looked up from his desk as the two agents entered.

"Hey, Jameson, what have you got?" asked Jax Monahan as he came into the office.

Monahan sat while Riley stood over the desk studying the latest pictures lying at the edge. One at a time, he laid out the gruesome photos along with the official fire report. A woman, tied to a bed, was found in the burnt-out cabin, with her torso slit open like the man in the woods but appeared burned beyond recognition. One photo revealed she had been dissected like a frog. Ribs are broken from being pulled apart with internal organs missing through charred flesh.

"What's the doc saying?" Riley asked.

"Not a word yet. Been in the morgue since she got here and hasn't come out."

"I think we should talk to Delaney again. Being on campus, I'm sure he's heard rumors of something. If he's the expert he claims to be, he's at least got to have a theory of some sort."

"You go. Maybe he'll talk to you since we didn't exactly hit it off the first time," Monahan said, looking at Riley.

"Works for me. I've been doing a lot of research on my own. I have plenty of questions that need answers and maybe I can see if he's hiding anything from the answers he gives me."

"So let's go over what we know so far," Monahan said. "We have two bodies now that resemble what may or may not be a ritual-type sacrifice, similar to the bones from a hundred years ago. We don't have enough information to form connections between the victims. No eyewitnesses as yet, a ghost hunter who may be a suspect or another victim. We haven't found or identified either individual in the video of a man grabbing a woman and then running. Were they able to get anything from the phone they found?"

"It took them a while, but it belongs to a woman named Katiya Cortez. She rented a small bungalow off the beach area. We haven't been able to verify her yet. The rental office said she inquired about the best hiking places, so she could be just about anywhere. I'm guessing she could be the burn victim since it was a female's phone we found. The cabin that burned was rented by Reese Michaels who turns out to be the name of our ghostbuster. He tagged his equipment bag like you would if you were traveling by plane. We haven't been able to locate him as of yet, which makes him a possible suspect in my book," Jameson replied.

Officer Danny Williams entered the office with papers he laid on the desk. "The doc will be here in about an hour, but she wanted you to have this before she gets here," he said, then turned to leave. Hesitating at the door, he looked back. "Sir? I'm not trying to overstep my role as an officer, but I feel I must say that this should all be kept quiet and please keep an open mind. You'll understand more when she explains." Closing the door behind him, Williams headed back to the morgue.

The three men looked both confused and curious. Bewildered, they directed their focus on the new documents. Jameson began reading the file out loud. There were several points of interest. Dr. Coletrain widened the investigation to surrounding areas, finding two similar deaths had been reported. A connection could not be confirmed without exhuming the bodies. The few samples lifted from the current bodies proved to have animal DNA of an unknown species. This statement alone raised questions in their mind.

"So she's saying the burn victim was attacked by an unknown animal too?" Riley asked.

"That's the way I read it. But that doesn't make sense. She was tied to the bed," Jameson said.

"We can't let any of this get out. It will start a panic with everyone looking for fantasy beasts," stated Monahan with a smirk-like grin. "And it will make us look just as crazy as some of our so-called witnesses."

"It's making me wonder about your expert pathologist," Jameson said, concerned.

The report further said the woman was sexually assaulted. The semen also held properties from both human and unknown animal. However, the difference between the two bodies was the missing body parts. Nothing was taken from her head, and it was still attached. The heart, kidneys, and liver were missing, but so were her ovaries.

"So she was raped by both a human and an animal?" Jameson asked.

"Okay, when did we enter the *Twilight Zone*?" Monahan blurted out. Realizing his reference, he waited for a smart-ass remark from Riley.

"Or the *Night Gallery*?" replied Riley, surprising both men. "I like old black-and-white horror movies. I'm a sci-fi junkie."

The men looked at each other and burst into laughter. "This is all too crazy," Jameson said. "How the hell are we supposed to take this seriously?"

"Use whatever makes you comfortable," Dr. Samantha Coletrain said firmly from the doorway. "Be it paranormal, supernatural, or sci-fi fantasy, you will have to come to grips with the knowledge that your beliefs have been limited to what you've been taught. There is more to this than you can imagine. Welcome to my world, gentlemen. Please allow me to enlighten you."

The doctor entered, followed by Officer Williams carrying two chairs. He placed one next to Detective Jameson and the other on the opposite corner of the desk and closed the door behind him.

Monahan was the first to speak up. "I'm Special Agent Monahan, and this is my partner Agent Riley."

"You're the agent that worked a case ten years ago not far from here," she replied.

"Yes, and I must admit, my curiosity was heightened when I heard you were specifically brought into this case because of your background, knowledge, and high-level security clearance. What exactly is your specialty? May I ask?"

She sat for a moment looking at each of the three men before answering. "I specialize in the unknown aspects."

Getting the usual strange looks from them, she proceeded. "Anything that cannot be explained with rational logic. My security clearance is higher than yours. However," she quickly added, "after I realized what this case involved and did a thorough background check on each of you, I required that same privilege be granted to everyone here. Officer Williams was a decision made after we had a chat when he was assigned."

The three men were a bit taken aback and turned to Williams who simply said, "She asked me if I believe in ghosts. She liked my answer," he said with a grin, shrugging his shoulders.

"You and I are going to have to talk when this is over," said Jameson.

"Everything you hear going forward is highly classified and will be difficult for you to comprehend or believe. Gentlemen, the world of paranormal, supernatural, or whatever word works for you, does indeed exist. Please take a moment to let this sink in. It's not a joke, and you must be prepared for what you will learn and witness. Danny, would you please get us more coffee? I think they're going to need it."

He nodded trying to stifle a full-blown laugh as he left the room. The men sat in silent thought until he returned. Samantha let them take a sip of their coffee before speaking again.

With all eyes back on her, Monahan asked, "So how does a pathologist become an expert in what's considered fairy tales, if you don't mind me asking? Or was it the other way around? You seem rather young for your position."

"Let me assure you, I am a scientist first and foremost. I do not come from a religious family. My mother is a science teacher, and with her guidance, I became fascinated with what could be learned from it. My father was killed in the Gulf War before I was born. When I was ten years old, my girlfriend and her family invited me to go with them to New York. My mother said no. She had a dream in which my father told her that something was going to happen, and if I went, I would die. She was scared and very adamant about me not going. I didn't understand why someone so rational could be convinced by a dream. My girlfriend and her family were touring when the Twin Towers fell. They died. Later, when I was in college, my mother was in a car accident. I stayed by her side the entire time. That's when I saw a man come in and whisper to my unconscious mother, smile at me, and leave. I sat speechless. He looked just like the picture of my father that my mother carried with her. At that moment, my mother woke. I told her I was afraid she'd never wake, and she told me my father came to tell her it wasn't time. That she needed to teach and prepare me for something. That's how I got into parapsychology."

"But what do ghosts have to do with this case?" asked Riley.

"Excuse me," Monahan interrupted. "As interesting as that may be, doesn't it take like eleven years to be a pathologist? That would mean you just started, yet you were the one chosen."

"I'm the only one in this field. I graduated high school three years early, and my degree in forensics in seven. I have an unusual ability to learn things incredibly fast. The government approached me because of what I discovered while I was doing my internship." Dr. Coletrain went silent in thought for a moment.

"Which was what?" asked Riley.

"A story for another time. Enough about me. It's important for you to understand what you are up against."

"Please, Doctor," Jameson said a bit sarcastically, "you have our attention."

"Thousands of years ago, before established religion, what you call magic ruled. Then it wasn't considered magic, more like the science of the natural order. When humans were more in tune with their surroundings, the universe, and nature itself, they relied on themselves, unlike today where technology rules and does everything for us. Humans, animals, crystals, elements, and even plants and rocks had unique gifts and purposes back then. They all worked together maintaining a balance between light and dark along with other realms and worlds interacting, communicating, and creating accomplishments that would put today's progress to shame. They were for the good of all, not the few. All were mere legends and myths now. Mankind went backward when religion took hold, stealing and adapting the old ways with the new to control the masses through fear for the sake of power and greed. The seed of personal desire and jealousy took hold in the heart of man. True evil was born and flourished, feeding the ego of the few and dominating the masses."

The men sat listening, with curiosity and disbelief, like children being told a scary bedtime story, anticipating the moment when she would say gotcha and give them facts. Only Williams seemed preoccupied clicking away on his laptop.

Dr. Coletrain looked at each of them before continuing. "Werewolves, demons, witches, even vampires exist within our plane. Some hid in our world before the veils between dimensions were closed. Only a very few of the oldest held knowledge of the past were, and still are, able to travel between worlds."

Startled by the phone buzzing in, everyone jumped slightly in silence. Jameson punched a button and said, "We're in the middle of something here. Can't this wait?"

"I'm sorry, sir," a female voice said. "But there's a gentleman on the phone who insists on talking to no one but you. He says he has important information about the case at the park, and it's a matter of life and death."

Glancing at the others in the room, Jameson said, "Put him through." Leaving the phone on speaker so all could listen in, he took the call. "This is Detective Jameson. Who am I speaking with?"

"My name is Reese Michaels. I'm the ghost hunter you're looking for. I think I have some information pertaining to your case that you need, but I need you to come get me. My life is in danger, and right now, I'm not trusting anyone."

The statement made everyone sit up in their seats. "Why do you think you're in danger?"

"Because someone already tried to kill me by tampering with my car. I've been out cold in a ditch for at least half the day from what I can tell."

"I'll send a unit right away."

"No!" Reese yelled. "It's got to be you or one of the FBI agents. I'm not trusting anyone. There's a white pickup truck that seems to show up everywhere I've been. The last time I saw it was at your station."

"Mr. Michaels?" said Williams. "My name is Danny Williams. If this is as serious as you say, it will raise suspicion if any of these men leave. Please allow me to come for you. No one will notice me leaving, and I'm very familiar with the case. I'm sure the others here will vouch for me."

The line went quiet for a moment. "As long as everyone else will confirm, I'll agree."

Jameson and Monahan both acknowledged they would vouch for Officer Williams.

"Mr. Michaels, this is Dr. Samantha Coletrain. I'm a forensic pathologist, and I know what we are dealing with. Are you hurt? Do you need medical assistance? I can come if you need me to."

"I don't think so other than a slight concussion and lack of sleep before the accident. You can check me when I get there. I think the less involved, the less get noticed and the less get hurt. No offense, Doctor, but I would prefer someone who is well-trained to handle a gun."

"No offense taken. I understand."

Jameson took the phone off speaker and handed it to Williams. As the information was being exchanged between the men, the others began discussing the new development and their next plan of action. Williams hung up. Without looking at the others, he opened the door to leave. Outside the door stood a uniformed officer.

Jameson looked up. "You need something, Sanders?"

"Ah, no sir, just passing by," said the officer and walked away.

The three men exchanged a look of concern. Monahan stood and walked out the door. Before closing it, he glanced in the direction Sanders went. "I need food. Doughnuts okay with everybody? Or should I get popcorn?" he said loud enough for all to hear.

Jameson smiled, replying, "Sure, doughnuts sound great."

Riley sat lost in thought. He'd always had an interest in science fiction and fantasy. It was his escape from reality, entertainment. But also, an understanding of the psychological aspects of the human imagination. To hear it had real possibilities was his fantasy coming to life.

Dr. Coletrain patiently sat back in her chair. "You still think this is funny. You won't when I'm done presenting my evidence."

"I'm sorry, Doc, but you must understand how this all sounds like an urban legend or a child's creativity gone wild," said Jameson.

"Please, don't call me Doc. I prefer Sam if we're going to be informal. Under the circumstances, we should wait until your partner gets back before I go further," she said, looking at Riley, as his phone rang.

"Hey, I'll take glazed if you don't mind." Riley got a serious look on his face. "Got it." He hung up. "He said Sanders is driving a white pickup and went the same direction as Williams. He's going to follow him."

Jameson pulled up his phone and placed a call. "Danny, it's Phil. Watch your back. We think you're being followed."

"I know. As soon as Mr. Michaels mentioned the white truck and I saw Sanders at the door, I had a hunch. I spotted him right after I left. He's about three blocks behind me. I'm just playing with him right now. Don't worry, boss. I'll lose him."

"You sure?"

"Boss, think about it. Did anyone ever catch or keep up with me? I drove you all crazy when I was in high school. You got me to be a cop with your threats."

Jameson smiled and hung up. Before Jameson could relay his conversation with Danny, there was a knock at the door as it opened. In walked the chief of police. Cole Tate was of American Indian descent and a rather big man that filled the doorway. In his late forties, he was the youngest chief of police the department ever had. Known for being strict, fair, and dedicated beyond doubt, he was respected by the entire community.

"Phil," he said as he closed the door behind him.

"Chief," Jameson replied with a nod.

After brief introductions, Chief Tate turned to Dr. Coletrain. "Please pardon my intrusion, Doctor, but I have information you will understand. I am familiar with your reputation and knew you'd be assigned when the FBI got involved. I also have connections," he stated respectfully.

Jameson and Monahan looked at each other, puzzled, while Dr. Coletrain sat quietly patient.

"Early this morning, I met with the sheriff from one of our neighboring counties. A local farmer called to complain about hearing gunshots, claiming someone was hunting on his property just before dawn. The closest officer available was one of his K-9 units and sent him. After taking the report, he headed to the area the farmer thought the shots came from. About a half mile from the house, his dog started getting aggressive, wanting something in the field. He said it took a few minutes to get him under control enough to leash him. Not the usual behavior of a drug dog. He pulled to the top of the hill where he found"—he hesitated—"a body," he continued, unsure of the words he would use next. "I thought it best to have them bring it to you. He put it in his trunk before calling his dad, the sheriff in that area, who then called me. I would have brought it to your attention earlier, but you didn't exactly give any leeway for interruptions." He smiled.

Dr. Coletrain smiled and nodded. "Yes, I do tend to shut out everyone when I work. Would this sheriff and his son be any relation to you?"

"Yes"—he smiled—"my cousin. How did you know?"

"The tone of your voice came from your heart. Where is this body now?"

"Actually, it's in our parking garage, waiting. If you hadn't come out when you did, I would have used more authority to get your attention. With all that's happened so fast, I'm sure you'll agree this is connected."

"Has this been reported to anyone else?

"No. I explained to them who you are and what you do. We agreed it should only come to you. This needs to be kept quiet. I'm assuming these men here have been cleared. Correct?"

Dr. Coletrain stood, smiling with a twinkle in her eye. "Correct. Please lead the way. You have piqued my curiosity."

As they approached the car, two men stood side by side. The relationship was obvious; one appeared to be a younger version of the other. Without introduction, the chief and sheriff gave each other a nod as he took a step back allowing his son to reveal the contents inside the trunk. There lay a distorted body with a bullet wound to the head wrapped in a clear plastic tarp. Riley and Jameson stood, staring in disbelief. The body looked half man and half animal. The nose and mouth extended out like a dog's muzzle. The hands were swollen and thick, covered in hair with claws for fingernails. Dr. Coletrain's eyes went wide, astonished by what she saw. Her attitude changed fast as she straightened her shoulders and back.

"Clear everyone out between here and the morgue. No one is to see this, not even the men guarding the doors," she stated in a commanding tone. Turning to the chief, she lowered her tone. "Now!" she insisted.

Chapter 12

Ky woke first, with Charlie's nose in her face. She kissed it before rolling out of the bed. He lay there, his wagging tail beating the pillow behind him, with his eyes still closed and a smile on his face.

"Okay, moose. Let's find you a tree and me a coffee," she said, now fully dressed.

Charlie jumped off the bed landing at the door, waiting. Rummaging through her bag, she found a belt to use as a leash. After checking his bandages, they started out. There were no lights other than around the motel office. Thick clouds filled the sky hiding the moon and stars making the world appear as an endless pitch-black canvas. Charlie knew where he wanted to go and pulled her in the direction of trees running along the parking lot. After marking a couple of them, he turned toward the road, barked, and hopped on his front legs with excitement. Rounding the corner of trees at the road's edge came a man. Ky, realizing she had no weapons, held tight to her makeshift leash, as Charlie tried to drag her toward him.

Persistent and strong, almost taking her to the ground, the man said, "Sit," in a low, stern voice. Both Ky and Charlie recognized the voice. It was Wolfe.

"What are you doing out here?" Ky asked.

"I smelled smoke, went to the road to figure out where it was coming from."

"I noticed it when we came out, but it was so light I just thought it was left from the bonfire at the beach last night."

"Not the right smell." He looked down at her and grinned. Laying his hand on his chest, he said, "Come on, boy." Charlie jumped up, stretching his front legs to Wolfe's shoulder, and laid his head under his chin.

"Well, aren't you two something?" she said sarcastically.

"You're just jealous."

"Of what?" she spouted with eyes wide open.

"You're no taller than an armrest to me. He'd knock you to the ground or tower over you with his head on yours." Wolfe moved, just missing Ky's kick to his shin. Both laughed as quietly as they could to not wake others in the motel; they heard a woman yell.

"Hey, you two. You got my coffee?" Ivy was up and dressed unusually early.

Charlie let out a low moan as he dropped to the ground and headed back to the rooms with Ky and Wolfe following. Sitting in front of Ivy, ears perked, he let out a soft howl.

"Does your leg hurt, or do you want attention? You're not limping," Ivy said, looking down.

"He hears something," Ky said, laying her hand on top of his head, and he went quiet. A moment later, they could barely hear sirens in the distance. Ky looked at Wolfe. "Guess you know your smoke."

"I'm going to check his wounds, then we're going for coffee. What's with the smoke?" Ivy asked, going back in her room with Charlie at her heels.

"Something's on fire," Ky replied.

"You think?" Ivy said as she sniffed the air, giving her a death look. As she pulled off the bandages, Charlie swiped her cheek with his tongue. "You're welcome. That's enough with the kisses. You smell like Wolfe."

Glancing up at the other two, standing there, watching over her shoulder, she said, "He's healed very well. No need for more ointment, but I want to keep it covered for today. Now can we go? I need my coffee, and it's not like we're staying in a hotel where I can make a cup. What time is it anyway?"

"Why are you up so early?" Ky asked.

"Dream made me anxious. I was having a tea party with dead people I didn't know. If they were family, I'd know a relative is about to die. Strangers inviting me to join them is new. It put me on edge just enough to get woke by this fat boy's bark," Ivy said, giving Charlie a stern look.

"Well, it's just a little after five. There's a truck stop close to the park. We can go there and get breakfast. I'll put Charlie's service jacket on him so he can go with us. I keep it in the trunk. Come to think of it, I have an extra leash and harness too."

"In your trunk?" asked Wolfe curiously.

Ivy put her hand on his arm. "I'll explain why on the way. You won't believe some of the things she keeps in there or, for that matter, hides and brings home."

*****

The truck stop was buzzing with truckers and some locals just getting off the graveyard shift. A waitress came by pointing at an empty table along the windows, telling them she'd be right with them. Sitting themselves, Charlie jumped into the chair nearest the corner between Ky and Ivy. Wolfe giggled at the sight; the girls just smiled. The waitress approached, wide-eyed seeing Charlie sit at attention watching the room and parking lot.

"That's different." She smiled. "Does he need a menu too?"

"No, he just needs to see the whole room and eat," replied Ky lightly. "We'll have steak and eggs. Steak as rare as the law will allow, eggs up, and french fries instead of hash browns if possible, and a small extra plate please, so we can share."

After taking all their orders, the waitress went to get their coffee, still grinning ear to ear over such a sight.

"You spoil that dog too much," Ivy said.

"He deserves a good meal after what he went through."

Ky reached out to pet Charlie, but he put his paw up to stop her. His eyes were focused on a table in the opposite corner. They all turned seeing a group of men and a couple of women. The group seemed ordinary but somehow out of place. Ky recognized one of them from the beach, pointing him out to Ivy and Wolfe. It appeared they were preparing to leave when one of the women approached with something in her hand. Charlie let out a low whine. His tail sticking out the back of the chair began to wag, making a thumping sound off both the chair and the wall. The woman looked at Charlie, closed her eyes, and bowed her head before looking up and coming closer. Charlie responded with a yip.

"My name is Athena. I went back and got this for you," she said, handing a small camera to Ky. "I don't know if there are more. I didn't have time to look. Good luck hunting." She nodded once more to Charlie and went back to her group.

"What was that all about with Charlie?" Ivy asked.

"I asked his permission to talk to you," Athena stated from halfway across the room.

Surprised, all three of them looked at Charlie who sat there with what looked like a smile on his face and tail still wagging.

"You can just settle down there, big guy. I don't think you're her type." Ky looked at Ivy. "She's definitely part wolf. Past that, I'm not sure."

"Well, she seems to have a thing for you. I saw a look in her eye."

"She was just flirting with Charlie," Ivy said, turning her attention to the camera.

"I think it's Reese's," Ky noted. "The one I told you I saw in the tree."

"That was awfully nice of her."

"Yeah," Ky said suspiciously. "Do you know how to view what's on this?"

"I can with a laptop. You have that in your trunk too?"

"No. It's in my bag back in the room," Ky replied with sarcasm, sticking her tongue out.

As they finished eating, Ky noticed the local news breaking on one of the TV monitors across the room reporting on a fire in one of the cabins. The look on Ky's face made Ivy and Wolfe turn to the screen. There had been a body found inside, but no details were given.

"So that's the smoke from this morning," Ivy said.

"Looks like they got control of it pretty fast," replied Wolfe.

"Except, that's Reese's cabin," Ky stated.

"Reese Michaels?" asked the waitress as she came up. Everyone's attention turned to her. "I met him yesterday when he came in for breakfast."

"What time was that?" Ivy asked.

"About seven, or seven thirty, I guess. I was hoping he was here for a haunting, but he's here to see a band this weekend. He said we'd have a drink together," she said, smiling. "You don't think it was him in the cabin, do you?" she said with her smile suddenly gone.

"No, it wasn't," said Ivy as she focused on her cup of coffee. Ivy and Ky looked at each other with suspicion. "We need to go," she said to Ky and turned to the waitress. "May we get the check and three large coffees to-go?"

Wolfe took care of the bill as the girls headed back to their vehicles in silence. Ivy was the first to speak. "How could he be having breakfast just a few short hours after making it sound like he was hiding?"

"I don't know. Have you checked for any more messages from him? I haven't."

"Yes, there's been nothing."

"And you're sure the body isn't his?"

"Yes. I felt it was a female. We need to see what's on that video before we decide our next move. You go by the station. See if you can pick up on whether she was human or not, and we'll meet you back at the motel."

"Where are you going?"

"To drive by the cabin. See if I can pick up anything else."

*****

Ky parked on the street beside a small park area next to the police station as a sports car was pulling out from the back of the building. Putting a leash on Charlie, they walked by the station parking lot. The first thing she noticed was the white pickup she had seen at the cabin. Charlie let out a low growl as the man she had seen before climbed into the truck. Ky bent down, checking his bandage while watching the man out of the corner of her eye. The truck left, going the same way the car had. As she stood up, another man came out. Watching the truck, he made a call, quickly went to his car, and went in the same direction. Charlie growled again as a car pulled in going straight into the garage.

"Well, I guess I'm going in," Ky said to Charlie. Walking to the nearest tree, Ky sat cross-legged. Charlie lay next to her with his head in her lap. Visioning her bubble of protection, her essence took a vapor form. Drifting to the garage first, she hit an invisible barrier that wouldn't let her enter. Rounding the building to the main entrance, she hit another. This one threw her back into her body hard enough to almost knock her over. Charlie lay next to her on full alert; a low rumble sound came from him with his eyes focused on the station. The hair on his back stood on end. Charlie was in attack mode. Ky shook her head trying to clear the painful fog clouding her mind.

"We need Ivy," she said, irritated as they both started back to the car.

Charlie's eyes never left the building, even as they drove off.

*****

The speed limit for the park was only fifteen miles per hour, perfect for Ivy to feel the area. As they got to the burnt cabin, only the fire chief and fire truck remained, with one squad car blocking the drive. Ivy placed her hand on her window facing the cabin and closed her eyes as a shiver ran through her. Wolfe drove a little further finding a small road leading into a fishing area. Pulling the truck around, he parked facing the direction of the cabin.

"You okay?" he asked Ivy.

"Yes. There's just a lot of energy here. Why are we parked?"

"I'm thinking of taking a walk."

"You saw something, didn't you?"

Wolfe just smiled. "Want to take a walk in the woods with me?"

Ivy pulled her handheld crossbow out of the back seat along with a small jar filled with a clear liquid. Taking three arrows, she dipped each tip into the solution. After loading one arrow into the bow, she placed the other two carefully in the sheath inside her boot and the bow in her bag.

"I'm ready." She smiled, seeing curiosity written all over Wolfe's face. "Don't worry. It's just a sedative."

"Well, I got us covered if it's not enough," he said, patting the hunting knife in his boot.

Wolfe was known for his ability to throw knives. Ivy remembered when he nailed a rat at fifty yards away. She could throw with accuracy, but he had her on distance. Wolfe put his arm around Ivy, pulling her in close as they walked across the road to the small grove of trees. Deeper into the wooded area, the trees became more spread out. Sticking close to Wolfe, Ivy reached out, touching some of them as they went by.

"You're talking to the trees again, I see. You told me once, the roots are their communication network. What are they saying?" asked Wolfe.

"Violence comes from many life forms, causing chaos to the natural order and is chasing the wildlife that find their home here away. The oldest says they haven't seen this type of chaos in over a hundred years."

"You've never told me how you know what the trees are saying."

"You learn to listen with your feelings, mind, and then your ears."

A twig snaps behind them. Dozens of crows swirled overhead screeching and dove toward the two of them. Wolfe grabbed Ivy, pulling her toward the ground when a large burnt-red wolf came running at the same time the birds passed. Letting out a sinister growl, it jumped over them both landing a few yards away. A smaller scraggly wolf stood snarling behind them facing off the bigger one for a moment before turning to run. Turning to Wolfe and Ivy, the red wolf nodded with a wink before running after the other.

"Did that thing just wink at us?" Wolfe asked in an unbelievable tone.

"Yes, I believe she did," replied Ivy with a smile. "If I'm not mistaken, that was Athena. We can leave now. She's taking care of whatever you saw."

Wolfe looked down at Ivy, admiring her calm, peaceful perspective. "I love you, baby girl. You blow me away at times the way you handle things."

*****

Jess sat at the kitchen table enjoying a glass of her special blend of iced coffee. Bear, Nala, and Tucker came running barking wildly, jumping in circles around her, for her attention.

"What?" she yelled over the commotion. "You just came in." She stood pausing for a moment.

All three lay on the floor with their heads on their paws instead of heading for the door.

"Really? What? You want another cookie instead?"

The sound of glass cracking came from the next room. The dogs jumped. Ears back; slow and quiet, they crept across the floor to the other room with Jess following behind them. Jess looked around finding nothing at first. The windows were all intact. Bear and Nala stood in front of her glass knick-knack cabinet. Inside was the picture of her, Ky, and Ivy. The glass cracked directly across Ky's face.

"Shit. This can't be good," she said, reaching for her phone and dialing Ivy. "Ky's in trouble," she said before explaining what had just happened to the picture.

"Got it. We'll keep an eye on her. Knowing her, she probably already knows something she's not telling us. Charlie is with her, so I wouldn't worry too much. I swear sometimes I think that dog is more gifted than we are," Ivy replied and hung up.

Jess took a deep breath to release her built-up anxiety. Letting out her breath, she looked down at three furry faces with looks of anticipation staring back at her; she smiled.

"It'll be okay. Aunt Ivy and Charlie will take care of her. Now how about a cookie?"

Chapter 13

Jameson, Monahan, and Riley stood around the table trying to understand what they saw—a man in a partial fetal position. He had one bullet wound to the head and one to the torso; he looked as if he had melded into himself. Hands, thick and padded, had taken the form of a paw with short sharp, protruding nails. His legs were elongated from the knees down with feet similar to the hands. But his face was the hardest to look at. It appeared as if some force tried to pull it through a funnel making his ears appear pointed with sprouts of hair. Bone cartilage pushed against the skin coming out from his lower back as a partially formed tail.

"Welcome to my world, Gentlemen. What lies before you is a werewolf in transgression." Dr. Coletrain turned to Riley. "You don't seem as surprised as I would have expected."

"Fascinating," Riley said as he studied closer. "I've always believed there had to be at least a note of truth in legends and myths. Even if the original perspective was distorted."

Jameson stood along the wall, speechless. Chief Tate, the sheriff, and his son gathered in a corner deep in conversation.

"I am a little confused though," stated Riley. "Myth says they turn human when they die. He's stuck in between. How is that possible?"

"You watch too many movies. Hollywood got part of it right. It's true. They do change. But catching them in the process can be tricky. Bitten, they change fast, but when they are born with the ability to turn wolf, they stay in the form they are killed in. Protecting the innocent is essential. Too much information tends to embolden fear into aggression," said the chief. "Most people would panic and create violent mobs and vigilantes if they knew the truth."

"That would lead to the mass killing of wildlife and the extinction of important animals to our environment as well as people being beheaded for the wrong reasons, like those suffering from hypertrichosis," said the sheriff. "The silver stops everything. Doctor, if you can take it from here, my son and I have many things to do under the circumstances. I'm sure you understand. If you need anything, you can contact us through Chief Tate."

"Thank you both. I will. We need to keep each other in the loop going forward. This case is highly unusual. Even I'm not sure what to think. Agent Riley? I believe I overheard you say you were going back to see Mr. Delaney, correct?"

"Yes. In fact, I think I should do that now. As much as I would love to be here for your autopsy, we need to get to the bottom of this quickly before we have any more deaths. I don't know how many more bodies the morgue can handle. Or how long we can keep this contained. With Monahan gone, does anyone have a car I can use?"

"Ride back with us. You can take my car. It's GPS-tracked. It's best if we know the whereabouts of all involved until this is over," said the sheriff.

"You are very wise, Sheriff. This is more than an isolated incident. There is no way of knowing how many are involved, let alone who," the doctor said, turning to Jameson. "Spread the rumor that the last body brought in was a decaying animal. Add that we are checking the stomach contents to verify if animals attacking humans is a concern or not. That should buy us some time. Are you okay with that?"

Jameson nodded that he understood.

The chief placed his hand on Jameson's shoulder. "Phil, I know this is a lot to take in. Do you want me to handle this?" asked the chief.

Jameson shook his head no. "We have to maintain standard procedure, or it will cause cover-up gossip. I know who the mouths of the city are. You need to stay out of it and watch our backs. Riley, you call Monahan. Have him get back here. We'll figure out a plan. I'll call Danny and tell him to hurry up and get his ass back here with our ghost-hunting friend."

"What about Sanders?" asked Riley.

"Don't worry. I'll handle him. You guys get going. What about you, Doc? Crap, sorry. I mean, Dr. Coletrain. You haven't slept since you arrived."

"I sent my team to the hotel earlier. When they arrive, Danny and I will shower and rest. I don't want this room left unattended, especially now, since we are not sure if we can trust the guards you assigned. Until further notice and unanimous agreement, we trust no one. By the way, I'll need strong chains made of silver. Just a precaution," she said, smiling.

"We have some," said the sheriff. "We've grabbed rogues for the local pack many times."

Exchanging glances with his son, they left the doctor to do her job. Detective Jameson and Chief Tate headed into the station while the other three men went to the garage.

"How far are we from your car?" Riley asked, turning to the sheriff.

"You won't be taking mine. You're taking my son's. I only said that because someone was outside the door listening. One of our hunters from the tribe is in the parking lot waiting for us and keeping watch. Now you go but make sure you stay in touch. The GPS will tell us where you are, but not the situation you may find yourself in. When you feel anything suspicious, call. Keep it in your breast pocket so we can hear clearly."

"How long have you known—whoa!" Riley exclaimed, taking a step back as a black wolf rounded the car.

"It's okay. He's with us. We've lived with them our entire life, for many generations. Not all wolves are bad. They help us hunt renegades. We help them with rogues. This is Night Wing. He's a shapeshifter. He's going with you for your protection."

"Shapeshifter? So what? He's a werewolf too?"

"No. Werewolves can only be wolves. Skinwalkers can only change to whatever skin they hide under of equal mass, like a bear or wolf. Shapeshifters can change to mimic animals, birds, even other humans, depending on their lineage, age, and experience. There are only four that we know of that still travel between dimensions.

They're the most powerful and oldest. They can be as small as a mouse or as big as a dragon. Hell, legend has it they can be an insect or even just a shadow in plain sight."

Handing Riley the keys, he opened the passenger door. Night Wing jumped in the back seat and laid down blending with its black interior. Riley couldn't tell he was there unless the wolf opened his eyes.

"How is a wolf going to go unnoticed?"

"Like I said, he's a shifter. You get there. Let him worry about the rest."

*****

"Phil, I need you to go back to your office and wait for Danny. Gather your notes and see if you can find a pattern, connection, or anything. Call the surrounding counties. See if they have anything unusual happening more than we've already learned. Make sure you don't let on that you know…this. Make it sound like we have a potential gang of killers we're looking into. And make sure you keep me posted. I'm going to get in touch with the tribe elders and see if they can give us some insight. Maybe if they've got any stories of this happening before, we can find out how they dealt with it." Chief Tate placed his hand on Jameson's shoulder. "You going to be okay? I know how hard it is to accept all this."

"Yeah, just give me a few minutes. I should wait for Monahan to get back first, and we'll figure it out together. I'm sure he's as confused as I am. I wonder how he'll react when I tell him what's in the morgue now."

Chapter 14

Ky chose to drive to the cabin and find Ivy. Knowing how enhanced werewolves' hearing can be, phoning her from the station would be giving herself away, especially not knowing who to trust. At this point, she even doubted whether Reese was in any trouble and had no clue about the meaning behind her vision of the dumpster. As she rounded the first curve, Charlie sat up in his seat. Into the second curve, Charlie let out one loud bark of warning. A large red wolf came busting through the line of trees at a dead run. "Athena," she said aloud.

Two black wolves and one brown came chasing behind her. Athena headed straight into a small outlet clearing made for fishing. She'd be trapped. Ky sped up, taking the last wolf out as he flew up and over the car, landing on the road behind her, not moving. Speeding into the clearing and throwing the car in park as she opened the door, she stepped out before it came to a full stop.

Sword in hand, she ran to Athena's aide. The first wolf took Athena down in a roll. Ky swung, cutting the tail off the second in mid jump. With a yelp, he turned to face her. Holding her sword with both hands like a baseball bat, she stood ready to take his head. Athena was in an all-out brawl with the other, rolling across the gravel as he tried to rip her throat. Her legs were strong with paws big enough to push him back as teeth snapped catching her fur. The second wolf paced, slowly circling Ky, sizing her up. He lunged only to be plowed to the ground when Charlie used him for a trampoline, catapulting to Athena, giving Ky the advantage to thrust the tip of her sword deep between his eyes.

"Go ahead, make a move," she said to him. He moved to the side. Ky rammed her sword, slicing his face and neck as her blade plunged through his shoulder deep, piercing the center of his heart.

Charlie landed on his target, sinking teeth into the back of the wolf's neck. It snapped as Athena ripped his throat open from the front. Ky turned, running back to the road, but the third wolf was gone. Charlie and Athena came running at full speed, side by side.

Charlie looks like a small dog next to her, she thought. Both took off across the road, up the hill, and disappeared in the trees.

"Damn it!" yelled Ky as she stormed back to the car. "There's no way I can keep up with you guys." Grabbing her phone, she dialed Ivy.

*****

Wolfe opened the truck door as Ivy's phone sang out Ky's ringtone.

"Hey," she said, then stood still in silence. "Stay there. We can get to the other side faster. We're close to the boat dock. We'll catch them."

Wolfe started the truck as Ivy hung up. He knew where to go from what he heard. "What happened now?"

"Charlie and Athena are chasing a lame wolf through the woods. They were in a fight."

Putting the truck in gear, he took off with Ivy, who relayed what Ky told her. They hit the docking area with the rear tires sliding into a slight fishtail. Not slowing down till Ivy yelled, "Here!" Wolfe slid to a stop on the side.

Ivy rolled down the window letting out a very loud and long whistle, then waited. Ivy waited a few seconds. When no response came, she whistled again. This time, they could hear a wolf howling deep in the grove, followed by a couple of barks. Both climbed out of the truck when Charlie came running. He was alone.

"Where's your new friend?" Ivy asked.

Charlie turned his head looking back toward the trees, wagged his tail, and barked once before climbing in the truck. Ivy and Wolfe stood there looking at him and then at each other.

"Well, I guess he told us." Wolfe laughed.

Ivy called Ky letting her know they were on their way and had him while Wolfe examined Charlie for injuries. He had mats of wet hair embedded with dried grass and twigs but found only one scratch across his nose.

"You're getting another bath, boy. You smell like bad breath. I hope you got him."

Charlie barked once, then slid his tongue across Wolfe's face, making him grimace and say, "Kisses aren't going to get you out of a bath."

*****

Ky recognized Ivy's whistle. Ky could project her voice up to four blocks, but Ivy's whistle could be heard a half mile away. Relieved when the response came, she walked back to inspect the damage to her car. It was still running, and the hook on Charlie's seat belt was bent beyond repair. He'd gotten out through her open door. With no visible damage to the front end where the wolf was thrown up and over, she knew she would have to get under the bumper to find any real damage. Ky opened the trunk to get the duffel bags, lined in disposable plastic, she used when hunting. Placing the bag under the tailless butt of the one she killed, she began sliding him inside. Disposing of supernatural bodies didn't happen often, but it was important to always be prepared.

"Need some help?" said a male voice.

Startled, she pulled the dagger from her boot, turning to find Damon standing over her. He didn't budge or flinch at the sight of the blade positioned close to his groin. He just stood there looking Ky in the eye, smiling. That was the second time he had snuck up on her and the third time she didn't feel anyone near. She definitely had to talk to Ivy about her protection necklace.

"What is it with you?" she said, putting the knife back in her boot. "Every time I see you, you ask me if I need help. Do I not look capable? Or are you some kind of stalker trying to play hero?"

"Maybe I'm just drawn to your friendly personality," he said sarcastically. "Besides, I think you're a little distracted because of your dog."

"Really? What makes you think that?"

"You forgot to cut his head off."

"No need. With my sword, they never come back," she said with conviction. "I'll bag them and burn them where it's safe."

"Nice. But my way will be faster and less messy," Damon said as he raised one hand. A blue flame formed a ball from his palm. As he tossed it at the carcass, the wolf disintegrated to dust along with her bag.

"Impressive, but I spent a lot of time designing that bag."

"Sorry. I can't bring it back, but I bet I can teach you to do it my way." He grinned as he tossed another at the second wolf. "Less mess."

"Maybe, but I don't plan on being here long." Ky picked up the other bag and headed for her car.

Athena came running across the road, straight to Damon, and sat. He looked back at the trees, then at Athena.

"She says he's with your friends but has a scratch on his nose." Athena looked up at Damon, wagging her tail.

"Now that's something I would be interested to learn."

"What?"

"Talking to the animals."

"That takes longer, which means…you giving up your phone number?"

"I'll think about it," she replied with a scowl. Ky climbed in her car mad at herself. She'd set herself up for that one and walked right into what she felt was a trap. Something about him made her suspicious and intrigued at the same time, but she was on a mission. There was no time for romance. *ROMANCE! Where the hell did that come from?* she thought, feeling her face turn red. "I gotta go. Thank you, Athena. You too, Damon. Maybe I'll see you again." Ky put the car in gear and sped to the boat dock to meet Ivy.

*****

Ky's car slid to a stop next to Wolfe's truck. Running to Charlie as he jumped out the window, she scolded him for taking off.

"We need to talk. Nothing is making sense, and things are getting crazy out of hand. You want the motel or a restaurant?" Ky asked.

"Coffee. Further in the city and not too busy. Privacy in public at least till we know we're not being followed," said Ivy.

"Followed?" asked Wolfe.

"Yes. While you were watching ahead, I was watching behind. Let's go."

"What about him?"

Ky looked at Charlie. "You stay in the car, buddy. Not taking you in looking like that."

Charlie let out a moan, going to the back of her car, panting hard and rapid. Ky opened the trunk looking for a bowl she could pour water in for him along with a harness to strap him into the second seat belt.

"Is there anything you don't have in there?" asked Wolfe.

Ivy and Ky looked at each other; both started laughing. Charlie finished and lifted his leg on her back tire.

"Don't get pissy with me. Get your ass inside," Ky said.

He lowered his head, got in the back seat, and laid down, still panting. "Stop pouting. I'm proud of you, but you are getting too old for this," she whispered, kissing his nose. "And I'm sure you made an impression."

He lifted his head smiling. The cut on his nose wasn't deep, but it was swelling up fast.

"Ivy! Come see this. Something's not right about his cut."

Ivy took one look at the welt and grabbed her bag from the truck. It had doubled in size in a matter of minutes. From her bag, she pulled a cotton swab and vial. She dipped the swab in the vial, covering it in dirty green goo. The smell made Ky and Wolfe cover their mouths. Charlie wrinkled his nose and sneezed.

"Hold his head still. This might sting a little."

"As bad as it smells?" asked Wolfe.

"Shouldn't. It depends on whatever it's up against." Ivy laid the goop over the wound.

Charlie flinched and sneezed again when the goo began turning black.

"That's not good. Guess we're picking up coffee. We'll meet you back at the motel."

*****

Ky pulled up to her room, finding Damon and Athena waiting for her. "What are you two doing here?" she asked.

Athena stepped forward looking at Charlie's nose. "Had to check on my knight in shining armor. He didn't get bit, but when Damon ashed the wolf, his claws sparked yellow. They were covered in a poison very few know how to use. It would slowly drive him mad before killing him after he killed you. Your friend was wise using that gunk. It won't save him, but it slows the process. Can't let anything happen to my new friend," she cooed.

"We tried to catch up to you at the boat dock. You had already gone," said Damon.

"What can you do for him? And how did you get here before me.

"If I told you all my secrets, we wouldn't have anything to talk about when…you have dinner with me." Damon grinned.

Ky scowled at him as she opened the door.

"Enough, Damon," Athena said sternly. "His heart rate is increasing."

Charlie jumped on the bed letting Athena sit with her arms around him tight, whispering in his ear. As he laid his head on her lap, Damon raised his hand just above the wound. Sparks flew between creating a bright blue-and-white sphere of light. Charlie tried to lunge. Athena tightened her grip. Charlie let out an ear-piercing cry, making Ky come running with tears in her eyes. Wolfe busted through the door with a gun in his hand. Ivy stood beside him with her crossbow loaded and ready only to say, "What the fuck?"

91

Chapter 15

Danny caught sight of Sander's pickup a few blocks away from the station. He hadn't gone far when he got the call from Jameson. Danny lived here his whole life and knew the city as if he had designed it himself. Continuing to drive, he knew exactly where to lose Sanders. After driving to the outskirts of the city, Sander's truck turned toward the lake. Danny, disappointed, was looking forward to playing the catch-me-if-you-can game. He hadn't got to drive like that since joining the force. Glancing at the rearview mirror, what he saw told him the game was over. Seeing the fed's car turn as well, he proceeded to the highway taking him to Reese.

Monahan followed the pickup thinking they were going to the lake until Sanders drove past the entrance. Instead, he took a side road. Monahan decided not to follow but made note of the sign sticking out of some bushes. "Redemptions" was all it said. Driving a little further to find a spot to turn around, his phone rang. Riley sounded a bit excited telling him to get back to the station. Pulling a U-turn, he slowed down going past the access road. The road went in quite a ways before revealing what appeared to be a parking area of a large two-story building. A balcony on the second floor wrapped around the corner of the structure was all he could make out through the trees. With no clear view of the main entrance nor the truck, Monahan headed back to the station.

*****

Sanders parked in front of the main doors to Redemptions. It was dark inside the large room, with just enough light for the average person's eyes to adjust quickly. The bar ran long down one side of the oversized room. In the center of the far wall was a raised stage, big enough for two bands with a dance floor to match, surrounded by at least a hundred tables. There was one bartender, a waitress, and a cook on duty. This time of day was generally the slow period with a half dozen people sitting at the bar. In the far corner, the darkest in the room sat a man. Sanders ordered a Coke and went straight to the table.

Jack Marsten was the one man no one messed with. At 6'2" and weighing 250 pounds of solid muscle, he could take down 4–5 men at a time. He wasn't good-looking by any means. In fact, to look at him, one would think he should be out on the open sea fighting sea monsters, not hiding in the dark in the middle of the midwestern Bible Belt. Sanders pulled out the chair opposite him and sat.

"They got the ghost guy. He's turning himself in, I guess. Not sure from where, but he called. They sent one of the guys working with them to get him. I'm sure he noticed me. He's one of our better cops, and I saw one of the feds following me. I'll be back in the station before they get there so I can get more information to you then."

"Good to know," said Marsten.

"What are we supposed to do?"

"Nothing."

"But we don't know what he knows or saw. I was going to follow him, but since I was sure they spotted me, I chose not to. The guys at the station think I'm at lunch."

"Didn't I tell you not to do anything without talking to me first?" asked Marsten with a low, threatening voice.

"Yeah, but everything was happening so fast there was no time. It's not like you carry a phone."

"I stay off the grid. I like it that way. I live longer. You, on the other hand, get too cocky for your own good. It's going to get you killed, maybe even by me, especially if you don't get your men in line."

"What's that supposed to mean?" Sanders said, glaring at him.

"A couple of your men got stupid last night, got drunk, and fought. One shot the other in midchange, then ran like a coward. A farmer called in about gunshots, and the county sheriff sent a car.

I listen to my scanner. One of my men found yours, still drunk, running off the mouth to himself. He's been dealt with, but by the time he got to the farm, everything was quiet, and there was no sign of a body. Whether he had the time to heal and get away is still in question. You need to make sure no one else screws up before this deal is finished."

"With all things considered, can't we move locations or postpone the timing?"

Marsten slapped his beer bottle on the table. "No. Why are you complaining? You feel stronger, faster than you ever have, don't you?"

"Yeah, and more so each time we eat what the master prepares. But I don't trust any man who hides his face under a hood. Those parts are pretty tasty though. You going to give up that recipe when we're done? Or we going to have to eat this male witch, demon, whatever he is, to get it?" Sanders said with a grin.

Marsten took a sip of beer ignoring Sanders's snarky comment. "We only have a few days left, and we're still short on…ingredients, shall we say. Send four groups of your men, each going a different direction. No less than fifty miles. Dispose of three of the bodies so they won't be found. The ones that head south need to get two. Get the second further out. Set them up the ritual style. That will lead your feds and the others to believe their suspects are headed for the state line. Now get the hell out of here."

*****

Monahan arrived at the station with three dozen doughnuts in hand. Dropping two boxes at the information desk, he told the sergeant on duty to let everyone have some. Entering Jameson's office with the other box, he found the detective on the phone tapping his pen on the desk in frustration. A moment later, Jameson hung up giving Monahan an update on the way to the morgue.

"You really bought doughnuts?" Jameson asked.

"Had to. Don't need everyone wondering why I left and came back empty-handed."

Jameson stopped at the door to the morgue and took a deep breath before opening the door. Dr. Coletrain had a computer webcam set up for recording. The body lay on the table with chains draped over the chest and ankles. Beside her was a tray of various equipment, typical of any doctor, except for what appeared to be a machete. The men glanced at each other, then back to the table. Next to it was a small bowl with the two bullets she had removed. Her gloves were covered in blood with little splatter on her lab coat.

"That looks like some kind of movie prop," snickered Monahan seemingly unfazed.

"We need to talk over drinks when this is done," Jameson said, looking at him curiously.

"I assure you it's not. However, you are just in time, Gentlemen. I'll need your help. If you'll be so kind," she said picking up the blade. "One of you will help lift the chains. The other must be ready to take the head off when I say…if it comes to that. I'd rather be prepared than taken by a silly, arrogant mistake. Your file says that you served in combat, Agent Monahan, so I can assume you can handle the knife, correct?"

"Yes," he said. Taking it from her like a man about to carve a ham at dinner instead of beheading a beast, he positioned himself at arm's length from the body.

"Wait, what?" Jameson exclaimed.

Chapter 16

Charlie appeared to be completely asleep, with his head still in Athena's lap. Ky stood over him with tear-filled eyes. Damon leaned against the small dresser with his arms folded. Ivy glared at him. He knew she wanted answers and wasn't hiding the fact she was pissed.

Ky spoke first. "It's okay. They saved Charlie from being poisoned and are leaving now," she said. Turning to Athena, Ky's facial expression told her, "Go. I'll handle this."

"Thanks to your green stuff. The poison didn't take effect as fast as it could have," Athena quickly said, seeing the insulted look on Ivy's face. She laid Charlie's head on the bed and stood to leave. "He'll stay asleep for at least another half hour. When he wakes, he's going to be very thirsty, but there won't be any other side effects, and the pain will be gone."

Ivy placed her hand on Wolfe's arm, lowering his weapon as she did her own weapon. They stepped aside as Damon and Athena made their way out. Still glaring, Ivy turned to Ky with Wolfe closing the door.

"What was that all about? What poison?"

Ky began explaining as Wolfe went to check on the dog. Ivy put her weapon away while listening. Ky and Wolfe waited in anticipation as she stood in silence for a few minutes, contemplating the events. Ivy's words could be viciously wicked when she felt her knowledge insulted.

"Get your laptop," she finally said to Ky. "Can you hook Reese's camera up to it? We need to see what's on there."

"What are you thinking?" asked Wolfe.

"That we need to start from the beginning and piece all this together. See if there are any dots to connect. Right now, it's as if there are several different things going on at the same time."

Ky set up the laptop and camera on a table near the window. The girls pulled up their chairs on either side, leaving room in the middle for Wolfe to see from the bed as Ky started the camera. They could see a woman run into view before stumbling and screaming as she crawled backward. Reese came running, picked her up, and they both ran. Ky was about to shut the video off when two wolves went running through the frame in the same direction. Before anyone could speak, Ivy's phone rang.

"Hey, Jess," she answered, looking at Ky.

They waited while Ivy gave a brief update. Hanging up the phone, Ivy turned to Ky, who was checking on Charlie as he was starting to wake up.

"Bear is fine and missing you both. Jess said it's time we file a missing-person report and to take Charlie with us. She didn't say why, just that she has a feeling."

Charlie, still a little sluggish, sat up swiping Ky's hand with his tongue. Wolfe picked him up and headed for the bathroom. "You ain't going nowhere. Not without getting cleaned up."

Charlie didn't fight, just groaned till the water warmed. Ky and Ivy discussed what story they could use without sounding crazy. Fifteen minutes later, the boys came out of the bathroom. Ky and Ivy were both ready to go with the camera footage on a flash drive in hand.

"Oh, hell no," exclaimed Ky when Charlie began to shake.

Charlie waited for her to get the hair drier and shook again when she got close, making everyone laugh as Ky got wet. Fifteen minutes later, they headed for the parking lot. Ivy explained to Wolfe what they were going to do and say once they got to the station. As Charlie got back up to speed, he jumped in the front seat.

Ky scolded him. "Back seat, mister. You broke the front hook, remember?"

*****

Damon and Athena were waiting in the parking lot of the station when they arrived. Ivy got out of the truck with attitude written all over her face.

"What are you doing here?" she demanded.

"I picked up a familiar scent when we left you. It led us here," said Athena in defense. "We had a hunch you'd be coming."

"We're backup to your backup," said Damon, looking at Wolfe with a nod of respect.

"Fine but keep quiet. We'll do all the talking," said Ivy, calming down.

Damon tied his hair back before putting on a baseball cap. Reaching into the trunk of his car and pulling out a shirt and plaid jacket, he took off his T-shirt. For a moment, Ky's eyes were focused on his perfectly naked T-shaped torso. His smooth caramel-colored skin stretched over a muscular build. Ky felt her face flush red with heat, looking away before he could see her staring. Wolfe and Ivy exchanged knowing looks, aware of Ky's reaction. Athena looked away to hide her grin. Damon, now looking like the locals, followed Athena to the bench shaded by a tree near the building, stating she'd keep watch, as the others approached the entrance. Upon entering the building, all hell broke loose inside.

Chapter 17

Riley looked in the back seat as he stepped out of the car. Night Wing wasn't there. He stood there for a moment, confused. How could a wolf, slash man, just disappear? Closing the car door, he saw a spider on his sleeve. As he started to brush it off, a vision came to mind—*Night Wing.* Was that even possible? After everything he'd witnessed since he'd gotten to this town, he chose to leave the spider alone, just in case.

As Riley reached the third floor, the students began filling the hall heading for their next class. Surrounded by so many young adults reminded him of his college days. He wasn't much older than the students, though it felt like he was. For a moment, he felt the thrill and anxiety of the hopes and dreams of opportunity they were living. He smiled to himself and thought, *Life is more like an adventure now.* Something he'd never thought it would be like. He knew being with the bureau would have its moments, but not the *X-Files* kind, making him wonder if aliens were next.

Delaney was gathering the papers strewn over the desk into the oversized briefcase he carried. "Agent Riley, I wondered when you'd be back," he said with his back to the door. "Have a seat. I don't have a class this period. We can talk here."

Riley took the chair nearest the desk as he studied the professor leaning back with his hands folded over his chest.

"How did you know it was me?" asked Riley suspiciously.

"Nothing magical, I assure you. I saw you enter the building from my window. Where's your partner?"

"Tied up on another lead."

"Another murder?" A small grin crept across Delaney's face.

"A man of your stature knows I can't talk about an ongoing investigation." One thing he knew was how to manipulate an ego. From the smile on the professor's face, it was working. "I was wondering if you could tell me more about cults and their rituals. Specifically, ones that are prone to human sacrifice."

Riley wrote in his notebook while the professor rattled on for twenty minutes giving only general information that was basic in any textbook. He made notes of Delaney's body language, tone of voice, and delivery, looking for clues to give him an edge of insight. He found plenty.

"You mentioned body parts having meaning. Can you be more specific?"

"The heart is the life and soul. The brain is knowledge. The liver strengthens with its nourishment to the blood. Eyes and kidneys are merely delectable to the taste buds, but the tongue is more. It's regarded in two ways—one being a tender delicacy and the other being the sword of words. It's removed, so the dead cannot speak."

"You seem to have a keen sense of human behavior, Professor. Do you know or have any suspicions of individuals or groups in this area that show any signs of this nature?"

"Do you want my opinion? Or are you just fishing, young man? I don't have time for games."

"I respect your opinion, sir. I take my job seriously."

Delaney looked at him long and hard before answering. "I've heard rumors that may be very hard to believe."

"I'm listening. You'd be surprised what I believe."

"What do you know about werewolves?"

"I know there is a certain amount of truth behind every myth and legend."

Delaney thought for a moment before speaking. "Well then, I have heard there are some wild werewolves in the area that think with a little help, from some devil worshipers, they can come out of the closet, so to speak," he snickered, waiting for Riley's response.

"So you're saying not all werewolves are wild?" Riley replied casually.

Surprised at the response, Delaney jumped at the chance to talk. "Yes, they have lived among us for hundreds of years. The good ones learned to evolve and adapt. The wild ones are more like renegades. They can't control themselves and become power hungry or bloodthirsty." He watched for a reaction but got nothing. Riley sat there as if he was listening to a history lecture with great interest.

"They tend to take care of the wild ones among themselves. It's rare that a human has actual contact. That's how the stories of myth were created. There was a time in history that was just as dark as the witch trials. When people were scared and accused of such outrageous acts, they were tried and convicted, whether innocent or not. Most fled, living in the wilderness, waiting for a chance to reenter society, while a handful hid in plain sight. Those that remained were the voice of reason, helping the truth become a fairy tale."

"Do any of the rumors you've heard indicate that's what's happening here?"

"Yes, but like I said, it's a little hard to believe. I've heard there is a small group that are devil worshipers of some sort. Everyone seems to be making this up as they go along, like campfire stories, trying to see who can out-scare who. That's the best I can give you."

"Anyone in particular pique your interest?"

"No, can't say they have."

"Thank you for your help, Professor."

"Anytime, young man, I appreciate you not coming with your partner."

Remaining silent, Riley smiled at Delaney as he stood to leave. "Word from the wise, Agent," said Delaney. "Be very careful. You have no idea what you're getting into. A place nightmares and horror stories come from can be deadly."

"I'll keep that in mind, sir, thank you." Riley exited the building and stopped when he hit the bottom stairs. The feeling he was being watched was overwhelming. He glanced up to see Delaney standing at the window of his classroom next to the same blond woman they saw on their first visit. Riley raised his hand and waved goodbye noticing a crow sitting on the windowsill staring down at him. Turning to the parking lot, the crow took flight.

*****

Dr. Coletrain and Jameson lifted the chains. To the men's surprise, the body began turning into a wolf form. Monahan raised the machete.

"Not yet. When it's done," Dr. Coletrain said, holding the chains inches above the body.

Horrendous crackling sounds of bones expanding in length and density and snapping new joints into place filled the room, stretching skin thickened with a pelt of fur. Vertebrates swelled before splintering in two, doubling in length, unfurling a thick fur-covered tail. The jawbone extended with the nose forming a muzzle. Protruding razorsharp fangs and ears shaped to a point lengthened as the body began convulsing. Arms, hands, feet, and legs, already covered in fur, quivered, stretching with the torso building to a massive size across the table. Gurgling growls escaped its throat choking on its own blood, fighting for life. The body lurched wide-eyed as the transformation was completed. Monahan swung. The blade hit straight through to the table with a thump, severing its head the moment the wolf took full form. Jameson stood there with fear in his eyes, frozen. Monahan laid the bloody blade down next to the body. Taking the chains from Jameson's hands, he helped Dr. Coletrain laid them on another table.

"Take him back to the office," she said to Monahan. "My team will take it from here. I'll join you in a few minutes." She went to her laptop, turned off the camera, and began typing her notes into a file.

Monahan led Jameson out of the morgue and found the guards gone. Loud voices and barking from down the hall brought Jameson out of his shock. They ran to the front desk where the guards stood. All officers, as well as Chief Tate, had guns pointed at a small-framed woman holding the leash of a growling, snarling dog. Around her were two men and another woman trying to calm everyone. Completely focused on the men behind the counter, the dog was ready to attack any minute. The dark-haired woman bent down and whispered something in his ear, settling him down. Ears back, teeth showing, and hair on his back still bristled, he never took his eyes off his target.

"We need to see the one in charge of the lake incident," said the redheaded second woman.

"What's with the damned dog?" yelled one of the officers at the desk.

"He smells fear," said the taller man.

"Fear my ass," he said, cocking his gun.

"That's enough!" yelled the chief, cutting him off.

"Put your guns down. I'm the one you want to talk to. Follow me," said Jameson. Turning to the two guards, he gave an order. "Get back to your post and, this time, stay there."

Everyone turned to the chief, who nodded as he lowered his gun. Quiet but cautious, everyone went back to their duties waiting to see how the situation would unfold. The officer and dog still glaring at each other as they passed stood their ground. Jameson led the way with Monahan taking up the rear.

*****

Danny came through the back door by the cell block. All the commotion could be heard before rounding the corner. Throwing Reese behind him, he pulled his gun. Dr. Coletrain stepped out of the morgue in front of him. Placing her hand on the end of his gun and lowering it, she motioned him to follow. Things seemed to calm down in front as they approached the lobby.

"Reese!" yelled both women.

"Ivy?" yelled the man standing behind Danny.

"I'm going to need a bigger office," Jameson said, shaking his head as he opened the door.

Chapter 18

Detective Jameson sat behind his desk listening as the redheaded woman bombarded Reese with accusations and questions too fast for him to respond. The dog sat beside the smaller dark-haired woman holding his leash as his eyes remained fixed on the door. Agent Monahan and Dr. Coletrain leaned against the window ledge behind Jameson while the other two men stood along the wall grinning. Danny went for more chairs.

Ivy glared at Reese standing there dumbfounded, waiting to get a word in, while Ky listened quietly. The questions came fast. What's with the text? Who are they that were after him? Where's he been? Why didn't he just call, and what the hell did he get involved in, followed by…

"Do you know how worried you've had us? We've been running all over trying to find your sorry ass. Now what have you got to say for yourself?"

"Plenty, if you're done," Reese replied and held his breath. Casting a quick glance at Ky, he was already regretting his words. He knew better than to argue or antagonize Ivy when her emerald-green eyes flashed flecks of gold. That's when she was the most dangerous. Wolfe was strong enough to hold her when pushed to her limit, but the relationship between Ivy and Ky was unique. Grounding tension to focus clarity through eye contact, they were each other's anchor, but at the moment, both were glaring at Reese.

Ivy closed her eyes and took a deep breath. When she opened them, the flecks were gone. Reese began to breathe again. Danny came in with chairs, completely unaware of what had taken place but could tell something had from the hauntingly silence in the room. Once they were all seated and the door closed, Reese proceeded to tell everything he knew, including about Katiya, ending with a question of his own.

"What text? I never sent anything."

Ky and Ivy looked at each other, then back at Reese.

Before either could get another word in, Detective Jameson spoke. "You three can argue later. The text is not my concern, the murders are. Ladies, now that your friend is found, you can relax and go back to wherever you're staying. You can pick up Mr. Michaels once we have the report and his statement. Please understand, you are not allowed to speak to anyone about what you've heard here, pending the investigation. We'll take it from here."

"Actually, we have information you need," stated Ivy with a tone of authority. She took control ignoring Jameson's dismissiveness. Ivy reached into her purse, pulling out a flash drive.

"This is from one of Reese's other cameras. It confirms what he's already said and has a clear picture of the woman for identification." As she looked toward Dr. Coletrain, she went on to say, "We know the type of wolves you're dealing with, and I believe you do too. We've dealt with them before."

Everyone turned as Dr. Coletrain spoke. "We haven't been properly introduced. I'm Dr. Samantha Coletrain, forensic pathologist," she stated, reaching across the desk to shake hands.

"My name is Ivy Meadows. I'm here with Ky Lang, and her dog, Charlie. The gentlemen are Wolfe and Damon. We are not ghost hunters like our friend, but you will find that we can be an asset. This isn't our first rodeo." Ivy looked toward Danny, who was busy taking notes. "You'll find we are well-known in small circles of the... unusual, shall we say."

"I'm Detective Jameson," he said, trying to establish some reprieve with Ivy. "And this is Special Agent Monahan with the FBI. His partner, Agent Riley, will be joining us soon. Please accept my apology. I meant no disrespect. I'm just beginning to understand. Standard protocol doesn't seem to apply here, and I must admit it's all new ground for me. So if you would, please enlighten me on how you can help."

Ivy smiled. "I'm the one the locals, in my area, call when their lives go sideways and when things from another realm interrupt their lives for whatever reason. Ky, on the other hand, is unique in her abilities."

"She scares the devil himself," said Reese.

Ivy bit her lips trying not to smile as Jameson, Monahan, and Danny's attention turned to Ky. With doubt written all over their faces, they studied the petite little woman. Ky stood there, unmoved, still listening. Being underestimated was something she was used to and used it to her advantage.

"And the men?" Jameson asked.

"Wolfe is my life-mate and bodyguard, so to speak. Damon, we just met." She turned to let him speak for himself.

He was gone. Wolfe, still leaning against the wall, stood up straight, looking confused. Ivy and Ky exchanged suspicious glances. Jameson, Monahan, and Danny sat straight up; they knew they had seen him. Reese's eyes widened, and Dr. Coletrain hid her frown. She hadn't seen him leave but had felt a moment of suspended time. The room went completely quiet knowing the door to the office hadn't opened.

"Where did he go?" asked Danny, breaking the cloud of silence. "Good question," Ivy said, disgusted. "Like I said, we just met, but I am confident he's not going to be a problem and will be there if needed. I'm sure we'll see Mr. Houdini again. He has a way of showing up when you don't expect him, but he's proved to be useful when he does."

"Well, out of curiosity," Jameson asked, "why is there a dog in my office? Is there a reason he's part of your entourage?"

Charlie jumped to a standing position, partially in front of Ky. Turning his attention to Jameson, a low growl could be heard. Ky's only reaction was a slight tug at the leash, making Charlie sit again but closer.

Ivy looked Jameson in the eye before she spoke. "It's not his first rodeo either. He's highly sensitive, more so than most animals, and very protective. Something triggered his instincts, or maybe someone doesn't like dogs."

"Now that we've established who we all are," Jameson said, "How about we start with how you obtained possession of the video footage from a crime scene?"

"Animals are wonderful creatures. They can track, sneak quietly, and retrieve pretty much anything. Your people failed to look up. Knowing Reese, we knew his equipment would be set up in different locations and angles. Unless the grid was lit up, your men wouldn't have known where to look. The battery pack is only good for a few hours. The grid's brightness will weaken as the battery goes down and can't be seen in lit areas. With all due respect, Detective, if you wish to learn more about the who, what, why, and where of things surrounding us, may I suggest you join one of my classes? Or we can get started hunting down your suspects." Ivy's direct, a bit snarky, diplomacy proved she was both serious and not intimidated.

The room went silent for a moment as Jameson contemplated his next move.

Agent Monahan spoke first, saving Jameson. "You stated we could identify the woman with a clear picture. Is there anything else you can tell us while we view the footage?" he said, taking the flash drive and plugging it into Jameson's computer as Ivy continued.

"Reese, when the wolves appear, I'll need you to enlarge the shot. I want to see their markings. As you can see, there is a clear picture of Katiya. The wolves come into frame one minute, thirty-seven seconds after they're gone."

"Stop there," Dr. Coletrain said. "That's our Jane Doe. I'm sorry, Mr. Michaels. Katiya is in the morgue."

"How can you tell?" Jameson asked.

"Facial bone structure," she said, looking at him.

Jameson began the video again, pausing as the wolves came into view. Reese enhanced the frame to get a better look. Their markings were distinct.

"The one on the left is dead. I killed him. I don't recognize the other," said Ky.

Monahan and Jameson's eyes went to Ky. Hearing her voice for the first time took them by surprise. Danny stopped writing in the middle of a sentence, raising his head. The sound of her voice, low, smooth, underlined in passion, making even the word *killed* seem sensual.

"I can't wait to hear this," whispered Monahan.

"A female was being attacked by three of your renegade wolves near the cabin Reese was renting. Charlie and I intervened. We took down two, and the third ran. Charlie followed him into the woods, end of story."

"Are you saying we have three dead wolves out there somewhere?" Dr. Coletrain asked in a concerned voice.

"No, two are ash. The third, I'm not sure. You'd have to ask Charlie, but my guess is there's nobody there either," she said, patting Charlie's head looking like he was smiling, tail wagging, and proud.

Danny sat there with his mouth open while Jameson seemed blown away in disbelief. Dr. Coletrain and Monahan exchanged looks, both thinking the same thing. *I like her.* The office door opened as Ivy's phone rang.

Riley walked in, looked around, and said, "I miss something?"

*****

"Every time you pull your disappearing act, you create a hornet's nest of questions," said Athena as Damon came around the tree behind her.

"Time to gather the others. Tonight we hunt before anyone else gets hurt."

"I think it's a little late for that." Athena pointed to the back of the police station as a plain black panel truck pulled into the garage. "I'm picking up two more dead."

"There's more to this than just a couple of renegades. Round the guys up. We need a plan."

Chapter 19

Jessica Carlisle sat at her computer searching for any type of related or unusual reports in all the news media outlets available across Illinois—newspapers, television, even blogs, and conspiracy theory sites. She'd been at it for what seemed like hours. Jess didn't like being left out, and no one checked in with her about how it went with the missing-person report. It wasn't until she saw a set of comments in a farmer-type community message board that she found any reference to wolves seen in the area. Most of the chatter surrounded packs of wolves roaming in fields and among trees lining the roads and highways since wolves weren't known to inhabit the area. The curious part was the fact that no animals were reported as missing or attacked, only that the packs were seen along with comments of their unusual large size. Taking a few notes, she pulled up a map of the area to pinpoint the sightings, then widened her search to other farm areas.

From the descriptions given, she couldn't tell if it was one pack or two. Only, that a group of four had been seen running through various fields, and a pack of five was seen around the highway and other small roads. Judging by the dates and times, they appeared to be headed toward Rockford from the northwest. The first sighting was over a week ago outside Sioux Falls. The most recent being within thirty miles of Rockford just twenty-four hours before the lake murder.

Jess stood and stretched. The house was warm. *Time to put the coffee away*, she thought. Placing her cup in the sink, she looked out the window to see the dogs looking up and circling one of the young trees she planted last year. She glanced up expecting to see one of her many squirrels, but instead, sitting on the top branch was a rather large crow. It turned its head looking at Jess, then spread its wings wide. Giving a very loud caw directed at the dogs, they all stopped in their tracks and laid down, still watching the bird. His wings were brought back tight to his body. Only sitting for a moment, as if surveying all that was his to command, he took flight to the east. The dogs watched until he was out of sight before moving to the door to come in.

"That was weird," she said, opening the door as the dogs ran straight to the snack jar. "Guess it's snack time." Giving each one their snack, they laid around her chair. *Time for tea as well*, she thought. As she filled her teapot with three cups of water placing it on the stove, she began to hum. Opening her cabinet, she spoke. "Guide my hand to herbs I need. Help me find that which I seek." With eyes closed, Jess floated one hand over her collection of herbs, repeating her chant three times, once for each jar she was drawn to. Closing the cabinet, she opened her eyes to study the jars. The first was rosemary. Placing her hand flat on its lid, she said aloud, "Astral travel." The second was marigold, again, repeating each movement. "Clairvoyance." The third was yarrow. "Enhancement." Jess never measured; her instincts were never wrong. Tipping each jar, she tapped its content into the palm of her hand, then into the teapot filled with water.

"Three cups, three herbs with three teaspoons of honey for taste," she said, smiling to herself. Jess walked to the window over the sink and raised it, allowing a small breeze to fill the room with scents of lilac and hibiscus from her flower bed. Satisfied with her choice, she sat petting each dog as she waited for her tea to brew.

*****

The sun began making its appearance as the garbage truck pulled up the alley behind the bar. Lifting the dumpster, the driver noticed someone lying on the ground behind it and stopped. He was used to having the homeless sleep there. Usually, the noise from the truck woke them, but not this time.

Great, another drunk, he thought as he climbed out.

When yelling didn't wake him, Cal went to the back of the dumpster to roust him. A man lay face down covered with a tarp for warmth. Gently kicking the sleeping man's foot gave no response, so he reached for the man's shoulder. Shaking him caused the tarp to slip from his partially covered face. Cal stood stunned seeing a pool of blood surrounding him. Taking a step back, he dialed 911.

*****

The Sutton boys followed the car for a few blocks when they slowed down, turning the headlights off giving more space between them. Jake Sutton watched, waiting with his little brother, John, as the car pulled around the back of the abandoned old warehouse. Jake looked at his watch; it was just after 3:00 a.m.

"You sure you want to do this?" asked John. "What's the rush? The full moon isn't for another week."

"I'm tired of waiting," Jake said.

"But the master is the only one that knows the ritual stuff."

"I'm hungry. I'm gonna prove all this magic is bullshit."

"How, by just eating?"

"Yes, now shut up. These two will be at it quick. We'll go as soon as they get naked. Her screams are going to be delicious. I might even do her before we eat."

"Damn, bro! I forget how sick you truly are. I don't want to eat her after you—"

"You won't. We eat him. I'm just juicing her up before collecting for this so-called master," he said, adjusting the tightening crotch of his pants.

*****

Paula Owens should have been celebrating her sixteenth birthday instead of packing her backpack with whatever would fit. Her abusive father went too far, and her mother was too blind with fear to listen. Tonight, it would end. Paula slipped out her window. Without looking back, she made her way to the highway. She had no idea where she was going, only that she wasn't going back to where she came from.

The terrain in the unfarmed country was rugged. Hitchhiking in this day and age was risky, so she walked the shoulder of the rarely used old highway. She knew it crossed a railroad track with a bridge over the river. All she needed was to get across the bridge to be in another state before her parents could file a missing-person report. After walking just over an hour, she heard a car slowing behind her.

"Are you okay, sweetie?" the woman asked from the passenger seat.

"Yes, I'm fine. Thank you," she said, continuing to walk.

"It's not safe out here, and you look cold. Let us give you a ride. My name is Val, and this is my husband, Stan. We're headed for Dubuque. We can at least get you that far."

Paula thought for a moment. They seemed like a nice middle-aged couple and chose to take the ride. It was cold out, and she had a ways to go. A ride would put more distance between her and her past faster.

"Thank you. I appreciate it. I couldn't afford a bus, so figured I'd hike home for spring break and surprise my family," she lied as she climbed in the back seat.

"No problem. We're glad to help. We remember being homesick and broke at the same time." She smiled.

*****

Jim and Scott decided to play sick. Fishing sounded much better than school. It was around ten o'clock when the call came in to verify they were home, so they could slip out. Reaching their favorite spot under a bridge, they got comfortable and cast their lines. Laughing about how slick they were for getting away was interrupted when the body of a teenage girl came floating up along the shoreline face down. The boys ran to pull her out of the water to save her from drowning. Flipping her over, both boys fell backward, kicking their feet trying to back away, seeing bloody holes where her eyes should have been and her chest torn open.

*****

Jack Marsten sat in the dark at his usual corner in the bar. Knowing everything was on the line, he also knew that's when things went wrong the most. Running his finger around the top of his glass, he contemplated a backup plan. An opportunity like this only comes once in a man's life. He wasn't going to let anything or anyone blow this one chance of achieving his ultimate goal or at least a good portion of it. The money alone would set him up for the rest of his life.

Chapter 20

Ivy and Ky chose to discuss the events over coffee and fries while Wolfe took Charlie back to the park to hunt. After exchanging information from all sides, the decision was made for Riley to take Reese to a federal safe house. The girls could help, as long as they didn't jeopardize the investigation. But the lines drawn with multiple unknown factors were a bit vague where the girls were concerned considering the circumstances.

"I know they aren't telling us everything, and I understand that. You never want to give too much information about an investigation for fear of alerting suspects or causing panic. And, of course, they don't know how much to trust us," Ivy said, dipping her fries in the glob of ranch dressing with ketchup.

"That works both ways. I didn't tell them everything either," replied Ky smugly, giving Ivy a disgusting look. "Wow, that looks like you slaughtered something in the snow or a pile of melted marshmallows or a basket of white rabbits that's been shot and stirred.

Ivy sat back giving Ky an evil look. "Stop changing the subject. Spill it, woman. What are you holding back?"

"Remember when we got there? Charlie went off, and the one guy got all bent out of shape over it?"

"Yeah, what was that all about?"

"Charlie picked up on me. That's one of the guys I saw at Reese's cabin. I'm not going to accuse one of their officers when I don't know who to trust or how deep this goes."

"You little minx, what's your excuse for not telling me?" Ivy asked, in an irritated tone directed at Ky and her smirky grin.

"I forgot. Between meeting Damon and Athena, what happened with Charlie, and me getting slammed back into my body after finding the camera, it slipped my mind. I didn't know who the guy was then anyway. Did you bring your cards?"

"Of course, I did. Why are you changing the subject again?"

"I'm not. I just need a question answered," said Ky, looking all innocent.

Ivy studied Ky's face for a moment. "Cut 'em," she said annoyed, pushing her tarot deck across the table.

*****

Riley would take Reese to a nearby federal safe house with Danny following behind as backup. The consensus among them was to follow what leads they had. Now that the woman in the morgue was identified along with the first male, local police would handle notifying their family members. Chief Tate would handle the press after Riley put together a speech for the media briefing. Riley would also be there to answer any other questions if needed. Monahan, Jameson, and Dr. Coletrain had more digging to do with the man-wolf lying beheaded on the slab. As they rose to go back to the morgue, Detective Jameson's personal cell phone rang. Glancing down at his caller ID, he raised his hand stopping them in their tracks.

"We'll be right there," he said, seconds after answering. "You guys take him and get right back here. We have two more bodies," he stated, looking at Agent Monahan and the doctor.

*****

The small morgue was filling up fast with the body count now at five. The new ones were different yet the same. All the same, parts were missing, but their bodies were covered with odd-looking marks carved into their skin and had identification on them. They were brought in, in secrecy after Chief Tate reached out to his closest allies in law enforcement and bloodline. He also requested them to look into cases that were overlooked, inconclusive, or hadn't been reported as found yet or were on a missing-person list from a few weeks prior.

"Guess we'll see if our new friends are everything they say they are," said Dr. Coletrain. "I'll send pictures of the symbols I don't recognize to Ivy. If she's familiar with them, it will save us time."

"Why the change in the MO? Are we dealing with more than one group of fanatics?" asked Jameson.

"More likely a diversion," said Monahan as he looked closer. "These carvings were done sloppy like they were in a hurry."

"Good observation. I agree. Definitely made with a knife, not a claw, and there doesn't seem to be any particular pattern. Have you found any connection between the victims other than missing organs?"

"No, we haven't. It seems to be random but also ones that won't be missed right away. I'll see what we have on file from their IDs." Monahan went back to the office leaving Jameson in the morgue.

"What should I be doing? I'm kind of at a loss here, Doctor," Jameson said.

"My team will be here shortly. I need you to act like business as usual. In the meantime, I would appreciate your help getting the bodies into containment, so I can finish my autopsy of our wolf-man over." They stood there facing a table of ash and chains. "Get those girls back in here and see if you have their disappearing friend on camera. I want to know how this happened and who got past your guards," Dr. Coletrain said, fuming.

*****

"Well, big guy, why don't you show me where you and Athena left your chew toy?" Wolfe chuckled, hooking a leash to Charlie's harness. Looking him eye to eye, he added, "I'm not Ky, so don't think you can get away from me."

Charlie dropped from the truck and headed into the trees. Going straight to the spot, he sat, barked once, and wagged his tail. Wolfe looked down to find a small pile of ash. Knowing Ivy and Jess as well as he did, he scooped up as much as he could into a small bag for analysis or whatever they might want it for. Halfway back to the truck, Charlie stopped letting out a low growl, and the hair on his back rose. Wolfe took a knee next to him, placing one hand around Charlie's neck, ruffling his fur as he spoke softly, and Wolfe's other hand reached for the knife in his boot.

"Easy, boy, we don't start fights. We finish them. Let them come to us."

A light breeze whipped around them, circling up through swaying branches and leaves, creating its own music. Charlie relaxed just as a crow swooped by and cawed. He sat looking up and let out a long soft, low howl as if to answer back. The breeze calmed slowly to an end. Charlie swiped his tongue across Wolfe's face once and headed for the truck like nothing happened.

"What the hell was that all about? Got your guardian angel there, do ya?" Wolfe said.

Charlie climbed in the back seat and sat, wagging his tail with a smile on his face, waiting for Wolfe.

*****

Ky cut the deck in two, laying each pile side by side.

Ivy picked up the first stack and turned it over in her hand. The bottom card was the ten of swords; she laid the pile face down. Turning up the second pile, she found the tower, a card of chaos and turmoil. Looking at Ky, she said, "Pick one," as her phone rang. Ky reached over turning the top card up in each pile. Ivy hated it when she did that, but it was Ky's way of figuring out which one would tell her what she wanted. With the first card being death and the second, the devil, Ky wanted both piles read. Ivy looked down as she hung up her phone and, in one big swoop, put all the cards into a pile before putting them away.

"We're going back to the station."

"What about the reading?"

"I don't like the way they feel. We'll try again later. I need to call Wolfe. He can meet us there," Ivy stated abruptly.

"So why do they want us back now? Is Reese okay?"

"They didn't say, just that they need our help with something."

"You may not like how the cards felt, but this doesn't feel right to me."

Her phone buzzed with a text with Dr. Coletrain's pictures. Ivy shoved it in her bag without saying a word.

*****

Darryl Ellis was proud of himself until he went down hard from Sanders's fist, hitting his jaw. "You said you wanted it to look like the ritual was moving south," he yelled, grabbing the side of his head. "I thought it would make it more realistic."

"That was your first mistake—thinking. All you had to do was your job. Instead, you get the idea of carving shit on them. Signs you Googled at random? That's not thinking. That's the act of a rebellious snot-rag kid painting graffiti, getting off by playing a catch-me-if-you-can game."

"The signs will make them stop looking for us. It'll create some confusion. They'll be looking in another direction."

"No, it won't. It gives them more clues and brings them closer to hunting us. That doctor they brought in—it's like…she's different. She knows stuff, and those other women? I think they're going to be trouble, especially that damned dog." Sanders turned away, clenching his fist with his anger rising. "Asshole, you're going to get us all killed."

"Well, what do you want me to do then?"

"Die," Sanders said, spinning around. With one swing of his arm, a clawed hand severed Darryl's head. His body crumpled to the ground as his head rolled to Sanders's feet.

"Take this piece of shit way south of town. Make it look like what we did at the lake. Unless you both want to die with him, I suggest you do it right. Understand?" he said, glaring at the two men who came with Darryl.

Both men nodded. Without saying a word, they picked up the two parts of Darryl, threw them in the trunk, and left quickly, fearing their fate would be the same. Sanders climbed in his truck and sat staring out the window, betting Marsten already heard. Marsten always knew somehow. This was strike 2 against his team. With any luck, Marsten would give him a pass for handling it himself. All he could do now was hope he wouldn't meet the same fate as Darryl.

*****

Damon looked around the table as he explained to his team what he learned at the station. They weren't dealing with a couple of rogue wolves; they were dealing with a well-organized renegade pack. Athena sat quietly near the window, watching everything and everyone that moved in the parking lot.

Colt Nickels sat tapping his foot on the floor in anticipation. He joined Damon's group hoping to find the rogue that killed his family and left him for dead. The local alpha of the territory found him turning while hunting the same rogue. Taking him into his pack, Colt was trained in both control and skill once the painful transition was over.

Jeremiah Justice, born a skinwalker and a turned werewolf as well, sat next to Colt. Known as JJ, he had been and still was one of the local alpha's best hunters and executioners in the country before joining Damon's elite party that could hide his identity through other talents he possessed.

Max Boucher sat between Athena and Colt. Max was the oldest in the group. A day-walking vampire whose talent lay in many areas. The most prominent was the power to manipulate anyone's mind into giving up information and truth as well as luring the corrupt into revealing themselves.

Miles Devlin was the most recent member recruited, with a shape-shifting father and a voodoo high priestess for a mother. An exceptional con man whose charm and personality could get them anything or anywhere they needed with little effort.

"We're going to need more information and help. Colt, you and JJ go see what the local pack knows. Make sure they understand their part in this. We need to figure out what this ritual is. Max, you work on that. The university should have a good-sized library. If not, I'm sure Miles's family can help. Miles, I need you to go hunting. Lure a couple of easy marks for tonight. See if you can get in as one of them. Athena, keep an eye on the two girls and their companions. We need them to be an asset, not a liability. I'll work on the hook. You guys just follow my lead. You good with that, Max?" asked Damon.

"I'm not crazy about revealing our identities to so many," said Miles, interrupting. "That's going to compromise us in ways even I can't con us out of."

"We won't have to," claimed JJ. "Our Alpha controls this territory and spent years building a secure coalition with high-ranking leaders for generations. We only have to talk to him."

"We're not after the renegade. They're following someone's lead. The local pack can take care of them. We're after the one who's giving the orders," said Damon.

"I'll need a few things," Max replied, casting a glance at Miles. "Just bring me your new friends. We'll meet back at the hotel."

Everyone nodded and went their ways.

"What about the outsiders, Damon?" Athena asked, still watching out the window. "Us getting involved with law enforcement is one thing, but we know very little about the *others*."

"Sarcasm? Really? I thought you liked the dog."

"He's a handsome boy with a big heart, sensitive to our ways of life, and brave but spoiled and overweight. The girls are just card-carrying, sage-burning, ghostbusters with a bodyguard. They could get killed. You willing to take that chance?"

Damon leaned back in his chair. "I agree when it comes to that guy Reese. The girls and the boyfriend are a different story. Ivy and Wolfe make a good team. Both are skilled in their own ways and have a good head on their shoulders. Ky is the one I haven't figured out."

"Falling for a pretty face, are you?"

"There is a lot more to her than what she lets anyone see."

"Good or bad?"

"That's the mystery. At this point, I'd have to say both. I'm just not sure which is the stronger."

"Just make sure you're thinking clear. Can't afford your lust getting in the way."

"What's that supposed to mean?"

"Only that when it comes to a pretty face, you tend to think with your dick instead of your head," she said, smiling.

*****

Jay and Ed pulled off the highway just north of the Shawnee National Park. It was the perfect place. Close enough to both the Missouri and Kentucky border, the law would have to pursue both as possibilities. The fields were partially plowed, indicating the farmer would find the body sometime later that evening while finishing his work for the day. They found a spot to lay out Darryl's body and proceeded to remove the parts that would either be served at that night's meal or at the full moon grand finale. They started the car as the sound of a tractor firing up could be heard in the distance. Driving slow enough not to kick up dust, they drove back to the highway. Pleased with themselves, not only for being smarter than Darryl ever could be, but also for knowing the power in numbers and their numbers were growing by the day. Tonight was the banquet-like gathering before the celebration feast they had been promised. They would get their final instructions. No more hiding from civilization or being hunted by their own kind. They would be in charge. They would be in control of their own lives and rule over others.

Chapter 21

Jess poured her freshly brewed tea over ice. Steam swirled up, circling like a small cyclone before dissipating, filling the room with its sweet, floral aroma. It was such a beautiful cloudless day with a light breeze she felt her journey should be outside among nature's bounty. The dogs followed her to a glass-top table on the patio. Bordered on one side were flowers creating a rainbow of colors in front of a row of three magnolia trees. A fifteen-foot dog pool lined the opposite side. This was her Zen zone, in between. Specially designed chairs around the table made sitting comfortable and could be reclined enough for relaxing with your feet up. Friends said it was a great way to tan without laying close to the ground with easy access to the table.

The dogs wrestled in the pool, playing tug-of-war, dragging each other through the sun-warmed water. Jess watched, enjoying their frolic, only leaning back as she felt the tea begin to take effect. Taking a breath deep into her lungs, she slowly let it out. Calming her mind and body, Jess focused on one word—*enlighten*. A small gust of air enriched with floral fragrances swept over her, filling her with a sense of empowerment. Feeling surrounded by protection in a golden orb, she spoke.

"Show me what I've come to learn. Remove the veil of lives concerned. So I may see what is unknown. That I may bring my loved ones home."

*****

Ky and Ivy got out of the car to find Wolfe already there waiting with Charlie sitting at his feet. Without a word, they headed for the station's rear entrance, finding Jameson holding the door open.

"I saw you from the window in my office. Dr. Coletrain needs to see you in the morgue right away," he explained.

The morgue was filled with three men and three women dressed in white coats. Two were on computers, two more were picking apart portions of a body, one stood over a microscope, and the other was filling a vial with something blue from an eyedropper. Dr. Coletrain stood over another body across the room taking pictures.

"Charlie can't come in," said Ivy, turning to find Wolfe and Jameson already entering his office with Charlie leading the way. "I forget how smart that dog is sometimes."

Ky winked at Charlie when he turned to her before entering the morgue. She noticed the marks carved into the man lying in front of Dr. Coletrain immediately. Crossing the room quickly, she bent down for a closer look to study a particular cluster of sigils down one leg.

"As you can see, we have a new development," stated Dr. Coletrain.

"Sliced with a knife unlike a werewolf's puncture and tear," Ivy observed.

"You recognize a knife wound. Impressive. Do you recognize the markings?"

"Some of them," Ivy replied as she studied the symbols. "Not all of them. Some are slightly off in design, like they weren't sure or the knife slipped."

"I do," stated Ky.

Both women looked at her, curiously surprised.

*****

Monahan was staring at his laptop when the others walked in having found nothing to connect the victims. Cameras around the station were interrupted with white noise at the time that Damon disappeared. With no last name, there was no way to determine how he played into this bizarre case, let alone how he left unseen. Leaning back, he looked at Jameson already behind the desk, then turned to Wolfe sitting in front.

"What do you know about this Damon?"

"He just showed up out of nowhere and saved this dog's life. Past that, you have to talk to the women." Wolfe shrugged.

"How about you tell us about these girls? What exactly do they do?" asked Jameson.

"Careful using that word around them. They may look like girls, but they are all woman. Strong-willed, skilled in ways I've never seen, and not the kind to flaunt what they know or do. You don't ever want to get on their bad side."

"How do you fit into all this?"

"Love, my man. Love brought me, and she accepted me. I've seen what they are capable of. I'm here to back my woman and keep her safe. Just like ole' Charlie here. When the two of them get focused on something, they don't always see what's coming from behind. But you'll never get them to admit that. So when they do their thing, we just make sure no one else gets froggy," Wolfe snickered as he scratched behind Charlie's ear.

Charlie stood and approached the window. Jumping up, he placed his paws on the sill and let out a short bark getting all three men's attention. Just outside a crow, sitting on a medium-sized bush, let out a caw as if answering him. When a second caw came, Charlie followed with a soft howl. Charlie returned to Wolfe's side when the crow flew away. Placing a paw on his thigh, he gazed at Wolfe with pleading eyes. He knew Charlie wanted something but wasn't sure what.

"What the hell was that?" Jameson spouted.

"Let me guess," Monahan said, looking at the dog. "You know something, we don't."

Charlie cocked his head toward Monahan, let out a short high-pitched bark, and wagged his tail as if he was answering him.

"You catch on quick," said Wolfe.

Jameson sat back in his chair speechless and confused, rubbing his temples from the headache that was forming.

*****

Jess felt herself drifting on the waves of a soft wind through cloudlike puffs of white and gray. As her vision became clear, black tail feathers of a large bird ahead led her through the thinning vapor. Appearing in full form was the biggest crow she had ever seen. The fog cleared into the darkness of a starless night. They were gliding over the treetops. Reaching the forest edge, they circled a group of three men crossing a large meadow surrounded by hills of tall trees and brush to perch on a high branch. Off to her left, crashing sounds of a stampede caught her attention.

The three men stopped. Turning toward the forbidding vibration, shaking the ground beneath them, they stood closer together in fear. A countless pack of wolves came thundering out of the forest, led by a massive black dog. Sparks rose from their paws as they charged down the hill toward them. One man took a deep breath, imagining what they would do to them. He closed his eyes accepting what was inevitable. An army of glowing eyes like golden globes of fire in the night could be seen approaching fast and furious. Reaching the group of men, the pack split in two. Flowing around the frightened men, rejoining again behind them, running into the trees on the other side. Curses, screams, and snapping teeth pierced the air as hidden adversaries were being ripped apart. The furry mass became a frenzy of fury, wildly enraged with chaos for what seemed like an eternity. A shroud of silence fell covering the horrific blanket of blood, bodies, and fur strewn across the floor of the woods.

Jess quickly sat straight up in her chair back in the peaceful surroundings of her home. All three dogs sat side by side in front of her watching silently while she panted her way out of a panic attack.

Fuck was the only word that came from her as she reached for her phone. She had to call and warn Ivy. Ivy would be able to interpret and rationalize the vision better than anyone. She knew Ky would see violence and go badass protector with no restraints without hesitation.

*****

Sanders sat trying desperately to hide his nervous fidgeting while Marsten answered the bar phone sitting next to him. A gruff, distorted male voice on the other end spoke loud enough to be heard by both men.

"Tell me you have your mess cleaned up efficiently, Marsten, or I withdraw my offer."

"Keep in mind who you are talking to. Without me, you're nothing. We have a bigger problem."

"I already know about the FBI."

"And the new party crashers?"

"Who?"

"Two women, a man, and a dog."

"And what, the great Marsten is afraid of females and an ordinary man with a dog? Sounds like you're getting weak."

"They're gifted, at least the women are. More up your alley than mine."

"They're merely women. Even self-proclaimed witches can be beaten. I say make them part of our ceremony. Tell your men they will only strengthen our cause and add a little spice to our taste of power."

"Your arrogance will be your downfall," Marsten said, handing the phone back to the bartender. "You heard what he said. Don't screw it up, or your men will be my men's final meal."

Sanders left without looking back. He needed a plan and quick. Sitting in his truck for a moment, he dialed his phone.

"Gather the men. Meet me at the hole, eight o'clock tonight. I want all of them there."

Sanders drove down the highway devising a strategy he hoped would solve all his problems, including Marsten.

Chapter 22

Charlie stood facing the door, wagging his tail. Detective Jameson, still bewildered, looked from the dog to the door along with Special Agent Monahan.

"Now what?" spouted Jameson.

"Momma's coming," Wolfe replied casually.

Less than a minute later, the door swung open. Dr. Coletrain stormed into the office with Ivy and Ky followed by Riley and Danny. The office was filled with tension as they all gathered seating themselves around the desk, except Ky, who stood at the door with Charlie. All the men stayed quiet, watching as they anticipated a cat-fight was about to begin judging from the women's attitudes.

Ivy took a deep breath to bring her agitation under control. "We're all here. Now talk, woman!" she spouted at Ky.

"Yes, please enlighten us as to why you won't tell us about those symbols, and why you destroyed them and the pictures I took," said Dr. Coletrain bitterly. "They were important documents for my reports."

"Be thankful the symbols were carved at random. They're from a dead language, older than time itself, and forbidden. Not of this world. Put together correctly would be worse than anything coming out of Pandora's box. It gives the one wielding them the power to annihilate not only mankind but heaven or hell, even the entire planet, and rebuild everything to their liking. It was alleged that it's the foundation of the universe as we know it," Ky said as if she were lecturing a history class.

As the room went silent, they all watched Ky who appeared lost in thought petting Charlie. A knock on the door made everyone jump, except Ky. Chief Tate entered, closing the door behind him with a grim look on his face.

"Calls have been coming in from all over the state. Numerous bodies have been found. They are keeping it quiet but need answers."

"Tell them the FBI is after a black-market ring selling organs and are about close in," Ky said to everyone's surprise.

"That's very good. We can establish a solid theory using current cases," Riley nodded, acknowledging Ky. "I'll work on a statement to buy them and us time. Which brings us back to how, with no more information than we have are we going to catch these guys?" Riley turned to Monahan. "Is it possible that we're chasing our tails with the ritual idea? We've done a lot of assuming that it's all about magic. What if we're wrong, and it is just a black market for organs?"

"No, though I wish it was," Monahan answered. "Not with the wolf element playing such a big part. They've gone through all the trouble to send us on this path for a reason, and it's not money. There's something about this case that, other than the bizarre realm some of us knew nothing about, doesn't add up. We have more questions than answers."

"Ritual-style murders, missing body parts, randomly carved symbols, werewolves—what more evidence do you need to show you this is a satanic group?" Dr. Coletrain popped off.

"I realize that's your expertise, Doctor. But from a logical and legal point of view, it's still a theoretical speculation. We need to eliminate all other possibilities to find the truth."

The chief nodded. "I thank you, Ms. Lang. I'll leave this to all of you. I have what I need. And with Agent Riley's help, we should be able to stay ahead of the many rumors. Please keep me posted. I'll report to you with any other information I get. Agent Monahan… Jameson," he said with a nod.

"Back to the sigils. It's got to mean something," said Dr. Coletrain.

"Right now, it means I have a fool playing with fire," Ky said, looking the doctor in the eye.

Monahan directed his attention to Ivy, who—he assumed—was the lead spokesman. "We need to figure out who this guy Damon is and what his involvement is. What's his intentions? Can you get a hold of him? He's a ghost as far as I can tell since we don't even have a last name or know if that's his real name. I can't even find him in the facial recognition database. Can you contact him? I want him brought in for questioning."

Ivy turned to Ky. "Good question. Can you?"

"No, but I think I know who can," she replied, looking down at Charlie. Ky went down on her knees, eye to eye with Charlie. "Baby, can you call Athena?"

Charlie barked once and went for the door.

Jameson's mouth dropped. Monahan stifled a laugh. Dr. Coletrain pressed her fingers to the bridge of her nose. Wolfe reached for Ivy's hand with a and-the-show-begins look glittering in his eyes. Ivy just shook her head looking down to hide her amusement.

"Wait a minute. What?" Danny said, confused.

"I have got to see this," Riley snickered, trying not to laugh watching this little woman have a conversation with a dog bigger than she was.

Ky stood with a no-big-deal expression. "We'll be right back, and from the look on your faces, to answer your question, no, I'm not kidding. Stay here. This won't take long, but I don't know how soon we'll hear back. I'm not a miracle worker."

Ivy and Wolfe sat in silent amusement as the others gathered around the open windows behind Jameson's desk when Ky and Charlie appeared near the parking lot. They watched Ky bend over and say something to Charlie who turned his head to the sky and barked three times. Within seconds, they could hear dogs barking in the distance, coming from all directions. He proceeded to bark two more times. Receiving the same response, he let out a long howl, changing its pitch as if he were trying to talk. Two howls could be heard from the north, one being further away than the other. Satisfied with himself, Charlie headed back to the station. When they returned, to the office, everyone was sitting in their chairs trying to look normal, except Jameson. He sat shaking his head.

"I'm never going to get used to this," he said aloud.

"Show off," Ivy said in a low voice, turning to her friend with a smile. "Can we go now?" she asked Jameson. "There's not a lot we can do from here, and it's going to be a while before we hear from the dog line."

"We all need a break and something to eat. We'll be in touch," Monahan said, motioning for the girls to leave.

Dr. Coletrain stiffened in her chair with anger; she wanted answers. Turning his laptop toward her and remaining quiet, he watched the others leave. On the screen was a file labeled "Arbitra" with Ky's picture and the words *proceed with extreme caution*.

"I ran the girls through our database. Both came back with clean records. Not even a traffic ticket. Ivy has some background in law enforcement, which explains a lot. Ky is a freelance photographer and trained in the martial arts. With help from facial recognition and a friend who hooked me to the dark web, we found this. I thought it might clear up a few things. Instead, it raised more questions."

*****

Athena roamed through the forest in wolf form, trying to pick up a scent around the first crime scene. When she heard howling in the distance. With each one getting closer, she replied with a long-drawn-out howl before taking off on a dead run. A gunshot blasted through the peaceful terrain. Athena felt the sharp pain of a bullet piercing her hind leg. Stumbling only for a second, she continued to run harder low to the ground as she began zigzagging between trees and brush. Two more shots rang out, barely missing her, hitting the trees before disappearing in the denser part of the woods.

"Damn it. I know at least one hit," yelled the man armed with a rifle.

"Yeah, but now we can track it and let JD know we ain't after no bear," said the other.

"How we gonna track it? That's a big damned park."

"Dogs, dumb ass. JD's dogs. It's hurt and bleeding."

"Sheriff's not going to let us hunt on state ground."

"Who said they need to know? We're just enjoying a day in the park, and the dogs were attacked. We saved the dogs."

"Walking through the park with guns?"

"No. We were still next to the truck when it happened. Now let's go before the trail gets too cold, and we lose the scent."

*****

Athena lay across the table of Damon's hotel room on her side in human form. "Sorry, didn't see this coming," she said, embarrassed.

"Be glad you got away, and it's not any worse than it is. JJ's on his way with everything he needs to get it out and patch you up. You'll be fine. This could be a good thing, depending on the ones involved and what they do next."

"Ha ha! What did you do? Go sniffin' around where you don't belong? My aim would have been better." JJ laughed, walking in. Setting his medical bag down, he began to clean and examine the wound. "You'll be sore for a day, maybe two. It's not that deep and in the fat, not muscle. This won't take long."

"It's not fat. You're just jealous of my muscle. Now get the lead out, Cowboy, before I show you how to hogtie an asshole."

"I'll update the others and see where we're at. Let me know when you're ready to go see your new boyfriend," Damon said, leaving the room.

"I'm leery about this," Athena called out.

"So am I. That's why I'm making sure we're ready for anything."

"Ow!" Athena yelled, glaring at JJ pouring vodka into the bullet hole grinning from ear to ear. "You're liking this way too much."

*****

Riley sat in his car waiting for Danny when his phone notified him of a text:

> Agent Riley, this is Professor Delaney. I have
> information that might be of interest. Meet me
> at my office at six tonight. Please come alone. I
> don't want to deal with your partner's ego.

Chapter 23

Jess sat fidgeting in her chair. It had been an hour since her call to Ivy went straight to voicemail. She didn't know what her vision meant, only how it felt—violent, bloody, horrific. Ivy would know the meaning better than Ky. Jess had the gift of seeing warning signs. Ivy had a knack for pinpointing interpretations down. Ky, always ready to go headfirst into the fight, could see the gray between light and dark. That's where it was most dangerous for her, where she was vulnerable and could go either way. Yes, Ky had a dark side, a side with no remorse.

Jess thought back to a moment in time when the three of them were having a coffee day. A man came to the table, troubled over the death of a friend. His friend was murdered leaving behind a wife and two young kids that he hadn't seen since the funeral. Passing Ivy a photo of his friend and family, she held it in both hands to get a reading of what she felt. The man wasn't the target. His wife was, and the kids were in danger. The man turned pale as he explained the kids witnessed their father's death and haven't spoken a word since. Rumors were the woman had gotten involved with a gang known for pushing drugs. Ky grew agitated the longer Ivy and the man talked. In the end, no one had a real solution or solid evidence. They moved outside getting ready to leave when Ky spoke up.

"Do you know where the kids are now?" she asked.

"Not for sure. She took off with them to hide. I heard a lot of people are looking for her."

"Do you know which gang is involved?"

"Sorry, I don't."

"I'll find them myself," she said, turning to get in her car.

"Ky!" Jess and Ivy yelled together seeing Ky's eyes change to a red dot surrounded by pitch-black.

Jess apologized to the group for Ky's behavior, telling everyone to stay safe at home over the weekend. Dark threatening clouds began replacing a clear blue sky. As Ky got in her car, a downburst of rain poured hard with a thundering lightning bolt. She watched Ivy quickly climb into the passenger seat trying to talk to Ky. A moment later, the rain stopped as fast as it came, and the skies began to clear slowly.

Three days later, the news reported thirteen known gang members were killed in what authorities were saying appeared to be a drug-related gang war. No witnesses, and no solid suspects.

Jess jumped, startled by the sound of her phone; it was Ivy. "It's about damned time!" she answered and began relaying her vision.

*****

Sanders descended the basement stairs where a dozen of his men were waiting. Placing himself at the head of the table, he viewed a mixed bag of emotions throughout the room. Word of Darryl's plight traveled fast. Some hung their heads with the loss of a comrade. Others in fear they could be next. A few were glad the idiot was out of the way.

"Because of Darryl's stunt, we have to divide to conquer. We'll separate the men from the women. Lure each into a trap. This time, we take the parts we want and make it look like two different attacks. The men need to look like a large animal attacked. Make the one woman look like a gang trying to copycat to cover a rape and murder. No one lives except the one with the dog. We want her for the final sacrifice. Got it?"

"Yeah, the cops go after gangs, and the park rangers, with the help of townspeople, will go on a hunt," said Hanson, leading the second pack. "My guys will take the woman. They deserve some fun. Besides, Cooper's men look mighty hungry. You got an idea on how to get them separated and where we want them?"

"Actually, I have. To get the one woman," Sanders said, pointing at Hanson, "grab the dog. Make her come to us."

*****

Riley arrived at Delaney's office a few minutes early. Sitting in a chair in front of the desk, he gazed around the room. It seemed typical for a professor, with shelves filled with books, and walls covered in plaques and degrees. In a corner, tucked away, was a coat rack. A raincoat hanging on the rack seemed odd. The weather had been sunny with clear skies for a couple of weeks. It also appeared to be bulkier than it should. Riley walked over to take a closer look. Something red hung hidden beneath. He lifted part of the coat enough to see a gold symbol when he heard Delaney's voice in the hall. Quickly returning to his chair, before the professor opened the door, he drew the symbol in his notebook.

"Agent Riley, glad you made it. I'm limited on time, so I'll get straight to the point. I've overheard a rumor of great concern." Delaney seemed nervous as he placed his briefcase on the desk. Lowering his voice, he leaned toward Riley. "I felt we should speak in person for a number of reasons. One for confidentiality," he said, looking over his shoulder at the door. "Though I can't confirm, I felt you should know. There seems to be a group trying to revive an old traditional blood hazing, one that was banned many years ago. Some sort of secret-society crap similar to satanical rituals, if you get my drift. Rumor has it they're meeting tomorrow night, somewhere on the far end of the lake. I'd have to say it's a prelude to something bigger with us so close to the full moon. That's the usual pattern with most fanatics. This generation of students may be tech-savvy but want instant gratification. They don't take the time to think things out. You should have no problem catching them. I would think. Now if you don't mind letting yourself out, I have papers to grade before meeting with the dean."

Delaney went to work, spreading papers across his desk. Riley, abruptly being dismissed, thanked him for his time and left the room. Closing the door behind him, he stood in the hall for a moment baffled over the change in Delaney's behavior. He was glad he came, or he never would have seen the cloak under the raincoat with a symbol that might be a clue. The entire event seemed oddly suspicious.

"Maybe Monahan will see something I missed," he said to himself getting in his car.

*****

Wolfe came out of the shower to see Ivy sitting on the bed, naked, with her laptop open. Putting his arm around her waist, he sat behind her. With his chin on her shoulder, he glanced at the screen and nibbled at her ear. Ivy tilted her face toward him for a kiss.

"We've got a little time you know," Wolfe whispered. "I'm betting Ky's curled up on the bed with her arms wrapped around Charlie, and her face buried in his fur sound asleep. Sounds like a great place to be, but I'm not tired yet. What about you?"

Ivy closed her laptop, smiling. "Neither am I."

Holding her against his chest, Wolfe laid on his back, taking her with him, holding tight as she rolled over to face him. She needed him as much as he needed her. The rest of the world could wait.

*****

Ky handed Charlie the last few cold fries left from the night before. Patting him on the head, she reached for her phone to call Ivy. Charlie ran to the door, tail wagging before a knock could be heard, and began bouncing on his front paws with excitement.

"Let me guess. It's not Ivy. It's your new girlfriend," she said. Pushing him out of the way, she opened the door. "Hello, Damon, Athena. Come on in."

"We heard you were looking for us," Athena said, carefully plopping down on the floor to pet Charlie.

"Your disappearing act got a lot of attention. There's new evidence, and they want to talk to you, Damon." Ky pulled her feet up, crossing her legs as she sat on the bed.

"How much trouble am I in?

"That depends on how helpful you turn out to be. Ever see symbols like this?" Ky handed him a pad of paper where she had drawn a few of the symbols from memory.

Damon studied the drawings, running his finger over each of them. "Yes, I don't know what they mean, but I've seen some like them before. It was part of a forbidden language, but these feel older than anything I'm familiar with. What do you know? How did you come by these?" he asked suspiciously.

Ky sat in silence for a moment studying Damon. Coal-black hair pulled back, neatly tied with a black leather strap, hung down the middle of his back. His golden-brown complexion and framed eyes looked like pools of melted chocolate. "Eyes are the doorway to one's soul" her grandmother would say, and his were deep in luring mystery. Ky wasn't sure if she could trust him or herself for that matter.

"You can find out for yourself. You're wanted at the station for questioning."

"I'm tied up tonight with other obligations, but I'm available around noon tomorrow. Will that do?"

"I'll let them know."

"You don't trust me?"

"I guess. We'll see." *Actions speak louder than words*, she thought.

"I'll make sure he's there," Athena said with assurance, giving Charlie a hug. "Right now, we have to go."

*****

Monahan clicked on one of the many files listed. Multiple pictures popped up of known or suspected drug lords, arms dealers, and human traffickers. Each with a woman resembling Ky close by in the background. Below every picture were times and locations over the span of a week. The FBI were still searching for the suspects even though they had fallen off the grid within a few years past. One picture partially showed the woman's face. Not enough to identify but enough for facial recognition to pick up as a possibility. Other photos were of ransacked rooms showing signs of a struggle. The multitude of pages ended with the subject as missing persons or presumed dead with no new leads.

Unsure of what to think, Monahan opened another file, then another, and another. Each had the same information. The same woman nearby and all reporting the subject was missing, presumed dead, or, in very few cases, the cause of death unknown. Subjects were both men and women, ranging from high-ranking officials worldwide and crime lords to local individuals with police records or suspects in ongoing investigations, all associated with violent crimes.

"I don't understand what this has to do with Ky, other than the similarity," said Dr. Coletrain. "It looks more like a military covert operation."

Monahan opened a file labeled with Ky's name. It began with a basic bio—freelance photographer, general information, and pictures of her in locations and timelines that matched each of the previous files.

"Well, whoever put this together thinks they're the same woman? There are too many files for this to be a coincidence," replied Monahan.

"The file says nothing about skills other than photography and martial arts. The only thing we have is the statements of how dangerous she is from her friends. We can't prove anything."

"Under the circumstances, do we want to?"

Dr. Coletrain looked at Agent Monahan, wondering the same thing.

"Do you know the source of where this all came from?"

"Each entry has a different IP address that's untraceable, which indicates an underground network. With all the files being people associated with criminal activity and the only reference to Ky as a photographer, I'd say they don't know either. After meeting her, I'm guessing it's more in line with your other realm. Wouldn't you?"

"I have to agree. I don't see any other possibility."

At the bottom of the list, Monahan noticed a file labeled *Secured* and clicked to open it. Suddenly the monitor went blank with the words *Unauthorized connection terminated* across the screen.

Chapter 24

Katrina Jones, simply known as Kat, pulled up to the side door of Redemptions at nine in the morning like she did every day. No one knew much about her, only that she showed up the day her grandfather died and inherited the bar. Sitting in her car finishing her cigarette, she looked around the tree line that surrounded the property. Something didn't feel right. It wasn't fear as much as an uneasiness of being watched. Taking the keys out of the ignition, she spread each one between her fingers making them a weapon. It was always better to be a bit cautious than reckless.

Kat was a robust black woman that nobody messed with. She could go from being everyone's mom to a venomous snake faster than flipping a light switch. Regular patrons all knew she kept a bat and a shotgun behind the bar and was not afraid to use them. Taking one more look around, she recognized a man coming from around the trees.

"She's here," he stated.

"I had a feeling, but this soon can't be good. You've seen her?"

"Yes."

"She knows?"

"No. Something else brought her here."

"And the other?"

"Still safe, for now."

"Keep an eye on both and me posted."

"Of course."

"Stay safe," Kat called out as he turned to leave.

"You as well," he replied without looking back.

*****

Detective Jameson's office was filled to capacity. Both FBI agents and Dr. Samantha Coletrain stood around the desk with Danny. Ivy, Ky, Wolfe, and Damon stood at the front, even Chief Tate joined the discussion. Ky grew impatient. The loss of innocent lives and body count in general was getting too high. Damon didn't lie when questioned but was obviously keeping something to himself. The only new information came from Riley based on speculation.

"Do you have a holding cell for more than one person?" Ky spoke up over everyone.

"Yes," replied Jameson.

"Is it empty?"

"At the moment? Yes, why?"

"I need room to set up."

Everyone turned to Dr. Coletrain for advice, who nodded her approval. Detective Jameson looked at Special Agents Monahan and Riley, shrugged their shoulders, and then led the group down the hall to the jail. Opening the largest cell, he stepped back. Ky entered, turning toward Jameson, she placed her hand on his chest nudging him away as she closed the door behind her. Ivy stepped forward and began to pour a heavy line of salt along the barred entrance before handing it to Ky. Ky poured a line across the only window before handing it back.

Placing her bag on the floor, Ky began making a large circle with chalk. Ivy and the doctor moved closer to watch. Riley, completely engrossed, stood to one side to get a full view. Danny took the other side. Agent Riley's research had created a deep curiosity in him. Danny was thrilled to be able to witness some truth to all the stories he'd grown up with. Monahan and Jameson stood back looking at each other with a this-ought-to-be-good grin on their face. Still struggling with wrapping their heads around werewolves and ghosts in this world, to them, all this magic business was pushing it.

As Ky drew sigils inside the circle, everyone could hear her mumbling. No one could make out what she was saying, only that it sounded like she was singing softly. Ivy took Wolfe's hand, locking their fingers together. Dr. Coletrain placed one hand around the necklace she was wearing. Behind her, Damon looked on with concern, knowing exactly what Ky was about to do and how dangerous it was. Ivy, Jameson, and Monahan's heart skipped a beat as the lock-down door at the end of the corridor opened. Wolfe didn't budge, not surprised; he was used to all kinds of strange things the girls were known for and heard someone coming.

Chief Tate entered with smudges of black and white on his face looking like a warrior or shaman; they weren't sure which. Chief Tate gave a quick nod of acknowledgment to the group taking his place at the door with his arms crossed over his chest. Remaining speechless, they turned their attention back to Ky.

From her bag, Ky pulled four colored candles, squared inside the circle, she walked counterclockwise, lighting them as she went. The first was white, then a blue one, followed by red, and the last one, black. Sitting down next to her bag, she pulled a stone bowl and three small jars and laid them in front of her. Mumbling something in rhythm, she placed a pinch of herbs from each jar in the bowl. Ky took a knife from her boot, slicing the palm of her hand over the bowl. Blood dripped over the contents while she stirred the mixture with the tip of the blade.

The candle flames shot to the ceiling making everyone jump back a step. Each burned in the color it represented before coming down. Chief Tate began mumbling a song in his tribal language in a repetitive pattern. Dr. Coletrain went to the floor sitting on her calves, placing one hand on the floor with the other still clinging to her necklace. Ivy's fingers entwined around Wolfe's tight. Both had confidence in Ky's knowledge and abilities but had never witnessed something like this and always feared for her life over the risks she was known to take. Ivy went stiff; her eyes became glazed over. Wolfe pulled her close to his chest, bringing her out of the trancelike state. The look in her eyes said they would discuss that later.

"What's she doing?" Jameson whispered to Monahan.

"She's making a ritual circle," Riley replied.

"So now we're going to summon a ghost?"

"No," Damon stated in a whisper. "Judging from those symbols, I'd say it's a demon."

Jameson, Monahan, and Riley's eyes widened while Damon and Wolfe stared ahead, not taking their eyes off Ky or the circle. Ky closed her eyes, still chanting, turning the palms of her hands up before looking to the center of the sigils. Her brown eyes became a shimmering silvery black as if they were marble orbs of hematite. A small whirlwind of dust came out of nowhere in the middle. Sparks in each of the colors grew taking the form of a large four-legged beast. Covered in a mix of black-and-red spiked scales, with eyes that looked like two small bonfires, the creature stood taller than Ky. Even its ears were long, jagged, and spiked. Sharp fangs hung out of its wrinkled snout, snarling and drooling. Deadly claws, long, razor-sharp, and curled like a sickle sparked against the concrete floor.

It lunged toward the bars of the cell, jaws snapping viciously. Bouncing off an unseen barrier, knocking it back to the center, startled everyone back in a gasp of disbelief and shock. Ky stood raising her hand as the creature turned rushing in her direction, only to be stopped again by the invisible wall within the circle.

"Enough!" Ky said in a stern but low voice.

Stepping to one side, its head shifted back and forth. Gazing first at Ky, then the others, and back again. Spikes down its back rose like the hair on a dog ready to attack, glowing a fiery orange and red. Wolfe tightened his grip in fear not knowing how far Ky's confidence was willing to go as Ivy stepped toward the cell.

"Settle down. Remember who I am," Ky stated in a loving voice to the creature. Looking him eye to eye, she reached out her hand, and he lowered his head. As the beast sat at her feet, Ky began petting it, whispering something. Not taking her eyes off his, Ky spoke. "The one you seek uses cunning charm to get others to do their bidding. They gain strength not from the killing but from the lies they are fed. Their souls are turned to do evil, appeasing an appetite of deception."

Ky laid both hands on the sides of the hellhound's head with affection. Closing her eyes and placing her forehead to his, she whispered again. Raising one paw, he gave her what appeared to be a bow. Lifting his head, she kissed his nose. Releasing her hands, the hellhound looked at Ky and, in shimmering sparks of tiny stars, disappeared.

Ky stood, with her palms up to the ceiling while chanting something in a whispered undertone. A slight crisp breeze could be felt throughout the room, blowing the candles out. The sigils melted into pools of liquid and absorbed into the floor like they were never there. All the salt lines flashed in a curtain of fire turning to ashen dust within seconds.

Ivy let out a sigh of relief as Wolfe kissed the top of her head. Chief Tate stopped chanting, nodding to Ky before joining his men who stood paralyzed in silent shock.

"A demonic hellhound. Really?" Ivy went off. "I'll never understand how you can do something like this and not believe in God."

"Hold on. If you don't believe in God, how do you justify what you just did?" asked Dr. Coletrain.

"Hermetic law philosophy. I don't have to believe in what you think to be true in order to understand how to get results. Be it magic, religion, or just science, they all have common denominators. Everything has its opposite to maintain balance. For every action, there is a reaction. Kind of like old math versus new math. Both are correct in their own right, whether the answers are different or not. A mind can manifest anything into truth if belief is strong enough. That's the power behind prayer, spells, or scientific theory. One plus one is two. But if you combine one and one, you get a third result. Thus, multiple realities become possible. I have an understanding that's hard to explain. To me, it's all pieces of a puzzle connected to a bigger universal picture of what is unknown," Ky stated like giving a lecture.

"Exchange academic debate later. What does the message mean? We need a lead. Time is not on our side," demanded Monahan.

"Whoever is behind this is not a werewolf. They're human," said Ky.

Dr. Coletrain left the room contemplating everything she witnessed, her mind filled with questions for the women and their companions. Monahan, Jameson, and Chief Tate spoke for a moment longer before Jameson and Tate left the room.

Monahan turned to the rest. "Show's over. Ladies, Gentlemen, thank you for your help. We'll take it from here."

*****

Ivy and Ky exchanged glances, both feeling insulted, being dismissed as they were led out the back door. No one spoke till they got to their cars.

"What the hell?" said Ky, looking around the parking lot.

"Don't worry. They will be calling us soon enough," replied Ivy.

"Not what I'm talking about. Where's Athena and Charlie? She better not be off feeding him junk food. He has issues with certain foods that give him gas that I classify as radioactive."

"Says the woman who spoils the shit out of him."

"Yeah, but I know what he can have. He can clear a civic auditorium when he has gas."

"We know." Wolfe laughed.

"She's not," Damon said in a low voice as he spotted blood splattered on the ground.

*****

Jameson entered his office carrying a large framed map of the park that he set up on the windowsill. Grabbing a dry marker from his desk, he made four circles.

"We can divide the area to watch for anything that looks like a group gathering. Each of us taking a position, covering all sides," Jameson explained. "Danny and I know the park well, so we'll take opposite corners. The chief has provided us with the ammo we need. It won't kill them, but it will slow them down."

"I wanted to go back to the university. I have more questions for Delaney," said Riley.

"Judging from what you've said, you would be better off following him instead. Is there anyone else you can trust to cover his corner?" Monahan asked, turning to Jameson.

"What about the chief's friend, Night Wing?" Riley asked. "He'd be better following Delaney than I would. He won't be recognized and can get closer than I can."

"Good point. Danny, go arrange it with the chief. We'll meet back here before sunset to coordinate any last-minute details," said Jameson.

"Excuse me, Gentlemen! Now that you all have your testosterone pooled in your balls, may I say something?" Dr. Coletrain stated in a raised voice, surprising the men. "Why have you dismissed the others so blatantly?"

"This is the only lead we have," Monahan replied. "We need results, not theatrics."

"You don't even know what you're up against."

"A pack of wolves and a leader that's not. What more is there?"

"You are assuming she's right about the leader being human. What if he's a demon or some other entity? How prepared are you for that?"

"You're our expert in that field. I'm not going to be responsible for getting untrained innocent people killed," Monahan said with a stern voice. "My concern is stopping more murders any way we can since none of this magic, supernatural stuff—I can't exactly put in jail."

"Then I guess you won't mind me getting the others involved," she shot back angrily. "I'm an expert pathologist, not a witch and not trained in fighting *in any form*! I deal with the dead, not the living. I would have thought you of all people could see you need them a lot more than they need you." Dr. Coletrain left, slamming the door behind her before Monahan could react.

Chapter 25

Dr. Samantha Coletrain returned to the morgue disgusted by the current situation. She knew her worth and had no tolerance for being used, then tossed back into a toolbox until she was needed again. Her entire life was spent searching for truth through science. Knowing, sometimes, ignorance succumbing to its own demise was inevitable, it was best to walk away. Having dished out her orders, the team packed up all the evidence they gathered. Everyone would head home except for Lee Akura. He would stay behind with her to tie up any loose ends. Lee was an exchange student and son of the doctor's most admired author of mythology, working his internship under her guidance. The team packed up knowing Dr. Coletrain had something up her sleeve. They worked with her long enough to know to get out of the line of fire if things went sideways. Each experienced such aftermath at some point. Now it was Lee's turn to watch and learn how to deal with arrogant bureaucracy and its consequences.

*****

"That was a bit harsh. I've never seen you dismiss anyone like that. What's going on?" Riley asked Monahan after the doctor left.

"We're after a dangerous group of men. This is not the time or the place for carnival sideshows. When Danny gets here, we'll coordinate tonight's stakeout," said Monahan in a cold, calculating voice.

Jameson sat quietly looking at the map while Monahan watched the girls in the parking lot. Riley began putting the pieces together feeling they were keeping something from him. For whatever reason, he knew not to ask yet. Right now, the girls and their friends had the full attention of Monahan, and it appeared something was going on.

All three men were drawn to the window when the sky mysteriously darkened.

*****

Ivy looked up at a beautiful, clear sky that suddenly grew darker from storm clouds forming directly over them spreading fast. Immediately she turned to see Ky pacing with shaking hands, trying to access the GPS on her phone. Ivy witnessed this behavior once before when a gang targeted a mother and her children of a rival gang as a warning. The weekend following that incident resulted in many gang members dying. Ky had zero tolerance for harming children or animals. Actions of that sort brought out the evil in her. Becoming the viciously bitch side of karma from hell came easy. Last time she was angry defending a family, this time it was personal. If Charlie was hurt, it would be a tortured, painful death sentence for all those involved.

"Take a breath, Ky, breathe." Turning to Wolfe, she said, "Keep her here."

Ivy bent down to pick up two small blood-splattered stones before running back to the morgue. Wolfe approached Ky slowly with one hand reaching out to her. In a low, soothing voice, he repeated Ivy's words.

"Breathe, little one. You have to breathe." Wolfe wasn't sure if Ky didn't hear him or was just ignoring him, so he tried again with a more direct approach. "Ky, if you act too soon, you're going to hurt Charlie too," he said more sternly. "You know that's not what you want. Take a breath, take a deep breath, and think of the consequences."

The flicker in her eyes burned a fierce intense flame. Wolfe laid his hand on her arm in the hope of getting her into a bear hug. When Ky looked up from her phone, Wolfe moved quickly wrapping his arms around her as a bolt of lightning shot across the sky.

Damon stood mesmerized by Ky. Her eyes were as black as obsidian with a flicker of red fire in the center. He could feel an intense sinister anger radiating from her thick black fog-like aura.

*****

Ivy burst through the doors of the morgue, startling everyone in the room. "Dr. Coletrain!" she yelled. "I need you to tell me if this blood is human or animal fast. Please!"

The doctor could see the panic in Ivy's eyes. Without hesitation, she grabbed the rocks throwing one to Lee and keeping one. Each went to work scraping what they could onto glass slides and into vials for analysis.

"Talk to me, Ivy. What's this about?" asked Dr. Coletrain as she began to work.

"Charlie and his sitter are missing. This blood was found on the ground next to the car."

"You're worried about Ky," she said, looking up and remembering the file Monahan found.

"It's canine!" said Lee, turning his computer around for them to see.

Thunder roared, vibrating the entire building. "She knows. Shit!" Ivy exclaimed as she ran out the door with the doctor and Lee close behind.

*****

Lightning and thunder hit fast and hard, vibrating the station, knocking all three men onto the desk. Everyone, taken by surprise, went running to the windows to see what happened.

Jameson, Monahan, and Riley stood confused and dazed for a moment before all eyes went back to the window. They could see Wolfe with his arms around Ky tight as she fought to get away.

Riley headed for the door when Monahan yelled, "Stop!"

Danny burst through the door out of breath. "I passed the doc and that Ivy woman in the hall rattling something about the dog being missing and finding blood. She said to stay here and was very demanding about it. What the hell's going on?"

They all turned to the only calm one in the room for an answer. Monahan, who still stood looking through the window, replied, "We are about to find out what the file on Ky isn't telling us."

Followed by the doctor and her assistant, Ivy faced off with Ky in Wolfe's arms. Lee stopped beside Damon standing off to the side. Placing her hands around Ky's face, Ivy pleaded with her to focus. When Ky's head dropped, the sky slowly began to clear. Wolfe picked Ky up, taking her to his truck, and making her sit there as she cried.

Chapter 26

JD released his dogs, Red and Bo, from the back of his truck. Four men joined him with their guns ready. Approaching the area the men said they shot the wolf, the dogs picked up a scent—a scent that made them anxious. Pulling at their leash as they were made it difficult for JD to maintain control. Both dogs went into a frenzy around the tree with an embedded bullet. Getting tangled around JD's legs brought him to the ground hard. It took all four men to help contain the bloodhounds and keep them from strangling JD like a snake with their leashes.

The dogs seemed confused as to which way to go. They ran back and forth from the tree in all directions when Bo picked up a scent that made him howl repeatedly. Red turned, ran to Bo, dragging two of the men with him. Now both dogs howled nonstop, pulling and fighting the leashes. Bo twisted his head out of his collar, taking off in a dead run. JD reached for Red's neck only to get bit as Red escaped his collar, running after Bo.

"Don't just stand there! Follow them!" yelled JD. JD pulled the pistol from his belt and headed into the woods with his men. Moving fast, with the howling getting more distant by the minute, the trampled underbrush made it easy to follow their path.

"They're less than a quarter mile away. You two go back and get the trucks. Meet us on the other side. Whatever they're after, we'll catch in the middle," JD ordered.

JD felt confident about catching the dogs and their prey between the small river running along Frank's farm on one side and the busy highway on the other. A few minutes later, the howling got louder and changed indicating they had something cornered. Slowing their pace and using caution, they approached spread out.

Getting closer to the uproar, the men stopped dead in their tracks for only a moment when the howls went silent. JD ran like he'd never run before with the other two close at his heels.

Clearing the trees lining the road, they could hear the engine of the truck coming fast. Trodden grass and weeds displayed dog tracks halfway up the incline to the farm. Muddy paw prints lay scattered in a small patch of road in front of them with no dogs in sight. JD and his men stood staring at each other befuddled.

*****

"We need to talk," Dr. Coletrain said, grabbing Ivy's arm and leading her away from the others. "What the hell was that? Who are you people?"

"I'm a sensitive, descendant from the Druid bloodline of Merlin," replied Ivy with pride.

"Merlin is a myth."

"Truth lies buried in myth and legend while religion rules the masses with fear. You know that better than anyone."

"What about her?" asked the doctor, pointing at Ky.

"Raised by her maternal grandmother, an immigrant from Poland. Said to be a witch from some rogue band of Gypsies."

"And her father?"

"Irish, German. Left after her mother died. I figure that's why she has a hairline trigger of a temper."

"So how do you explain what she just did?"

"I can't, not really. I'm not sure she can. There's a fine line between good and evil. She can wield power in both, equally. That's what makes her so dangerous and unique."

They watched Ky melt into Wolfe's chest. With his arms wrapped around her, she shed tears of anger and frustration, letting out a heartbreaking scream. Ivy pulled up the GPS app on her phone to track Charlie. The signal was coming from a farm on the north west side of the park. Now she had to decide if Ky was ready to listen without going over the deep end again.

*****

Chief Tate reached to hang up the phone when he heard a second click. Someone had been listening to his call with the county sheriff from within the station. It made him wonder if the call before it had been overheard as well. *Only one way to find out*, he thought and headed to Jameson's office. Not bothering to knock, he entered finding the men still gazing out the window. No one seemed to notice him until he stood behind them to see what had their attention.

"What's going on?" he asked.

Monahan gave the Chief a brief rundown, never taking his eyes off the scene outside. He already shared the file labeled Arbitra with him earlier.

"So it's begun. Are we ready?"

"I haven't told these two yet," said Monahan, referring to Danny and Riley.

"Make it quick. We have more problems," Tate stated. He proceeded to tell them about the call explaining the sheriff had more bodies. Two girls were found by a couple of farmhands. There was no way to keep this one quiet. The sheriff said they appeared to be like an animal attack, but certain aspects appeared as if they had been raped first. With the body parts still intact and tire marks in the area from motorcycles, it looked like an attempted copycat crime without all the facts. He was going to handle it as such. The fact the call had a listener on the line was a bigger concern. It had to be one of their men currently in the station. Danny and Riley looked at each other dumbfounded, listening.

"The chief got an anonymous call earlier saying the girls were the next target," Jameson explained looking at them.

"Did you warn them?" asked Danny.

"No."

"You intend to use them as bait," claimed Riley in disbelief.

"Yes," Jameson and Monahan said simultaneously.

"And the two girls are probably a planned diversion or mistaken identity. Anything is possible right now," Monahan went on to say. "So we're going to let it play out like we don't know anything. We'll leave here like we are setting up our stakeout. Halfway there, we're meeting other agents where we'll switch cars. They'll take our place."

"The elders of my tribe have made arrangements to follow the girls. That's the two pickup trucks you see parked across the street. You'll meet up with them a mile behind the girls so you'll have to move fast. They will relay the directions as they go by phone. We're only using the radios to keep everyone coordinated in our diversion."

"Once the decoys are in place around the park and the suspects are off our tail, Tate's men will join us. Night Wing is on Delaney, so he's covered. We don't know how many are involved so we want to be prepared for anything. We may have surprise on our side, but not knowing what we're getting into is against us. Once we're there, we'll have to play it by ear," Monahan explained.

"I'll be here watching to see who gets froggy. I have my suspicions and have three on duty I trust to back me," said Tate.

Monahan watched the doctor and Ivy approached Ky. After talking for only a few minutes, Dr. Coletrain returned to the morgue. Ivy and Ky left in Ky's car with Wolfe following in his truck. A moment later, the two pickups followed. Damon disappeared unnoticed again.

"Shouldn't we get going?" Danny asked.

"Not yet. They need a head start, or it'll look suspicious. We don't want this blown over simple mistakes. There's too much at risk," Jameson replied.

"Damned it! Did anyone see where that Damon guy went?" cussed Monahan.

They all peered out the window. He was nowhere to be found.

*****

Athena woke groggy, bound with silver handcuffs. Knowing the sting in her neck was from a tranquilizer dart, she shook her head to clear her mind and vision. A man was sitting on the floor over Charlie with a black bag next to him. Charlie lay there, not moving.

"What have you done to him? Leave him alone," she snarled, fully alert.

"I'm trying to help him. He got hurt."

"Yeah, by one of you!"

"I'm not like them. I would never hurt a cousin, which is what he is. When you two got grabbed, he still had enough in him to bite one of the guys. He hit him in the nose. I'm making sure it's not broken. Besides, I'm worried since he hasn't come to yet."

"What do you want with us?" she asked with calm suspicion. "They want the two women. This was the only way they could think of to get them away from the cops. You're here because they think you're the one they're after."

"Why them? They aren't even from around here."

"But they are here and made themselves a part of this, thanks to their friend being in the wrong place at the wrong time. Now they're in the way. They don't know what they're involved in, any more than these guys know who they or you really are. Your group was supposed to handle this before it got out of hand," the man said, still tending to Charlie. Turning to look at her, he said, "I know who you are, Athena, and I know what Ky is. We call her Arbitra."

Athena sat confused and full of questions, but the man put his finger to his lips, indicating someone was coming. She lay back down and closed her eyes when the door opened with three rough-looking men entering.

"He going to live?" one asked.

"Yes, but he's old. It's going to take a bit for him to come around. You hit him too hard."

"He's lucky I didn't kill him. I don't know why the boss wants him alive, for now anyway."

"I'll let you know when he's up and functioning. You dosed both of them heavier than was needed."

"Just do your job, Doc. We'll do ours how we see fit." With a snarky grin, the man spit on the floor, and the three left.

Chapter 27

Night Wing chose the form of a crow as he sat patiently in a tree across from the building Delaney taught in. Delaney came out heading straight to a delivery van with a fresh fish logo on the side, parked a few feet away. A man got out handing him a small cooler from the back. As the van pulled away, a woman walked up kissing Delaney on the cheek. Arm in arm, they went to the school parking lot. After talking a moment and getting in different cars, they drove off in the same direction. Night Wing took flight staying just above the trees, going higher when they picked up speed on the freeway. Hovering at a greater altitude gave him an advantage. After a few minutes, the cars exited, entering a neighborhood and into the driveway of a modest, well-kept property. Night Wing landed on the roof and hid behind the chimney.

*****

Recognizing the men, Damon watched as the pickups left following the girls. As members of the tribe, they befriended during previous engagements in the area, he knew the girls would be safe for now. Damon called his troupe while heading for his car, giving them a brief update and instructions. They were going hunting. Wherever the dog was, Athena was too and not by choice. If she had gone of her own free will, she would have left a sign or at least taken the van, leaving him without transportation.

Walking a half block, he climbed into an old beat-up green van and waited. He wanted to know what the law was planning. Events that had taken place only moments ago piqued his curiosity. Damon admired Ky's independence and her skill with a sword. When she fought the wolves, it was like watching an artist dance. How she handled the hellhound with such intimacy expressed her compassion. The storm that brewed from her anger displayed how dangerous she was to the likes he had never seen. To see her breakdown over a dog conflicted with her overall persona of strength and intelligence. Love for the animal gave her strength and weakness when used as a weapon against her. Hidden within a guarded heart, it made Ky vulnerable. All this wrapped up in an extraordinary, petite, and pretty package had him feeling drawn to her. It was not what he was used to and wondered what the consequence would be if he got too close, but Damon wanted to know more.

Damon's thoughts were interrupted when the men came out of the station. Jameson, the two agents, and a man he didn't know drove off in different directions. Choosing to follow Monahan, since he'd be the one giving orders, would tell him everything he needed. Damon would join his troupe and the girls as soon as he got some answers. Knowing Ivy and Ky had plenty of backups gave him some comfort. *But if they hurt the dog, it'll be a bloody massacre*, he thought.

*****

Jack Marsten sat at his usual table with a fresh, cold glass of beer waiting for the bar's phone to ring. His goal had been achieved as far as he was concerned, and he was ready for the final act. The quota had been filled. *With the chaos of an upcoming war achieved, it is time to collect*, he thought as the phone rang.

"Everything is in place. Loose ends are being handled this evening. All be done before the banquet. You ready at your end?" Marsten spoke when he saw the caller ID.

"Your payment is waiting for you. It's been a pleasure doing business with you, Marsten."

"I'm a man of my word. Just make sure you are." Marsten hung up, guzzling the rest of his beer before approaching the bar to return their phone and pay his tab. Katrina came out of her office when he handed the bartender his money.

"See you tonight?" she asked. "The band's back you know."

"Not tonight. Been here long enough. The roads calling my name. I'll see you in the fall."

"Starting early this year, huh?"

"A little. The weather is supposed to get warmer soon. I need to get to the mountains before the temperature gets hot." Jack smiled to himself as he walked out.

Marsten rode his motorcycle to the back lot of a mom-and-pop grocery store where the fresh-fish truck was unloading. The driver handed him a small cooler as he pulled up beside him, still passing boxes labeled fish to the store employee. Making sure he wasn't being cheated, he opened the cooler. Stacks of cash were piled to the rim. He lifted a stack from the middle, thumbing through it to ensure it wasn't blank paper. Satisfied, he closed the lid, riding off without saying a word.

*****

Monahan and the others drove off to meet their counterparts. Monahan would swap cars with Sam Hidelbaugh, a senior agent in the area. Jameson met with Will Green, Sam's partner. Danny and Riley exchanged places with Beka Pilkington and John Vasques. Sam's team would cover each corner of the park, keeping in contact by hand radio. Monahan and Jameson would relay what was needed by the car radio so no one knew they had changed places.

Monahan's team would coordinate with the men from the tribe members following the girls before planning their next move. They all knew the chances they were taking. The element of surprise was on their side, but many unknown factors made the situation extremely vulnerable. No one had experience in battling supernatural monsters other than the girls.

*****

Night Wing watched as Delaney and the woman entered the house. Repositioning himself to a tree branch off the side of the driveway, he could see into the front and back of the house. The woman went to the back of the kitchen. Placing the cooler on the counter, she turned on the stove and reached for a pan. Delaney went upstairs to what looked like a bedroom and began to undress.

The woman took four wrapped items from the cooler. Placing two on the counter and two others in the freezer, she began to cook. Everything seemed to be a normal night for any couple. Delaney went into another room, naked with towels in hand, apparently to take a shower. The woman placed a phone call as she pulled something out of her purse, sprinkled it over the food, then placed it back in her purse. She then pulled out a small insulated bag. Taking more items out of the cooler and placing them inside the bag next to her purse.

Delaney came into the kitchen dressed in a red ceremonial-type robe trimmed in black. The woman emptied the food into a large plastic container and handed it to Delaney. He in turn put the food into another insulated bag designed to keep things warm. After a short conversation and a kiss, he left. The woman placed the utensils in the sink, picking up her purse and the bag as she left. Night Wing took flight following Delaney.

*****

Chief Tate sat behind his desk watching from his office as Sanders paced the lobby trying to look busy, frequently glancing up at the clock. When Sanders's phone rang, he took a quick look around the room before announcing he was going outside for a smoke. Tate went to a window, where he could keep an eye on Sanders, noticing his face turning red in anger. He lit a cigarette as he paced, trying to keep his voice down.

"Where are you?" Sanders said angrily.

"One of my guys recognized the car you described. We tracked her to the motel she's staying at. We had it staked out when Cooper called. He said his guys got the dog and the girl and were taking them to the farm. She's not a witch. She's a wolf," Hanson replied.

"He got the damned dog sitter! We're going to need a diversion before the feds figure out what happened and try to back her up when she comes for them. Get on it."

"That's already screwed up too. Cooper's men took out two couples traveling through town. Said they were tired of waiting. Told you they'd be trouble, just like Darryl. You should pick your friends more carefully."

"Wasn't my choice," Sanders spouted as he hung up. Marsten made him take Cooper and his men to increase their numbers. Darryl had been one of them. He knew he was set up to fail.

*****

Ky followed Ivy's directions that she was seeing on the map from the tracking chip in Charlie. He was at a farm ten miles north of town. Wolfe stayed close behind keeping an eye on his rearview mirror. Two pickup trucks took turns in the lead spot allowing the other to fall back so no one could get suspicious. Neither would get close enough to be identified, but Wolfe wasn't fooled. He knew they were being followed. Ky parked a quarter mile from the farm in a wide ravine with overgrown brush off a dirt road with Wolfe directly behind her.

*****

Monahan arrived first with the others close behind. It was an unexpected convenience that the owner knew they were all coming. Apparently, Chief Tate figured out where they not only could see the girls but also knew the farmer and notified him before calling Jameson. The team of agents was only a few minutes away with orders to cover the opposite side to surround the area. Positioning themselves in the house, he sent Danny and Riley to the barn. Monahan made his call to the local office where the other agents gathered in two groups of thirty waiting for orders. Each team was ready to move on a moment's notice and were given a copy of Riley's report. The press release would state they were working with the local police in apprehending a gang involved in organ trafficking and murder. It appeared their plan was coming together. Soon they'd close the most bizarre case they had ever worked on and would never be able to talk about. A few minutes behind, the pickups drove to the farmhouse atop a small hill where Monahan and the others were waiting.

They watched as the girls and Wolfe loaded up with weapons from Ky's trunk and the back of his truck. Ivy and Wolfe spread out on either side staying back long enough for Ky to appear alone as she headed for the house. Monahan was about to give the order for his team to prepare to move when Beka came over the radio.

Chapter 28

Everyone was in place waiting. Beka parked in the picnic area. Sitting at a table with an open book, appearing to enjoy the outdoors while reading, she had the perfect view of anything that moved. A family with a dog, closer to the docks, began to wrap up their outing when another car pulled in. Two men got out carrying long medium-sized bags and headed into the trees. As the family loaded their car, two more vehicles entered. One car parked with two men getting out alongside a van letting one man out and then leaving. The man joined the other two, all carrying similar bags, and entered the woods. When the family began pulling out, their dog stuck his head out the window, barking wildly at the men. Beka grabbed her walkie-talkie relaying to Monahan that guests arrived at the party and brought the fireworks.

"Stay where you are till the others arrive. You are not going in without backup. Do you understand?" asked Monahan.

"No disrespect, sir, but just cuz I'm a woman, I'm far from being a rookie."

"That's an order. It's called safety in numbers. You know that," Monahan stressed.

Sam broke in. "Will and I are the closest. We'll go in together. John is going to take longer. He'll have our backs. We'll keep an eye on the situation while the other team gets set up."

"Remember, if you have to fire, head shots only," ordered Monahan.

"You make it sound like we're going after zombies. You ever going to tell us why?" asked Beka as the line went silent.

*****

Damon didn't follow Monahan down the dirt road. Being familiar with the area, he chose to drive further to circle round the back side. Positioned far enough away not to be noticed, he could see the rear of the house as well as the road running across the front. Having told his men already what to expect and alerted to the location, the farm would be surrounded. They needed to get in and back out before the law got too close. Damon only had to wait a few minutes before Colt Nichols pulled up beside him. Colt began his report.

"JJ picked up the scent first. He's coming in from the east. Max is covering from those big-ass trees by the barn. We're ready when you are. The pack is prepping for the rush on the main group as soon as we give them a location. They're pissed and in no-prisoners mode. The FBI has its groups on standby. I'm not sure how much they know or were told"

"Ky's over there to the southwest with the other two. Everyone else is a little under a quarter mile further west setting up their command post at the house over there on the hill. Let's get this party started before they get antsy. I want to be there when Ky makes her move," Damon stated. He was concerned for her safety from the renegades as well as their own from her.

*****

Ky loaded up with weapons—mostly knives and throwing daggers—and put her sword in its sheath on her back. Wolfe loaded both his rifle and shotgun, placing two handguns and a hunting knife in the side of his belt. Ivy packed arrows in the quiver on her back slinging her crossbow over her shoulder, then chose an HK VP9 automatic and filled her pockets with extra clips. They knew they were about to walk into a trap and were ready to go to war—a war that wasn't about just a dog. It was about family, and to Ky, it was justice for the innocent. Ky knew they would expect her to sneak up on them. She wouldn't; she was done playing. This is what her grandmother trained her for. She was Arbitra, and court was in session. The verdict of guilt had already been established. Punishment had two options, imprisonment or execution, and their opportunity for choice was pending.

*****

Sam Hidelbaugh and Will Green arrived at the same time. Parking next to Beka, they joined her at the table to wait for John Vasques. They would coordinate the surveillance before entering. Will had extensive military training. Tracking these guys through the forest would be tricky but not impossible. John was six minutes away when they heard a man scream, followed by a gunshot. The sound came from further down where the park edged a small road along a farm. Jumping into their cars, Sam informed John they were going in hot and to get there fast. Monahan was listening, informing the backup team to move, via the car radio, to the station.

Will was first in line. He slammed on the brakes, skidding to a stop as he came upon a small ravine between the road and the clearing. A group of wolves were attacking two men about a hundred yards in. Will, Sam, and Beka watched them scatter, leaving a man on the ground. Approaching with guns in hand, Sam took the lead position. Before he could stoop to check vitals, the man got up. Will and Beka came up from behind, stunned to see the man was fine taking a few steps back with a smile on his face.

"Welcome to the party," he said. His body shifted under crackling sounds of bones breaking and reformed stretching skin that sprouted fur. Slime oozed from needle-sharp fangs as his nose and jaw extended to a muzzle spewing the odor of decomposing flesh. His ears grew pointed above his eyes turning to bloodred oval slits of pure evil.

The three agents stood together, shocked, speechless, watching the transformation when a growl behind them drew their attention. The wolves surrounded them, circling wide, snarling. There was no time to understand; they had to get their heads back in the game. The agents stood with their backs to each other realizing they had walked into a trap. Hidden in the folds of black-and-red robes, two cloaked figures emerged from the trees facing Sam Hidelbaugh. One was tall and husky; the other slightly shorter with a medium build. Wolves between them separated to make a direct path to the agents.

"You are out of your realm, Gentlemen, and my friends are hungry," came a low, burly voice from the taller figure.

Sam Hidelbaugh glanced around the circle sizing up the situation as the pack crept closer. Five wolves crouched for attack surrounding them on three sides. He needed a plan fast. He knew their chances would be slim and wondered if he and Will Greene could fire fast enough once they attacked.

"Guess we know why Monahan said to aim for the head. Take the back two out first," Sam said to the other two just above a whisper. "I'll aim for the three on my side. That will be your opening, Beka. You high-tail it to the car. Go straight to John. Don't look back."

"I can take two," Beka whispered.

"No," Will said, "Sam's right. You're faster than us. We'll take these animals. You just run."

Beka eyeballed the distance to her unlocked car. It looked to be about fifty yards to the ditch and knew she could easily jump it. She thought about the shotgun inside her car for a moment. Even if she could get to it fast enough to get a shot, there was a chance of hitting one of them. Beka cursed under her breath at the thought.

"Now!" yelled Sam.

Gunfire rang out. Beka took off on a dead run when the first wolf went down. Will took out a second one. Another jumped, knocking Will into Sam, ripping his throat out in one bite. Sam fired off two shots. One shot took out the wolf in front of him. Aiming the second shot at one of the men in robes hitting one in the arm. The last wolf lunged from behind. As it locked jaws into Sam, he heard the snap of breaking bones as teeth went deep into his shoulder. Sam hit the ground hard, face-first, his body being viciously torn apart. Beka heard screams. Not looking back, she jumped the ditch with ease, reaching the car in two strides as John skidded to a stop and leaped from his car. John pulled his gun hearing shots ring. Beka hit the front of her car; brains, hair, and pieces of skull bone sprayed across the hood as her body slid to the ground.

John couldn't believe what he was seeing. He dove behind the car where Beka lay. John raised his head behind the back of Will's car to see five bodies on the ground. Two wolves and two men in robes were running to a dark-colored van just up the hill. John began to fire, but the man beside the van turned toward him, firing twice from a rifle. The first shot barely missed John while the second took out the back window before driving away. He ran into the clearing. The scene was grossly intense, looking like a scene from a horror movie. It was nothing like he had ever seen in his entire career making him drop to his knees, vomiting profusely. John, emotionally and mentally devastated, radioed Monahan out of sheer instinct and training.

Chapter 29

The farm was unattended for a few years after the owner died, leaving a mountain of debt. No one wanted the house; the neighbors were afraid of it. Rumors of it being haunted circulated rapidly after the old man died under mysterious circumstances. His closest neighbor saw him out in the field in his combine that morning. Later in the day, it was running but not moving for over an hour when he decided to see if he could help with whatever was wrong. He found what was left of the man that appeared to have been ground up by the blades. It looked as if he had been put through a wood chipper instead of chunks of flesh and bone sliced through a shredder. There had been very little left to identify past his head, which was stuck between the blades.

When someone finally showed interest in the property, the bank chose to do repairs to bring it up to code. Cooper was one of the first to bid on the job and obtain the contract. Now he and his men sat around the kitchen table having a beer. Proud they captured the dog and the girl, who was locked in the basement, they patted one another on the back.

"Wish I could have seen the look on Hanson's face when he heard we beat him to the punch," said one man.

"Yeah, I'll bet he was foaming at the mouth mad," said another, laughing.

"I don't get why we can't just kill them both and get it over with. What's so important about keeping them alive when we're going to kill them anyway?"

"They're going out in style," said Cooper, walking in. "They're part of the ceremony, some kind of sacrificial ritual as the finale, a dessert, so to speak."

Cooper's phone rang. "How's it hangin', Hanson? Catch anything good lately?" he said. Cooper stood in silence for a few minutes; his face went from smiling to angry. Hanging up the phone, he threw his bottle of beer across the room, shattering it against the wall.

"It's not her. We grabbed the damned babysitter. Kill them both now."

Another man came running in. "A chick dressed in black is coming up the drive. What do we do?"

"You two get in the basement. Guard the door. The rest of you, get to work. Remember, we're contractors," Cooper ordered.

*****

Monahan's backup was in place on the other side of the farm not far down the road. He and Jameson watched Ky from a second-floor window. Danny kept an eye on the barn off the side of the house and surrounding areas. Riley was in the rafters of the barn at their location, his scope and sniper rifle set up and ready. With a partial view of the living room but a clear line of sight into the kitchen across the way, he radioed Monahan that there were six men inside.

"I think we should be closer," Jameson suggested.

Monahan radioed the other team. "Move in. I want a fifty-yard perimeter from the house at your location. Stay low, stay quiet. Enter on my command."

Jameson and Monahan were halfway across the field by the time Ky reached the entrance of the driveway when John radioed news of the ambush. Everyone stopped dead in their tracks as shock set in. Immediately, Monahan ordered his first team to converge on the park to John's location.

*****

Ivy and Wolfe distanced themselves from Ky and each other. They circled around the front and one side of the house hiding low in the tall, overgrown prairie grass. Ky hadn't gotten far when what looked like the large black-and-silver German shepherd she met on the beach loped out of the tall grass. He just sat there looking at her as she raised her hand to the hilt of the knife hidden beneath a knee-length black jacket. Ky could feel the werewolf in him. A loud caw came as a crow swooped down circling her twice before landing on the dog's head. He looked up, let out a low grunt, and shook the crow off his head. In turn, the crow cawed in his face and then flew toward the house.

"Friend of yours?" she asked.

Shaking his nose with a snort, he looked at the house, then back at her.

"I'm going in. Don't get in my way, okay?"

He stood up facing the house, turning his head toward her as if he was waiting. He didn't move till she was beside him. They were going in together. At that moment, she knew Damon wasn't far away.

*****

Cooper peered out the window. "You didn't say she had a dog with her."

"I didn't see him. Are there two sets of women with dogs?"

"How the hell did she find us?" asked one man close to the window.

"Just play your part. For all she knows, we're contractors fixing the house."

"If she's the witch, she'll know what we are," said another.

"So we act like we're part of the local pack just doing a job. Follow my lead."

Cooper opened the door when Ky got close.

"Hi. You must be one of the people looking to buy this place. The bank said someone might come out. My name's Joe. My men are working inside. We still have a lot to do, but you're welcome to come inside and look around," he said with a smile.

"Yes, that would be nice. Thank you," Ky replied. Ky entered the ranch-style home with the shepherd at her side. All the men stopped what they were doing, turning to look at her, when Cooper closed the door. The shepherd let out a snort, glanced up at Ky, and preceded to the kitchen. Her mind began receiving images of the local pack passing judgment on the men, followed by Athena and Charlie being in the basement with three others. Ky looked at the shepherd understanding why he was here. He was either sent by Damon or was Damon; she wasn't sure now, only that the images in her mind were another talent of theirs she was unaware of.

"So what can we do for you?"

Ky made a mental note of the position each man was in before speaking.

"You can turn over your hostage and the dog to receive some leniency. Go to jail like men, or I can leave you to the local pack. If not, you die. You fight, you die. If the hostages are hurt, you die. You get one chance to make a choice. Make no mistake. I will kill you."

"That's an awfully bold statement from such a little girl who's obviously outnumbered," said Cooper, laughing.

Ky drew a deep breath as Cooper grabbed her by the neck, lifting her off the ground. Looking into her eyes, his grip tightened. Ky didn't flinch. She pulled a blade from under her jacket, jamming it into the underside of his arm, tearing in length right down to the bone. Cooper screamed, losing his grip from the severed muscles and pain. Ky went to the floor on her knees reaching for her sword. The two men, one on each side, jumped into action but not before her blade came down slicing Cooper wide open from chin to groin. Blood gushed in all directions like a geyser, covering Ky, ceiling, and floor; his internal organs spilled into a pile at his feet. Each man grabbed one of her arms as the third came up from behind with a hammer in his hand. He swung toward her head when the front window shattered. A bullet through his eye blew out the back of his head, splattering brains, scalp, and skull fragments against the wall behind him like abstract art. Still holding her arms, the other two stared in shock with their mouths open for a split second before anger and the taste for blood took hold.

Ivy turned toward Wolfe when she caught movement, out of the corner of her eye. In the tall grass about fifty feet to his right, she fired her crossbow. Though the arrow passed Wolfe by only inches, he just smiled, not taking his eyes from the scope of his rifle. To her surprise, the man in the field stood holding the arrow, throwing both hands in the air. It was Damon. Ivy gave him a catlike smile, signaling for them to move toward the house.

*****

Monahan, Jameson, and Danny heard the shot ring out bringing them out of their shock from John's call. Riley immediately relayed what he could see. The shot came from Wolfe, and Ky just gutted a man in one swift move. He was in awe as he watched her move with such precision and skill. The second team announced they were on the scene with John at the park and would take it from there. Monahan gave orders to the team in the field.

"Secure the perimeter. Jameson and I are going in. Wait for me to give the signal."

"It looks like they have her pinned. I don't have a clean shot," announced Riley. "Her friends are approaching the house fast."

"Keep your eyes on the basement," said Monahan.

Hearing all the exchanges, Jameson stared at Monahan for a moment. Danny kept focus on the house as they moved in.

"Why aren't we rushing the house?" Jameson asked. "What are you waiting for? They're going to kill her."

"They'll kill her quicker, along with her friends if they see us. We'll have a massacre on our hands if we all get caught in the crossfire."

*****

The shepherd was crouched at the basement door when the shot rang out. Turning to the living room door, he saw one man go down with the other two holding Ky at arm's length. Cooper's blood continued to flow across the floor, rapidly creating a slick pool beneath them. He lunged at the closest man in one jump, driving his face into the end of Ky's sword like a toothpick through an olive. The momentum of his fall into the increasing pool of blood took them all off-balance falling to the floor. Both hands of the one still holding her turned to sharp razor-like claws piercing her arm. Long deadly fangs protruded from his jaw as he transformed. Wolfe and Ivy busted through the front door; Damon, through the back. Ivy slipped on the blood, shooting her crossbow as she went down on her ass with the arrow hitting the ceiling. Wolfe stepped over Ivy, firing his rifle at the man's heart at the same time Ky's blade split his head open like an axe to firewood.

"Cutting it a bit close there, aren't you, little one?" Wolfe smiled. "I had it under control till someone decided to butt in," Ky said, pointing at her new companion.

The shepherd curled the side of his lip like he was smiling letting out a short snort and went back to the kitchen where Damon stood waiting beside the basement door.

*****

The two men behind the basement door listened to the shots and screams with guns in hand. One jerked his head toward the room where Athena and Charlie were being kept for the second man to run down the stairs and guard the other door.

"Kill them both," he said as he put his hand on the doorknob. Turning the knob slowly, he opened it with his gun ready. He stepped out to a low growl just beyond the door and took aim.

A shot rang out through the kitchen window, knocking the gun out of his hands and hitting the basement door. The shepherd looked up, snarling viciously before attacking. Riley, surprised, took a step back from the scope on his rifle, swearing the dog looked him straight in the eye for a moment. Going back to his scope, he saw the man go headfirst down the stairs with the dog riding him like a surfboard.

*****

Charlie was awake. Still groggy, he tried to stand, growling. Athena hushed him when the guard rushed in slamming the door behind him.

"Out of the way, Doc," he said to the only one standing between him and his targets.

"You don't want to do this. They'll kill you without hesitation." "I always knew you were a coward. I'm dead either way, and I'm taking them with me," he said, then backhanded the doc hard into the wall knocking him out.

Athena jumped, tackling him as he fired. Falling to the ground hard, she wrestled for the gun as it fired. Damon kicked the door open, crashing it to pieces. Wolfe rushed past, grabbed the man's wrist, and broke it, taking the gun. With one punch, Athena knocked him out. Ky pushed Wolfe out of the way with Ivy right behind her. Ky froze halfway across the room. Charlie lay there panting heavily in a pool of blood with a bullet in his chest.

Chapter 30

Night Wing followed Delaney to an old run-down house on the out-skirts of town. He recognized the package Delaney took from the car as the one the woman gave him. The man answering the door had the appearance of a derelict, weak, scrawny, and old. What Night Wing noticed most was an older model sports car, well taken care of, and very clean, parked in the alley behind the house. Delaney pulled the food container from its thermal casing. Smelling the food, smiling, and thanking Delaney, he closed the door.

The aroma of the food drifted in the breeze to Night Wing. It was liver and onions, but there was something odd about the way it smelled, something he couldn't identify in his current form. Delaney's phone rang as he was leaving. He sat in his car talking to the caller for a few minutes. The man in the house came out the back door, leaving in the sports car. This became a dilemma for Night Wing. Follow Delaney, report to Chief Tate, or follow the sports car. When Delaney pulled away, he took to the air high enough to track both vehicles as long as he could.

Delaney drove to a small estate on the edge of town near the campus. It looked as if it could have been an old frat house with a large garage where he parked inside with several other cars and entered through a back door. Night Wing flew to a tree closer to the house landing on a low branch that gave him a good view through the windows. One room he could see was big enough to hold a small crowd with a large table surrounded by high-back chairs. Along with normal electric lighting, candle lanterns were hanging spaced around the room. When Delaney walked in speaking with another man dressed in a different type of robe, he felt it was time to report in.

*****

Sanders got off work going straight to the bar. He wanted to talk to Marsten before things got any more out of hand. Hanson was already there with his guys drinking and playing pool to blow off steam before the night's festivities. The first thing he noticed was Marsten's empty table.

"Where's Jack?" he asked the bartender.

"Haven't seen him, but my shift just started. Heard Kat say something about him hitting the road. Ask her. I think she's in the back."

Kat came out of the kitchen doors loaded with food. He waited for her to serve a group of men drinking heavily. She turned to find Sanders watching her with anticipation,

"You're not here to give me a hard time about the band playing outside tonight, are you?" she scowled.

"No," he said with a grin. "I was wondering where Marsten's at. He's usually a fixture here this time of day."

"Heading for the mountains. Said the road was calling him early this year."

"That's too bad. I'm sure tonight will be a blowout. It's been a while since these guys have played here. I enjoy when he gets up and tries to sing," Sanders said, slightly laughing.

Walking over to Hanson's table, he thought about how odd it was that Marsten chose to leave town with tonight being such a big deal. Marsten never missing a Road Rats show made him feel uncomfortable and leery, especially since it would be the first time they meet Marsten's teams considering all the screw-ups his men had done.

"Have a seat, Sanders. You look stressed. Need a drink?" Hanson asked.

"I'm not staying. Have you heard from Cooper? He's not answering my calls."

"Not since this morning when the little prick called to gloat."

"I want you to go early tonight. Check out Marsten's men. If there's any hint of something hinky, make sure Cooper dies by your hand. Make it known you and your men are not the idiots, but Cooper and his men are."

"With pleasure," he said, smirking.

*****

Athena held the man with his arms locked behind his back as everyone rushed into the room. Wolfe made a move toward Charlie when Ivy stopped him.

"Ky?" called Ivy in a soft, affectionate voice.

Ky turned, swinging her sword into both hands like a bat before they knew she moved. Her eyes were black like shiny onyx stones. Damon stepped forward.

"Stop!" Ivy cried out. "Don't move. She's out for blood."

"She got it," said Athena.

They all looked her way as the prisoner's head slid from his shoulders to the floor, bouncing as it rolled and stopping at Wolfe's feet. Blood erupted from his neck like a geyser spraying everyone except Ky and Charlie.

"*Eww*, yuck," whined Ivy.

As the man against the wall began to stir and come to, catching Ky's attention, she took a step toward him.

"No!" yelled Athena. "He helped us!"

Ky cocked her head, sizing him up, when Charlie let out a weak yelp. Ky straightened her stand but didn't move. Charlie yelped again. Ky, consumed with grief and shock, didn't move till Charlie tried to wag his tail in vain. A moment went by before her eyes returned to normal, and Ivy relaxed a bit. Placing her hand over Ky's, lowering her sword, she walked her over to Charlie. The pool of blood was expanding. Ky fell to her knees as he looked up at her with eyes full of love, not fear.

"I can save him!" Athena spouted. "If you'll let me." "How is that possible?" asked Ivy.

"She's blood born to the werewolf," stated the man on the floor, now fully conscious. "A blood transfusion will have healing properties. He's losing a lot of blood, so we must work fast."

Damon moved in closer, setting the headless body to fire and ash. Walking over to the head, Ivy jumped up to stop him.

"I promised I would bring at least one if not two back to Dr. Coletrain."

"Some things are not meant to be known," he said, raising his hand.

Ky leaped in front of him before Wolfe could react. Placing the tip of her sword against the skin under his chin, warning him not to move, surprised everyone.

"Ivy always keeps her word," she declared in a low, venomous tone.

"I suggest you back off," Athena said to Damon. "We have more important things to worry about right now. You two love birds can fight later. We have a life to save." She bent down to look Charlie in the eye, placing her hand on his face. "You aren't going anywhere, my friend."

Damon put his hands up, taking a step back. Ky's eyes told him she was serious.

*****

Monahan, Jameson, and Danny took off on a dead run hearing the muffled sound of a gunshot coming from inside the house. Riley radioed everyone was in the basement. The backup team verified they had the perimeter secured within the fifty-yard boundaries on the other three sides awaiting orders. Monahan took the front while Jameson and Danny took the back. With both doors already open, they stormed in, armed and ready for anything.

"What's that smell?" Danny asked, curling his nose up.

"Burnt flesh," Jameson replied calmly.

Monahan saw there were no signs of bodies, only piles of blood and ash on the floor. Puzzled, he moved toward the kitchen. Wolfe came bursting through the basement door taking them by surprise.

Without paying any attention to the guns pointed at him, he began rummaging through the cabinets. Finding a big stock pot, he placed it under the faucet. While the pot filled with water, he lit the pilot lights of the stove.

"Don't just stand there gawking, find me some towels. These guys have been living here. There has to be something we can use even if it's sheets off the bed," ordered Wolfe.

Danny took off to the other room. Jameson hesitated only seconds before following.

"I'll call an ambulance," Monahan said.

"Don't bother. There's no time and no need. We got this."

Wolfe placed the pot of water on the stove and went back to the basement with Monahan on his heels. Ky stood off to the side where Ivy held her tight. A man digging through what looked like a medical bag knelt next to Charlie. Monahan caught sight of Ky.

"You're bleeding," he said, walking toward her.

Blood was dripping from her where the claws penetrated her jacket and arm during the fight. She looked down as if it was nothing. Ivy reacted quickly, pulling off Ky's jacket, exposing puncture wounds. Ivy caught a jar of salve the man threw at her and immediately began smothering Ky's wounds.

"Is she going to turn? Don't you turn if you get scratched or bit?" asked Monahan.

"Bitten, yes. Scratched depends on how bad. She'll be fine," Athena answered.

"I'm ready to get the bullet out. I need the rags and water. If you're ready, I want to hook you up for the transfusion," the man said to Athena. Looking down at Charlie, he laid his hand on his head, saying, "I'm sorry, buddy, this is going to hurt."

The German shepherd came bounding down the stairs with a dark-skinned man in his midfifties behind him. Athena smiled. Ivy recognized him from the restaurant sitting at the table with Damon. Ky looked up when her mind received a picture of the man turning into a crow and then back again. Realizing he was the dog's friend from the driveway, Ky wondered, *Who in the hell are these guys?*

"It's about time. Thank you, Max," Damon said, stepping out of the way.

Max went straight to Charlie. Crossing his legs, he sat in the blood. Leaning down, he raised Charlie's ear and whispered something. Placing both hands on Charlie's head, he said, "Get it done, Doc. I got him."

Danny yelled, "The water is boiling."

Jameson added he had rags. Ky went to the floor in Ivy's arms, chanting under her breath. Everyone in the room heard Monahan's radio sound off. His men were awaiting orders.

"Get rid of them," Damon said. "There's too many involved already."

Monahan gave the orders. "Go help the other team. There is nothing to find here. The only one shot is a dog. The whole thing is a false alarm."

Ivy looked at Athena and the man they called Doc. "Can you save him?" she said, her eyes tearing up.

"In theory, yes. We'll know soon enough," he replied as he began to work.

*****

Sanders paced the kitchen of his home with a glass of whiskey, contemplating his situation. He wasn't sure what to do; running wasn't an option. He'd lived in Rockford all his life and always been a good man until four years ago when he met a man at a party. They hit it off so well they planned a monthlong camping trip to the mountains that summer. Little did they know it would turn into a nightmare. Both being the adventurous type, they chose to go hiking high in the Appalachian Mountains where they were told to take careful measures. Both liked the idea of the isolation, though there had been reports of animal attacks, some fatal. Authorities tried closing off the area but were met with such opposition that it wasn't long before it reopened.

After finding a cliff overlooking the vast forest surroundings with a wide view of the city off in the distance, they set up camp to watch the sunset. It was the most beautiful scenery either man had ever experienced. Seeing the city light up after dark was a sight to see. Some of the lights made the streets look like a roller coaster running through a carnival. The men laughed as they exchanged stories and enjoyed the sounds of nature late into the night. Deciding to turn in, Sanders noticed dark clouds building. A storm was moving in over the edge of the city. Lightning flashed across the sky with thunder echoing over the mountain as the storm covered the city, drowning out the spectacle of lights. Only lightning could be seen going in all directions before roaring its thunder. Yet above their heads in the night sky, the stars were immense, looking like sparkling diamonds sprinkled across the vast velvety darkness. Sanders and his new friend sat watching in awe from above for hours as the storm passed. It was an amazing first night.

Every morning, they would hike in a different direction, exploring the terrain of nature's bounty in all its glory. Full of sounds and color, the paths led to small caves, ponds, and creeks. Each day was a new discovery. They bonded like brothers in a matter of hours. It was on day 4 that the nightmare ensued. The two of them sat beside the fire drinking, enjoying the quiet, peaceful night when his buddy entered the woods to take a leak. A moment later, he let out one bloodcurdling scream after another. Sanders ran to the woods grabbing his rifle and a flashlight, finding his friend ripped to shreds. A deep, menacing growl rumbled behind him. He froze with fear. Something hit him from behind. Dazed, he heard a gunshot as his head slammed into the tree trunk, and everything went black.

He woke wrapped in bandages lying in a bed of what looked like a cabin. The man sitting next to him tending his wounds introduced himself as Jack Marsten. As he lay there, Jack told the story of werewolves and how he was out to kill the wicked ones, as if there was a difference.

Sanders's phone rang, bringing him out of his memory.

It was Marsten.

Chapter 31

"We didn't need the hot water?" asked Wolfe concerned.

"Yes, but under the circumstances, we couldn't wait," said the man hovering over his patient. "We'll still use it to clean up afterward."

Max kept Charlie in painless status as the man they called Doc put the last stitch in his chest. The room went quiet waiting for his diagnosis. Ivy cocked her head giving Ky a strange look, listening.

"What's she saying?" whispered Wolfe.

"She's singing that song she wrote for him," she replied in wonderment. "The one about having a moose dog."

The man referred to as Doc checked Charlie's blood pressure and heart, then sat back taking a deep breath. As he began disconnecting the transfusion tubes, Athena spoke first. "Well?"

"We'll know in a few minutes, but so far so good. I'd like to move him upstairs as soon as we know. Can someone get something we can make a bed out of to keep him comfortable?"

Danny flew up the stairs to find blankets. Charlie half wagged his tail once making Ky stop singing. Max looked up smiling, giving Ky and Ivy a nod. Everyone in the room sighed in relief when a crow abruptly flew down the stairs landing in front of Charlie's nose, startling the men. The crow cocked its head side to side as if making its own assessment. Taking a couple of hops toward Ky, it looked up at her, cawed once, then left the way it came, leaving everyone bewildered. Charlie let out a low yip and appeared to be smiling. Ky broke free of Ivy's grip. Putting her arms around Charlie's head and neck; she pressed her forehead to his, holding him as tears erupted.

"You are the strangest people I've ever met," sighed Jameson, shaking his head. "I take it that was a good sign? Another friend of yours?"

"Definitely theirs," said Doc, pointing at Ky and Charlie.

Ivy thought of her conversation with Jess about the dogs and the crow that spoke to them. Realizing who sent the crow, she smiled, giving Wolfe a look that said, "Tell you later."

"I think we can move him now," said Doc. "Upstairs will be comfortable and cleaner. Then I can get a better look at the wound."

"I got him," said Wolfe as he placed his hand on Ky's shoulder. Charlie went completely limp in Wolfe's arms when Max released his hold. Ivy grabbed Ky's arm. Wolfe looked like he was about to reach out and kill Max when Damon suddenly appeared between them.

"He's just asleep!" Max said, quickly backing up. "Moving him would cause unnecessary pain."

Everyone gathered in the kitchen as Riley came in the back door. Monahan, Jameson, Ivy, and Doc sat at the table while the others made themselves comfortable on the countertop or leaning against it. Ky sat on the floor with her hand on Charlie, tracking his breathing and comforting him as much as herself.

"So you want to explain what happened here?" Monahan asked Ivy.

"We take care of our own," Ky stated.

"You can't take the law into your own hands."

"But you can use us as bait?" she snapped. "Yeah, sorry to disappoint you, but we aren't stupid. You knew we were the target and didn't tell us. Why?"

"We didn't know it was going down so fast. There wasn't time to coordinate a plan with us spread out in different directions. Besides, from what I've learned, I knew you could handle it better than we could," said Monahan.

"Then why follow us with all the backup?"

"Our cover story is a gang of organ traffickers, raping and killing just as you suggested. I was hoping to arrest a couple or at least get a clue as to why all this is going on, who's behind it, and how we stop them."

"Arrest a werewolf? Really?" Ivy exclaimed.

"I can help with that," said Doc. "My name is Cyrus Montgomery. I'm a member of the local pack," he said, looking around the room, then to the shepherd. Facing Ky, he went on, "I'm also a member of a local order of—watchers, so to speak. We observe, document, and try very hard not to get involved unless the natural balance of things are sabotaged."

"I wouldn't call any of this natural," said Jameson.

"No, it's supernatural," said Ivy, smirking.

"Yes, we got that," said Monahan, turning to Doc. "Now how about telling us what this is all about and why these three and their dog?"

"They weren't supposed to grab the woman, only the dog since no one was told what Ky looked like. It was to lure her out. Another team was supposed to grab her. They're afraid of her and think she's a witch and would add power to their last ceremony."

"Ceremony for what?" Riley asked.

"Someone they call the Master promised them strength and power through some kind of magic to not only take over all the packs but to be able to take over mankind and not hide anymore."

"Is this even possible?" Monahan asked Ivy.

"Nothing is impossible, only improbable. Magic or not, you have a major problem on your hands. The possibility of a potential war with a world the public can't know about is a threat all its own. Just think about the chaos and panic caused during the Salem witch trials, not counting the Inquisition, and the Dark Ages. Just from fear of the unknown can cause major devastation. History has proven that over and over."

"The ceremony is supposed to take place during the full moon shortly after midnight," Doc informed them. "It's being held at a venue just east of town. The place closed down a few years ago when the owners couldn't afford the upkeep with business dropping over the years. Not that many people today go in for barnlike settings anymore. Most people prefer the glamour stuff nowadays. There is a banquet beforehand. It should be tonight from the way they talked."

The room went quiet as everyone let this new information sink in. All eyes went to Monahan as he went to the sink and filled a bowl with water, deep in thought. Turning, he set the bowl near Charlie's head. Ky watched with a questioning look on her face.

"He's going to be thirsty when he wakes. I know what he's going through," he said, going back to the table. "Chief Tate has his ties with the tribe as well as connections with the local pack. As soon as he's able to be moved, I want the rest of you to go home before sundown and take your friend Reese with you. We'll handle it from here. Cyrus, you're coming with us in handcuffs for your own protection. Until we know who we can trust, I don't want anyone to know you're helping. Do I make myself clear?"

When no one said a word, Monahan cuffed Cyrus and walked out the door with his team. Max and Athena looked at Damon. He nodded toward the door.

"Guess we're done here. Your dog will be fine. He just needs some rest for a day or two," said Damon.

"That's fine with me," said Ivy. "I'm all for going home. I've had about all of this state that I can handle."

"Hold on a minute," Ky stated, slightly panicked. "Charlie is being healed with werewolf blood. What are the side effects? Is he going to turn?"

Athena bent down, kissing Charlie goodbye on top of his head. Placing her hand on Ky's, she smiled. "No worries. The organism that causes the change is in our saliva, not our blood. That's why you weren't affected by being clawed. He has enough blood to heal faster, but that's all."

When Damon, Max, Athena, and the German shepherd were gone, Ivy turned to Ky. "We are going home, right?" asked Ivy.

"You two are. You can hook up with Reese and go. I'm sure Monahan will have him ready by the time we get back to town. Take Charlie to Jess when you get back. She'll know what to do."

"You aren't seriously thinking about getting involved, are you?" Wolfe asked.

"She's not thinking. She knows she is," Ivy replied, irritated.

A loud sudden caw made Ivy jump from her chair. The crow was standing on the sill outside the window looking in. Ivy glared at it as it stood there, obstinate and knowingly. After a moment passed, it let out a long caw, followed by a short one in a tone she had never heard a crow make before. Charlie opened his eyes, turning his head enough to swipe his tongue across Ky's elbow.

"He's awake," said Ky, smiling, as the crow tapped the glass three times and flew off.

Wolfe turned to Ivy. "I'd have to say that's a messenger from her late husband," she whispered with a grin.

*****

"Before you make a decision, there's something I need to tell you," Athena said, stopping Damon. "That Cyrus guy called your girl Arbitra."

Looking up from thought, Damon said, "I thought that was an urban legend?"

"We all did."

"That does change things. Max, I need you to find out what the cop's plans are. We're going as planned but staying on the sidelines unless things get out of hand. Where the hell is Colt? Why wasn't he here?"

Chapter 32

"You're sure about this?" Dr. Coletrain asked.

"Positive. All the test results are the same," replied Lee.

"Pack it up. All of it, including the head. Take it all back to the institute and tell no one. I'll deal with these guys and call the girls. They need to know."

"What about you?"

"I'll join you in a day or two. Right now, I want you and that head gone before they start asking questions."

Once packed, Dr. Coletrain watched the hall as Lee slipped out the back. She gathered her bags and waited in the morgue to give Lee enough time to be well away before confronting Jameson and Monahan. She felt comfortable confiding in Danny but had not seen him since they got back from their mission and decided to call Ivy first.

*****

Ky sat quietly drinking her coffee as Reese and Ivy discussed plans to get home. Ivy was ready to go without stopping, but Reese wanted to stop along the way, saying something about a haunted house he wanted to check out in Iowa. Ivy was arguing she wasn't about to stop. Once they got over the state line, he was on his own. Reese started to protest when her phone rang.

She looked and answered quickly. "You found something?" then went silent, listening. "Thank you." Ivy looked at Ky as she laid her phone down. "That was Coletrain. Lee found massive amounts of steroids in the head and is going to warn Monahan, but we don't know how many are attending this so-called ceremony or how many others may be on the drug too. So before you go off like you're ten foot tall and bulletproof, tell me what you're planning, woman!"

"I knew she would find something," Ky said calmly. "I could smell it and taste it when I licked the blood off my lips after the fight at the house."

"You licked your lips?" Reese exclaimed wide-eyed. Shaking his head and putting a little distance between them, he went on. "The more I know you, Ky, the more you scare me. I hope I never get on your bad side. I don't want to have to move to another planet to hide."

"Can we get back to my question, please?" said Ivy, taking control of the conversation.

"I intend to be there. Justice will be served. Jameson and Monahan will have a plan. I'm going to tie up any loose ends."

"You have no intention of letting them arrest anyone, do you?"

"Of course not. It's our job to protect one world from the other but also maintain balance. They committed violent premeditated murder. I have to clean up the mess before it gets worse."

"What if there's a chance of even one man being innocent? For instance, Cyrus. How are you going to know?"

"I'm bringing Garmr, my favorite hellhound." Ky smiled. "If their aura doesn't tell me, he will. After all, he's able to see past the aura to the true soul, as most canines do. It's going to be too dangerous to have you or Charlie there. Besides, Garmr can't be seen unless he wants you to, and he is the ultimate weapon. He's the next best thing to a dragon against an army. What more would I need?"

"Fine, but what are you doing with them?"

"I'll leave them to their peers if they cooperate. Cyrus said, his pack is in this area. They can hold their own court. If not, they answer to me."

"I think I'm ready to go home and get as far from all this as possible," claimed Reese. "I'll chase ghosts, but evil is your job, not mine."

Ivy looked at Wolfe, who just shrugged his shoulders. "I go where you go," he said.

Outside, Ky heard barking. Charlie was asleep in the back seat of Wolf's truck. She peered out the window to see the white pickup truck next to her car. Sanders was leaning against it.

*****

With the help of Chief Tate and Cyrus, the plan was set. No one unfamiliar with the world of werewolves and magic would play a part. Monahan was making sure no one would freeze from fear or shock. That would be the key factor in getting too many innocent souls killed. A chance he wasn't willing to take; he'd already lost three good agents. He also felt it was going to be a bloodbath. There could be no prisoners, not of their kind, not in this world, just the cover-up. Just the thought made him sick, torn between the rule of law and outright murder, which was against everything he believed in. He sat thinking how bad it might get and hoping they were all up to the challenge when Dr. Coletrain rushed in.

"I have new information," she stated. "The remains that Ivy brought show very high levels of steroids. You could be up against more than you know if the others are anything like this one."

"You didn't notice that in the first one?" asked Jameson.

"Drugs weren't something we were looking for."

"Werewolves on steroids. Interesting," muttered Cyrus.

"And magic," Dr. Coletrain said in a low voice.

Jameson looked at the doctor. Their eyes met, thinking the same thing. *One thing is bad, but together is terrifying.*

"Have you forgotten the Master? A human, not werewolf, dealing out power through magic. How do you plan to deal with them?" asked Dr. Coletrain.

The room went silent with all eyes on Monahan expecting an answer. Monahan looked at Dr. Coletrain. "You tell me," he said. "We don't know if he's going to be there before the ceremony, do we?" he asked Cyrus.

"No, and we also don't know if it's a he or a she," replied Cyrus. "I don't even know who's in contact with them or who all is involved.

I'm just the one they call when someone gets hurt. I've been trying to find out, but so far, no luck."

"How did you come by what you know?" asked Riley. "I have very good hearing. That, and a few talk when given drugs for pain." Cyrus smiled. "The pack was working on a plan to handle it, till the idiots went and got you guys involved. They can't afford to be exposed, so now, they figure they'll clean up any after-math, anonymously, of course."

"How do the girls fit into all this?" asked Monahan.

"That was an unfortunate glitch. The watch group is monitoring them very carefully. Their reasoning, I'm afraid, is above my status. So I can't help you with that. If I have to guess, I'd say because they're outsiders with skills that are unique and got caught in the wrong place at the wrong time."

"So I guess the question now is, if we take out the gang, we'll stop the potential war and more murders, but what will be the master's next move, Doctor? Any ideas? Criminals, I can profile, from crazy to downright evil minds but magic? That's a new crazy pile. We need your help, please, educate us," Monahan said with respect.

"There are as many different chapters to magic as there are in any religion. Many of them cross over the same way. I've called Ivy in hope that she and Ky can help narrow it down."

"I sent them home for a reason, Doctor. I didn't want them involved," spouted Monahan.

"We don't have a choice if you want answers that I don't have," she spat back. "Ky is the only one that recognized some of the symbols. I didn't ask them to stay, only some help with information. What would you have me do? It's not like you can Google something like this. Even on the dark web, it would be difficult, and time is not on our side."

Monahan closed his eyes, lowered his head, and began rubbing his temples. His tension headache was on the edge of a migraine.

*****

Ky approached her car while the others watched from the window of the diner. Taking her eyes off Sanders for a moment, she looked at Charlie. Pressing her finger to her lips, he stopped barking, sitting quietly in the truck staring at Sanders. Ky turned her focus back to Sanders and leaned against her car. Crossing her arms, hiding both hands, she gripped the daggers strapped under her jacket. Standing eye to eye, Sanders shifted from one leg to the other nervously. Ky could feel the fear underneath his lame attempt to look confidently dominant. She played this game too many times not to know, the first to speak would lose, and she had patience on her side.

"I didn't come to fight," he said, lowering his eyes to the ground. "I came to talk."

In silence, giving him no indication of her thoughts, she waited calmly and quietly. Sanders kicked a rock with the toe of his boot sliding his thumbs into the pockets of his jeans before looking up again.

"I didn't kill anyone. I need you to know that first, before, why I had to go along with everything if you'll let me explain," he pleaded remorsefully.

"I'm listening," said Ky, flatly easing her grip around the blade's hilts slightly.

*****

Ivy sat in silence with Charlie after Ky gave them strict orders to go home, and that she was headed to the police station. Without giving any details of her conversation, she kissed Charlie on the nose and went back to where Sanders was still waiting beside his truck. Ivy watched Ky drive off, following him. Wolfe and Reese stayed quiet seeing the wheels turning in Ivy's head at a rapid pace pondering her next move.

As the waitress made her way down the row of tables toward them, Ivy raised the empty carafe of coffee. "One more refill please," she requested, pulling out paper and pen to write. She passed the note over to them after Charlie went under the table and laid on the floor once Ky was out of sight. It read:

We need to find Damon.

"Why are you writing?" asked Reese confused.

Ivy and Wolfe gave him a look that told him to shut it. "He can hear us and understands more than you know," she replied as Charlie's tail began to wag, banging against the table legs. "I suggest you get yours to go. It's time for you to head home, isn't it? You'll be there by sunset if you leave now. You'll just have to see your band another time."

"Under the circumstances, I think I'll be just as happy watching their show at home on my computer. Call me. Coffee should be interesting when you get back," he said, smiling.

Ivy waited till Reese left the table before writing again, with Wolfe reading over her shoulder as she did. Nodding, he smiled and said, "Good plan. How do we find him?"

Ivy smiled back pointing under the table. "We send out a call on his private line."

Chapter 33

Ky called Dr. Coletrain from the parking lot of the station, with explicit i`nstructions to gather everyone involved to the office along with the chief. She wasn't going to give them time to argue their way out of the meeting. They were going to listen, and she was prepared to take drastic measures if they tried.

Walking in with Sanders beside her, the officer at the desk pointed to the chief's office. Sanders led the way with his head hanging low. He wasn't looking forward to what he was about to endure. Everyone was there, including Dr. Coletrain's assistant and the newcomer, Cyrus. To Dr. Coletrain's disappointment, Lee hadn't made it out the door before getting caught by one of the tribe's informants. Chief Tate's office was much bigger than Jameson's, so it didn't feel as crowded. Ky closed the door behind her while Sanders stood next to her with his hands in his pockets, looking at the floor.

"I believe I have found a way to solve all this, but first, you have to hear what this man has to say," Ky clarified.

Sanders looked up long enough to see all eyes were on him. He closed his own eyes, took a deep breath, and began to explain.

"The idea was to gather renegades together to stage a coup and attain their own territory, figuring they would fight among themselves and kill one another. Bad wolves taking out bad wolves takes the blood off the good guy's hands, so to speak. Three weeks ago, things changed. Somebody called the master wanted body parts and promised power and strength to conquer all. Who and how he got involved, I don't know, but that's when the killing began. It didn't matter who they were, only the body parts for some kind of ritual were important. Things got so out of hand that anyone who didn't go along was killed and added to the sacrifice. Marsten figured this was an advantage to draw everyone out together in one place. We could take them out all at once, fulfilling his vendetta long overdue."

From that point, Sanders laid out his story of the mountain, meeting Jack Marsten, and how he got involved. To Ky's surprise, they listened intently without interrupting. Chief Tate sat listening, torn between turning him over to the tribe or the local pack. He had known Sanders since he was a kid, watched him grow up, and recognized something had changed in him over the last couple of years. Sanders became quiet, aloof, and angered easily, but wouldn't talk about why to anyone. He stopped hanging around his childhood friends and coming to any functions the department was involved in. Everything began to make sense now.

Chief Tate was the first to speak once Sanders finished. "What's your plan?" he asked, looking at Ky.

"First, I need to know everything you haven't told me," she replied with her eyes on Monahan.

*****

Cole woke up disoriented and in some pain. Most of his wounds had healed while he was out cold, but the knot on his head was thumping in rhythm with his heartbeat. Running his hand through his hair, he could feel the crusty dried blood surrounding the swollen lump. He could tell it wouldn't need stitches, though it bled profusely like most head wounds. Taking a couple of deep breaths, he remembered running toward the house when the gunshots went off. Not paying attention to his surroundings, he inadvertently fell into an old well that hadn't been capped properly was his best guess. The ground felt cold and slightly damp, but the area seemed bigger than a well should. Sitting up, trying to get his eyes to focus, he noticed the rim of the hole he fell through was a good distance above him. Lying flat as he was meant, the walls were wider down here. What little light there was couldn't be more than fifteen feet above him, though the opening wasn't much bigger round than himself.

"Crap," he said, his voice echoing through the chamber in two directions. "I fell down an air shaft?" He wondered if he was in a tunnel—the kind used to hide and relocate escaped slaves.

He knew from high school history that the Midwest was riddled with caverns as well as underground tunnels made during the Civil War. What he didn't know was which one he was in or which direction they went. Pain in his head made it hard to think or concentrate. Feeling along the walls gave evidence of it being both natural and manmade. He would have to rely on his sense of smell and hearing, keen eyesight wasn't going to help in this muddy darkness. He looked up once more, trying hard to see which side of the shaft was the darkest. The shadows from light would at least tell him the sun's position. He knew he had been in the field to the northeast of the farmhouse. Hoping the tunnel ended somewhere near there, he went right. Keeping his hands along the walls wasn't telling him much. They were the same as the floor—rough, cold, and damp.

Cole's hand bumped something sticking out from the wall after walking what seemed like an hour, though he knew it probably wasn't. Running his hands across it told him it was a torch of some sort. Remembering he had a lighter, he reached into his pocket, finding it and his cell phone. Feeling encouraged, he turned on his cell only for it to say, "No service," and his battery was at 53 percent through a cracked surface. Cole inhaled deep, making sure there were no flammable gases in the air before using what light he had to ignite the torch and save his battery. Seeing better meant moving faster. After a quick look around, he could tell the tunnel had been carved through a natural cavern. He ventured even deeper into the endless void, for what seemed long and endless, then came a sign of hope.

The scent of fresh air lifted his spirit even more, making the pain tolerable. In the cool breeze, he could feel and hear water. Quickening his pace led him to a cave where short stalagmites bordered the flow of a small stream. Clean air coming in from above the water source had pinlike points of light shooting through a caved-in entrance. Cole studied the obstruction for its vulnerability. Finding a spot where rocks could easily move without further damage, he started digging.

Removing each rock gently, he listened for any shift in the barricade making a hole big enough to get his head through. Overgrowth of trees and brush proved he had traveled further than he'd hoped. Backing up to move more debris the soil seemed to displace, sifting down over him. He waited for it to stop. Studying the structure more, Cole grabbed his cell getting as close to the opening as he dared.

"Yes!" he said aloud, relieved he had service, and called Damon.

Chapter 34

Jeremiah Dunbar was a lean, limber, handsome man of five foot, ten inches. Light-brown hair hung to the middle of his back, and hazel-green eyes gave him the appearance of someone in his late twenties or early thirties. For a man who was actually more than ninety, slow aging was just one advantage of being a werewolf. His skills in leadership and diplomacy as well as fighting were extensive, making him the most powerful and influential alpha in the western hemisphere. Sitting at his desk, he studied the map that lay in front of him, surrounded by photos of renegade wolves his pack had been watching—all rogues, some local, and others from all over the country. The few he was familiar with chose not to join the pack; some wanted to live their lives the best they could in a more solitary style. None had been a problem until recently. Then there were those that other pack leaders had been hunting for various violations of the rule of pack law.

Jeremiah looked up as the double doors to the study opened.

Kelsey Sawyer, his second-in-command and mate, leaned in. "They're all here. It looks like we have a small army," she stated.

"Good, bring in all three alphas and their seconds. Feed the rest."

"They're already in the kitchen," she said, leaving the door open.

Jeremiah laid the pictures side by side across the table in the middle of his vast library. His strategy needed to be precise so as not to cause any exposure to their kind and to protect all wolf packs. With law enforcement being involved, they would have to be extremely cautious to remain anonymous. The plan would consist of members from each group to infiltrate as one. The rest would be waiting for their signal, hidden outside. Jeremiah laid out old maps of the area showing the underground tunnels. Getting around the humans was the bigger problem. They needed more information, but his mole was in the custody of the sheriff's office. As his allies entered the room, Jeremiah's phone rang. It was Cyrus, hopefully with news he could use.

*****

Chief Tate sat at his desk staring at the mound of paperwork slowly building over the last few days. All minor cases, in comparison, falling behind from being involved with the FBI that he had no control over or jurisdiction. The situation weighed heavy on his mind as he thought about all the consequences of various outcomes and scenarios. Tate always knew the day would come when the two worlds would collide. It had once before according to legend, before the settlers came, causing a warlike time of fear and death before the werewolves went into hiding. Lost in thought, he jumped when the phone rang.

"This is Chief Tate."

"Hi, I was walking my dog this morning after the trash was picked up when my dog went crazy trying to get to a can lying along the curb," a woman's voice said. "I figured some food fell out of the can or something, so I wouldn't let her get too close. For all I knew, it was poisonous or spoiled. As we got closer, I saw what she was after. I couldn't believe my eyes! It looked like a human eyeball. At first, I thought maybe it was one of those candy things they sell at Halloween, but it looks too real! With all the craziness going on right now, I think you should check it out."

She relayed the address and hung up before he could ask any questions. The call took him by surprise. Information about missing body parts had not been released to the media or public. Verifying where the call came from proved to be a local gas station. Without saying who he was or why, he asked the attendant if the woman with a dog was still there. They said no and had not seen a dog since only service dogs were allowed in the building. Tate would have to see their security footage to get a good description. How to do that without raising questions was going to be tricky. Choosing to search the address she'd given first made him sit up straight. Martin

Delaney's residence. Buzzing Jameson's office, he reached for the bottle of aspi-rin in his desk.

*****

It had been just over an hour since Ivy took Charlie for his walk when Damon and Athena pulled into the restaurant.

"Took you long enough," she spouted when they got to the table. "Thought you'd be long gone by now," Damon responded with a touch of sarcasm.

Athena lowered her head to hide her grin. Charlie laid his paw on Ivy's lap attempting to calm her. Wolfe sat back with his arms crossed, waiting for the fireworks. Ivy and Damon, each having that look in their eyes, faced each other off. Damon broke first, looking at Wolfe as he put his hands in the air.

"I'm not the one you have to worry about. She handles her own light work." Wolfe laughed.

Damon looked back at Ivy for a moment longer, then smiled. "Truce? After all, you called us."

"Remember your place, and we'll have a truce."

Damon just grinned. "What do you need?"

"Charlie to be safe when Wolfe and I go tonight."

"We're not in the business of dog sitting. Try doggie daycare."

"They could never hold him if he catches wind. I need your friend to put him to sleep like he did before. Can you handle that?"

"I can ask."

"Oh, so you don't have any power over your minions?"

Athena's hands went to her mouth to keep from laughing out loud. Damon stood quiet, choosing his words carefully. "I'll overlook your sarcastic arrogance and tell you they're my brothers. By choice."

"Sarcastic arrogance?"

"It was better than what I was thinking," he said, smirking.

Charlie moaned, plopping to the floor in exasperation.

"Careful where you tread when it comes to a redhead," Wolfe warned lightly.

Chapter 35

The barn was smaller than average and easily heated when electricity was connected. It could hold about seventy-five people with a table and chairs. Small doors next to the usual large ones were at either end with a nice-sized loft down two sides overlooking the main floor. Stalls had been taken out leaving the support beams in place with a kerosene lantern hanging from each. Bales of hay stacked three high in a stair-step fashion stood in each corner, covered in red fabric trimmed in gold. Two long tables down the center banquet style was set with tall candles running through the middle as four covered food pans kept warm over steno burners lined each side. Two were prepared meat with a variety of vegetables mixed in, and two were slabs of various raw meat. At the end of the table was a large tub of beer on ice.

Hanson and his men arrived to find some of the others already there. A quick look around at the parked vehicles told him Cooper and his men had not shown up yet. Trying Cooper's phone again, with no answer, he picked two men to stay outside ordering them to watch for Cooper and call when he did. The plan was to ambush Cooper's band of misfits once inside the door. Surround, condemn, and kill to show others the level of punishment for loose cannons that could jeopardize the mission's goal, which was a serious offense.

Riding high on his ego-confident arrogance with three of his men at his back, he studied the room, sizing up the other members of their newly formed society. Three groups of six, each divided into their cliques. Judging a book by its cover, he had them pegged as punk gang members from their behavior and the way they were dressed. His ego inflated more, feeling his team the greater, as they were. He fashioned them as elite rouge missionaries. Military trained and skilled as a fine-tuned unit as good as any government could ask for.

Two groups glanced their way without interest while a third bunch eyeballed them, making their assessment as if they were, at minimum, equals. *Those*, he thought, *are the potential rivals to make allies.* Four men and a woman moved surrounding their designated leader as Hanson approached. The man was as big as he was tall with an authoritarian essence about him. It was his chance to engage and negotiate while waiting for Cooper and his chance to show off his men.

A noise came from the loft above. Everyone in the room looked up. Six men stood leaning against the rails, watching. A couple were average-looking farmhands, strong, dressed in flannel, T-shirts, tank tops, all in jeans. Others were more clean-cut, bulky in size, but had that big city-dweller appearance, all acting relaxed as if enjoying the view. Hanson, along with his counterpart, were the only two paying any attention to the newcomers. Giving each other a quick knowing glance, without hesitation, slowly moved their men to a more strategic advantage. Each team casually spread out in the stalls under the opposite loft while keeping an eye on the new observers. Hanson smiled at his counterpart with a bit more respect. The mutual adversary formed an alliance without confrontation.

Meanwhile, the two men stationed outside were becoming restless. Leaning against one of the cars, they could smell the aroma of fresh meat coming from inside. Their stomachs growled from hunger after all the drinking they had done. Caught up in their bitch session, they didn't notice they had company coming up the driveway.

*****

Chief Tate sat in the back of the unmarked car with two men in front of the house next door to Delaney's. Another unit was parked ahead on the other side. The eyeball had been retrieved and secured in an evidence bag and was now at the station with Dr. Coletrain. That was enough for them to get a search warrant. Now it was a matter of finding proof inside to connect him so they could make an arrest while the others were staking out the barn. Back at Tate's office, they had all come to the conclusion, that the professor was the mysterious magician. As to why he would call Riley, to tell him about the ceremony was another question. Was Delaney trying to throw them off his track? Did he have another motive? Something wasn't adding up, but they weren't taking any chances. Either way, Delaney had to be involved somehow.

The squad car he sent to the university confirmed Delaney left and appeared to be on his way home. Everyone involved had been briefed on the idea they were helping the FBI in an investigation of an organized black-market ring for body parts. Delaney was a connection and suspect. So many pieces to the puzzle, each changing the picture in different ways, made any outcome uncertain. Some just had them chasing their tails.

Chief Tate looked up as Delaney turned the corner. "Stand down. We wait till he gets out of the car," he radioed.

*****

The sun had been down for over an hour. Clouds drifted through making the sky shadowy with only the moon shedding a little light from behind them. Ivy and Wolfe lay in the tall wild grass at the edge of the field with the barn's big front doors in full view. Ivy's crossbow, loaded and ready. Wolfe looking through the sight of his sniper rifle, equipped with a custom-made silencer, relayed any details he could see to Ivy. He watched the two guarding the doors leaning against a car while Ivy kept an eye out for Ky. They looked like typical door bouncers—one large, the other slender, but both muscular in size, wearing T-shirts and jeans.

Ky knew what she was up against and came well prepared. Her braided hair wound in a bun was held by two silver needle sharp hair picks. Two short swords crossed her lower back with her favorite, slightly longer sword, down the middle. Tucked in her pants on each side were double-sided knives hidden under her lightweight, oversized leather jacket. Easy cover with the nights still chilly. Three-inch heeled boots coming up to her knees held several daggers in each. Walking up the drive dressed in her usual black, she remembered telling Ivy blood doesn't show up on black and laughed when Ivy gave her a dirty look. Ky could sense her and Wolfe. Looking to one side, she smiled knowing Ivy was watching not too far away and mouthed, "Wench, stay down, stay out."

Ky turned back to the barn stretching one hand out, stroking the air at shoulder height before proceeding. Wolfe watched as she appeared to be waiting for someone to take her hand and kiss it.

"What the hell is she doing? I never took her to be the prissy type. Didn't think she could even pull it off," he snickered.

"She's petting that damned demon dog," replied Ivy.

"I thought he was supposed to be bigger?"

"He is. Her hands on his back."

"Wolf, not dog," growled loud in Ivy's head.

"Pardon me. You didn't have to yell," Ivy murmured aloud.

"I didn't say anything," Wolfe replied.

"Wasn't talking to you, dear. Apparently, Garmr heard me. I stand corrected. He's a wolf, not a dog and apparently both telepathic and sensitive," she said teasingly.

"Now, now," Ky said as she blew Garmr a kiss, "settle down. After all, you are canine and damned. She just doesn't know you the way I do."

"Her silly. You, me, equal mean. All say us best team. Respected," Garmr stated, turning to her. "Play now?"

"Yes, we play now. Careful with the semi-innocents. This game is new to them. We want to save them from the others."

"No hurt. Scare," Garmr grumbled and shimmered into full view for a short glimpse to those paying attention.

"Woah!" Wolfe blurted at the sight. "That's…that's—"

"Impressive. Glad he's on our side." Ivy's eyes went wide seeing Garmr for the first time.

*****

Jameson and Monahan positioned themselves behind a pile of wood off to the side at the back of the barn. Both watching Ky approach noticed three wolves sneaking up close to the ground on their opposite side.

"Friend or foe?" Jameson asked.

"They're watching the barn. I'll guess friend," Monahan expressed with relief.

Brothers John and Jake came out the back laughing. Approaching a small flower bed, they pulled at the zipper of their pants making rude comments about watering the garden.

"You smell that?" John said.

"What? Flowers or the booze we're pissin'?" Jake laughed.

"It's a flower all right. A delicate female in heat kind."

He turned to his left to see two gold-colored eyes staring back at him. A husky red female wolf seemed timid as she backed up a few steps. Turning to leave, she paused for a moment to look back. Lowering her head slightly, as if to beckon them to follow, she scampered off into the dark field.

"Ever do a wolf while in human form?" Jake sneered.

"You are one sick mother, Bro," claimed John as he followed.

Monahan and Jameson eyed each other with disgust. Sounds of something hitting the ground followed by a muffled gurgle caught their attention. The red wolf and a large silver German shepherd came into view. Both had blood dripping from their muzzles as a small ball of light burst a short distance behind them. Giving a quick nod to the men, they bolted into the dark.

"Was that who I think it was?" Jameson asked.

"Our mysterious allies? I certainly hope so. Two down," Monahan said, refocusing on the barn.

"You don't think we need them inside?"

"We could, but they weren't going to be here at all, so I'll take what we can get. Besides I'm more worried about us. We're in their realm, not ours. That's why I sent Danny and Riley with Ky. They're safer with her."

"If she's everything that file says she is, I'd be more afraid of her. I have to admit, I'm kind of curious to see her in action. Aren't you?"

Monahan looked at Jameson for a moment, realizing he was working beside a small-town cop. "Stay behind me and wait for Ky's signal," he said and began working his way closer to the barn.

Pressing their bodies against the wall on each side of the door, they waited, armed and ready. Neither wanted to acknowledge the fear creeping through their minds. Knowing they had a job to do, they listened waiting for Ky's signal.

Chapter 36

Danny and Riley worked their way up to the barn, keeping pace with Ky, hiding behind cars one at a time. They hesitated when Ky appeared to be talking to herself with her hand held out as if she was waiting for someone to take it. Watching confused as she stroked the air, both men gasped when Garmr flickered into view for a quick glimpse before disappearing.

"Whoa, what the hell?" Riley whispered, almost stumbling over Danny.

"Fascinating," Danny said under his breath with eyes wide, amazed at the spectacle.

"That's nothing like what she had in the jail cell." "It was just a hellhound. This is way more," Danny said with admiration.

Positioned between cars, to have a clear view of the two men, they waited for Ky to make her move.

"With a beast like that, why doesn't she just let him take care of the whole group?" Riley wondered softly.

"She can't let him loose. Legend has it that he is, literally, the apocalypse and can destroy everything all by himself. Quick history lesson—he guards the gates of hell. He sends the guilty to their demise and keeps the innocent out. I read up a little on him after she explained her plan. Nothing in-depth, saving that for some late-night reading. Heads up, she's ready."

*****

Ky approached the men at a casual gait with her thumbs tucked into the front of her pants, while her fingers wrapped around the daggers under her jacket. With a slight swing in her hips and smiling, Ky grabbed their full attention. Once sure their eyes were on her and nothing else, she knew her next move was going to be easy.

The slender man stood straight with his chest out trying his best to look impressive. The other larger man rubbed his hands down each leg, when his pants tightened, attempting to loosen the grip on his groin. Standing just inches apart, each radiating lust like heavy cologne, both inhaled the sweet scent of tender, youthful human female.

"Dessert before dinner?" asked the big man as he shoulder-bumped the other.

Ky sashayed within arms' reach of them. "I hear there's a party. Care to escort me in?" she asked in a low, seductive tone.

"And why would we do that?" growled the big man.

"I'm the life of the party. I'm here to entertain you."

The men glanced at one another. "How about you entertain this," he said, gripping his groin in one hand.

Ky looked him up and down. "Momma always said, 'Embrace the moment,'" she said, smiling.

Raising her hands, she slit both their throats before they could react. Ivy and Wolfe lowered their weapons.

"Crap. This is going to get messy," said Ivy.

"No worries, darlin', not my first rodeo with you and Ky. Packed plenty of lemon juice and seltzer," Wolfe said, smiling.

Ky stepped between them as they fell sideways, feeling Garmr's warm, rough tongue take a swipe at her cheek.

"What was that for?"

"Clean face."

"You just like the taste of blood," she said.

"That too."

Dan and Riley were still staring, surprised at the scene they witnessed when Ky stopped directly in front of them. "Remember. Don't come in, just grab the ones that come out. Oh, and please put these two out of sight for now."

"Got it," Danny said as he ran to the other side dragging the silver net behind him.

"Time to open the doors," she said, giving Garmr a quick pat.

"Grand entrance."

"Gently please, don't break them."

"No fun," he grumbled.

*****

Nervous tension built inside the barn among a handful of guests once Garmr was inside. Not knowing why, some felt the need to separate from their groups. An overwhelming feeling of doubt and fear compelled a few to gather near the front doors. Mixed energies charged the atmosphere in the barn. Some felt relaxed; some, comfortable. Others felt emboldened with power. In the loft, the air seemed to spike an electrical charge causing their hair to stand on end. No one noticed as they backed up from the rails and transformed out of instinct, ready for what was coming.

Ky stood waiting in the center of the drive as the big barn doors slowly swung open. A small circle of men near the entrance tightened rank with ideas of flight over taking all previous thoughts and ambitions. Hanson felt the change and began to survey the room. Not sure what to think, his first thought was maybe the master had arrived. Considering everything he'd been told, he believed they would feel the master's power ahead of him. Seeing Ky was not what he expected. He was sure this little girl could not live up to the reputation of such strength. His eyes searched the area around her assuming she had to be one of the master's followers, a concubine maybe or, on second thought, entertainment. He smiled to himself. Gloating in his arrogance swelling inside, as well as between his legs, lasted for only a moment. A soft whiff of fresh blood made him look around again. His men were gone.

Ky got closer glancing at the few gathered in fear. "Go," she mouthed as she walked by. Not taking their eyes off her, they slowly passed. Once outside, they turned running down the drive getting caught in the net. Danny and Riley hung on tight to the ends, not sure what to do now since they were only told to catch and hold. Both were rather surprised at how little their captives fought. It was as if the net had somehow drained the men of their strength. From the surrounding darkness came four rather large men each holding several pairs of handcuffs made of silver-covered steel.

"We'll take them from here," one said. "Join your friends in the bushes over there."

Nodding to Ivy and Wolfe, they marched the small group back into the dark from which they came.

Danny and Riley quickly reset the net as Ivy and Wolfe snuck closer. Hiding behind the cars, Ivy and Wolfe split up, one to each side, with Ky in full view as they readied their weapons. The barn was crowded enough they couldn't get a good count of how many were inside. Above in the loft were even more.

"Keep the net close but get your guns ready," ordered Ivy. "From the look of things, we're a little outnumbered."

"You think?" popped off Danny. "I thought we had friends on the inside."

"We do. The problem is figuring out who's who. All we can do is protect our own and hope the others are as good as we're told they are," whispered Ivy as they knelt and watched.

A cocky young member of the group, filled with alcohol-induced courage, approached Ky as she entered.

"My, my cherry pie, my mama always said dessert was best when served fresh, and you look delicious."

"She should have said, 'Don't bite off more than you can chew. You'll choke,'" replied Ky. Surveying the room, she realized the operation was bigger than they had expected.

A few of the others began to laugh as the young drunk wolf felt the indignation. The look on his alpha's face told him to shut up and stand down. He took a step back, but alcohol fueled his anger more. They were gathered to acquire power as a team to rule, no more hiding in the shadows, and he was being dismissed like he was insignificant. Downing the rest of his beer, he threw the bottle across the room, just missing Ky's head as it crashed against the wall.

Chapter 37

Ivy crouched behind a pickup truck waiting for Ky's signal when Danny gasped. Turning toward him, she felt hot breath warm her neck as a large black-and-gray snout lay on her shoulder nudging her ear, pushing her lightly to move over.

"Well, aren't you just a sneaky shit," Ivy swung her head in Wolfe's direction in fear that he would shoot only to find him smiling. Sitting beside him was a beautiful silver-tipped wolf with its head resting on his knee as he patted the top of its head. Two more, one on each side of the lot, came into view between the cars ahead. Sounds of glass shattering brought their attention back to Ky.

*****

Monahan heard the bottle break. Opening the door slowly, he could see everyone had moved toward the front giving Ky their full attention. He and Jameson slipped in the back, unnoticed. Armed and ready, they split up taking opposite corners. Both men scanned the layout of the room. *Ky standing front and center of the big doors looks more sexy than deadly*, thought Monahan. In the loft above Jameson, between the rails, he could see six black noses with six pairs of golden eyes focused on the center of the room. At ground level were the rest, all closely gathered on either side around the long table. Two men stepped through the crowd toward the front stopping at the edge, one on each corner. One younger man, closest to Ky, wavered slightly in his stance indicating his intoxication and anger. Ky appeared relaxed as she moved her foot slightly to the right keeping her eyes fixed on the two that had come forward.

The young drunk screamed a howl and began his transformation. Ky whipped a six-inch blade from under her belt on the left side, flinging it with her right hand, directly into his forehead without so much as a glance in his direction. Everyone froze in shock as he fell to the floor. Some stared at him, others at her.

Hanson could tell she was more than an average human, especially for her size but wasn't sure how powerful she might be and spoke first. "That's one hell of a first impression you made there. Now how about telling us who you are and what you want."

"Well, since you asked, I heard something about a pack of renegades taking over the world with a little help from magic. I take it you're the leader of this ragtag bunch of misfits?"

Hanson looked over at his new friend as he took another step forward. "We all have our roles to play. I'd be careful calling anyone here names with your spitfire attitude as tiny as you are."

"Yes, well, you know what they say. Dynamite comes in small packages."

"So does bubblegum, little girl," he said, making a few in the back giggle.

"And nitro even smaller," she said, curling one side of her lips up, smiling to antagonize him. "Your murderous ways have not gone unnoticed, and I'm here to bust your bubble for being a bunch of fleabag fools."

"Enough of this bullshit," said one of the females. "She wants to party? I'll be glad to show her how."

Ky cocked her head to one side. Sizing up her opponent, she smiled, saying, "Let's dance," as she shrugged off her jacket, pulling one short sword from behind.

The female spread her arms. With hands open, fingers extended into razor-sharp talon-like claws. Everyone spread out for a better look, surrounding the women in a half circle as they sized one another up.

Hanson and his equal leaned against the table with arms crossed. "Got to love a good catfight," he said with a light laugh.

Monahan and Jameson glanced at each other, shrugging their shoulders. Both were also interested in seeing what was about to happen. Climbing the bales of hay, stacked in the corners, giving them enough height to see over the crowd and an advantage like shooting fish in a barrel.

Everyone outside by the cars watched with anticipation. Ivy shook her head and grinned, calling Ky a show-off accidentally out loud. When the others looked at her, a bit confused, she said, "Just watch. She likes to play with her prey sometimes to warm up."

Ky lunged one foot forward and back quick, making the woman take the first swing. One clawed hand swung where Ky's face had been as Ky went to the floor. As she swept the woman off her feet with one leg, her sword took the woman's head off in one continuous move. Silence fell over the room, again.

"Next?" she asked, standing up with the ease of a ballerina's poetry in motion.

A second later, all hell broke loose. The group moved forward as one, surrounding Ky. Ivy shot first as one of the guys toward the outside started to transform. An arrow stuck out the back of his head with dead-on accuracy, right between the eyes. Wolfe, Danny, and Riley each took out three more trying to get in behind Ky. Jameson and Monahan downed four more from the back before anyone knew they were there. Taken by surprise, a few in the back split off to defend the rear. Wolves in the loft jumped crushing one of the tables to the floor, showering everyone with its content of raw meat and prepared food.

Monahan fired rapidly. With so many gathered in the center of the room, they were easy targets along the edge. As he moved closer, a pack wolf jumped from the loft landing on another about to attack taking him by surprise. When he turned toward the noise, another lunged. Jaws clamped down on Monahan's shoulder and neck, severing the main artery and taking him to the ground. Another from the loft leaped, rolling the one on top, leaving Monahan lying there, spewing blood profusely. Two more landed beside Monahan, dragging him out the back door. The rest of the wolves above jumped into the fray in pairs. The first would take one down as the other severed their spine at the neck.

Before Hanson could move, his counterpart jumped at Ky with two of his henchmen. Ky swung her sword in front of her, slicing him in half. With both hands on the hilt, she shoved it into a second coming in behind her. Ky didn't see the third one as he backhanded her hard, tumbling her through the air. Landing on the table beside Hanson, it crashed to the floor with her on her back gasping for air. Four more came at her from the side. Ivy nailed one in front as Danny took out one in back. Ky sat up with a short sword in each hand, slicing the guts of the other two at the waist, spewing intestines like an open can of worms spilling out on the floor.

Jameson turned, aiming for another, as a fist thrust into his chest breaking through his ribs. He stood frozen, watching as the werewolf pulled his heart out and squeezed, splattering it like a ripe tomato in his grip. His world went dark as his body collapsed.

Two of the pack wolves outside ran in taking down any in their path along the sides. The fight, now looking like a free-for-all, became too hard to tell who was who as so many turned. Both wolves remaining outside stayed close to the doors. Anyone trying to run wasn't going to get far. Ivy could only hope the back side of the barn was covered as well as the front since none of them could see Jameson and Monahan over the mayhem.

"Aim for the ones attacking Ky," yelled Ivy, firing another shot.

Ky was hurt from the fall and needed protection. Ky, engulfed in rage, went wild further into the crowded room. Ivy and the others had to stand on the cars for a better view, but Ky was short. All they could see was blood and fur splattering like an old movie Mafia massacre. It was impossible to tell the enemy from friend leaving them no choice but to trust the pack wolves on their side and stop firing.

Time felt like an eternity with every minute they waited before the intense chaos began to subside.

Danny asked, "Where's Jameson and Monahan? Anybody see them?"

When no one answered, he leaped from the car on a dead run with the others following close behind. Reaching the barn, two wolves guarding the door stood blocking their way.

One ran out of sight beside the barn, returning in human form.

"There's no need for you to go further. Your part here is done," he said. "We thank you and your friends for helping us bring this to an end. It won't be forgotten. If you are ever in need of our help, we'll be there for you."

Before anyone could say a word, Ky came stumbling out over the pile of bodies. She looked worn, bruised, and covered in blood. Ivy and Wolfe ran to her as she collapsed to the ground.

"How bad are you hurt?"

"That depends on what part of me you're asking about."

"Fine! Where are you hurt the most?" Ivy asked, heated.

"My pride and ego for getting knocked into the table," Ky said, smiling.

"Good, you needed to be knocked off your high horse."

"Be nice. I still have enough in me to knock you off yours. I told you to go home."

"You two can argue later. Where's Jax and Phil?" Riley interrupted.

"Gone."

"Gone where?"

Ky looked up at Riley without saying another word. Riley dropped his head while Danny dropped to his knees.

Ky turned back to Ivy. "I told you guys to go home. I'm grateful you didn't, but—where's *my dog?*"

Chapter 38

Delaney sat, hands clasped in his lap, nervously waiting for the chief to return. He couldn't understand why he was a suspect brought in for questioning. After all, he was the one who gave them all the information he had to try to help. He was a well-known, respected professor, the top in his field. Being treated like a criminal when he knew he was innocent both angered him and scared him. He took a deep breath to calm his rapid heartbeat. This wasn't the time to have a panic attack and needed to keep his mind clear, his thoughts focused.

When the door opened, the chief entered with two others. One was taller, slender than Chief Tate and seemed younger. Well-dressed in tailored clothing, he appeared to be government without the suit. The other was much older, definitely of Indian descent, and high-ranking by the way he carried himself. They sat themselves across the table from Delaney while Chief Tate leaned against the wall near the door. No one said a word. Sweat began to bead up across Delaney's forehead.

*****

Wolfe headed back to the motel to relieve Athena from her dog-sitting duties. Ky and Ivy went back to the station with Riley and Danny. The ride was quiet; no one knew what to say. As they pulled into the station parking lot, Ky collapsed on to Ivy's lap with her hair falling across her face.

"Ky?" Ivy whispered. Brushing Ky's hair back, Ivy felt wet blood hiding a lump that fit in the palm of her hand. "Ky! Wake up!" she said, nudging her gently.

Dr. Coletrain stood at the window in Jameson's office. When everyone arrived, the look on their faces and two of them missing told her everything. Ivy was tending to the unconscious Ky in Riley's arms. Danny ran to open the door. Dr. Coletrain ran to the back, yelling to the chief they were back. Stopping only for a second, she hollered, "Incoming," through the door of the morgue as she passed. Lee quickly went to work transforming the room to an ER the best he could.

Ivy, still trying to wake Ky, told Danny to grab her bag from the car and to call Wolfe. Once inside, Riley laid Ky gently on the table. Lee immediately worked on cleaning her up for Dr. Coletrain to examine her.

After a quick assessment, Dr. Coletrain turned to Ivy. "It's a mild concussion. When did she pass out? How long has she been out?"

"Not till we got here, so only a few minutes." Ivy investigated the room for things she would need, but there was nothing.

Dr. Coletrain opened her bag, handing it to Ivy. It was like a holistic pharmacy.

"You should find most of what you need in my bag. I never leave home, unprepared."

"Impressive. We can combine what we know," Ivy replied. "You get her awake. I'll take the wound. I've worked on Ky before. I know what her body will respond to."

Both women pulled various vials and containers from each bag mixing several solutions of their own. Lee had Ky cleaned up as if she were about to go into surgery. He watched the two women working with precision and determination waiting for further instructions. To him, it was like watching a ballet as the two moved in perfect harmony, synchronized as if they worked together their entire life. Ky was in good hands without a doubt. He smiled to himself thinking how his father would be pleased to hear about his unique opportunity to work and learn from two women with such capabilities in holistic knowledge. It only took a minute for Ky to wake seeing the doctor standing over her.

"Can you two make my head hurt any worse?" Ky said, coming to.

"You know I can and will if you don't lay still," Ivy replied, pressing a poultice she made into the cut along the lump.

*****

Riley and Danny left the women tending Ky to collect their thoughts and brief the chief before filing their reports. Chief Tate sat waiting in Jameson's office with his head in his hands. He'd already gotten the report from his fellow tribesmen. As Riley closed the door, Danny broke down. Jameson had been his mentor. At times, he had been a big brother; other times, a father figure. He remembered all the times Jameson chased him down for racing, the many lectures given before convincing him to join the force. He was the only person Danny knew who gave him a second chance, repeatedly, that believed in him.

Riley sat staring at his pad of paper. So much to do, so much to process, his mind caught in a relentless whirlwind. The death of his partner and friend was bad enough, but how do you explain to the home office that Monahan was killed in the line of duty by werewolves? Ky told them the pack was doing the "cleanup" and would contact them later. *What does that mean? If the pack brings back the body, how bad is Jax Monahan going to look?* So many questions with no answers.

Chief Tate sat quietly giving both men time to pull themselves together before he spoke. It was hard for all of them. He and Jameson worked together for over twenty years. They became friends while going through the academy together. The force was Jameson's whole life, his only family after his wife and son died during childbirth. This was a great loss to the force and all the men whose lives he touched. He heard Danny take a deep breath. It was time to move on.

"You both need to know. Delaney isn't behind this. He's innocent," the chief said. "This is far from being over."

Both men looked up baffled.

Chapter 39

Wolfe went straight to Ky's room only to find it empty. Pillows and blankets had been tossed around as if there had been a wrestling match on the bed. A note lay on the table simply saying, "Went for a run. Be right back," signed Athena and Charlie along with a drawing of a paw print.

"Well, he's not going to get away from her, and he needs the exercise," he said aloud to the empty room.

Picking up the bedding from the floor, he heard the door opening. Charlie rushed in past Athena, jumping on Wolfe, knocking them both onto the bed dripping wet along with Athena.

Thankful the bed cover was between them, Wolfe curled his nose and said, "You smell like dead fish."

Charlie let out one bark before shaking the excess water off, splattering droplets across the entire room.

"Housekeeping is going to have a fit. You need a bath Again!"

"We both do," Athena laughed. "We'll take one together. We went swimming in the lake to cool down after the run." It wasn't until then she noticed the look on Wolfe's face. "Ky and Ivy, are they all right?"

"They're both fine. Charlie would have known if they weren't. We'll talk after your baths." Wolfe looked right into Charlie's eyes. "Get in the tub," he said sternly.

With one sloppy swipe of his tongue across Wolfe's face, Charlie jumped down traipsing off toward the bathroom wagging his tail with Athena right behind him.

*****

The house was still and dark. There was no car in the driveway or the garage. A simple ranch style designed for a couple with a brick here and there, showing signs of crumbling, giving away its age.

Sergeant Malloy gave his men last-minute instructions before surrounding the house of Delaney's girlfriend. They had been dating only a few weeks. Orders were to apprehend a middle-aged woman, blonde, approximately five feet, seven inches tall. She was a person of interest, wanted for questioning in multiple murders including a police officer. Real name was unknown and went by the name Marie Pentacoss, a nurse by profession. Records showed she died six months ago at the age of fifty-five from cancer. Three officers spread out on each side of the house with four more closing in at the back. Malloy and three others took point on each side of the front door. There were no sounds heard from inside. Malloy beat on the door hard, yelling, "Police! Open the door, Ms. Pentacoss. We'd like to ask you a few questions." He pounded on the door a couple more times before signaling his men to enter, then kicked the door in.

Flashlights in hand, they searched the house, garage, and basement. One of the men flipped a wall switch, lighting up the kitchen. A small card table with one chair and a coffee cup in the sink that had been washed and dried was the only evidence of anyone being there. Even the trash was gone. No furniture or signs of anyone having been there; except the kitchen, the house was empty.

Malloy radioed the station while his men taped off the property as a crime scene. Outside, one of the officers cursed. His foot slipped on something that felt squishy, almost causing him to fall when he heard a pop. Lifting his foot, he froze in place. His flashlight shone down at red-and-white goo. Something egg-shaped with a small blue circle in the center that resembled a candy eyeball was seeping out ooze. Untying his shoe and slipping his foot out of what was now possible evidence, he asked one of the others to get the sergeant.

"Damn it, I just bought these yesterday," he said to himself.

Malloy came out with a phone to his ear. Looking closer, he said, "We've got something, Chief. Not sure what, but it does look like someone lost an eye."

*****

"Do I need stitches?" asked Ky as Ivy removed the poultice so Lee could close the wound.

"We don't do that anymore." Lee smiled. "We just glue it together, so you'll have to be careful when you brush your hair."

"'Cause it will open it up again, I suppose."

"No. It'll just hurt like hell."

"How are you feeling? You think you can stand?" asked Dr. Coletrain when Lee finished.

"I'll be fine. We need to check on how the guys are holding up and see if Tate had any luck on his end. I'm interested in how they're going to spin this to the public." Ky's legs wobbled when she tried to stand.

Lee grabbed Ky around the waist placing her arm over his shoulder. "You only get one concussion a night."

"Please be gentle. My ribs and back are sore. Probably bruised," she said, grinning.

Lee gently pulled her close. "Don't worry. I got you." He smiled back.

"Are you done flirting with the cute guy, or are you going to milk this attention some more?" Ivy asked, rolling her eyes.

Ky looked at Lee with a smile. "Sorry, handsome. Work first, dance later. She's such a killjoy."

"Get your sorry butt moving already," Ivy said, heading out the door with Dr. Coletrain.

They entered the office as Chief Tate was hanging up the phone. From the look on his face, the call couldn't have been good. Danny and Riley seemed both confused and frustrated. The women each grabbed a chair. Riley offered Ky the only comfortable chair that wasn't behind the desk and sat in one of the folding metal ones.

Chief Tate folded his hands on the desk, taking a deep breath before he spoke.

"My heart is saddened over the loss of two good men and grateful for all the effort the three of you have given as well as the fact we didn't lose any more than we did. Ladies, you have done an extraordinary job, to say the least. It's obvious we could not have done this without you. Thank you for seeing this through. I'm sure you are all looking forward to returning home. All that's left now is police work."

"You're right on all accounts. However, we will not be dismissed so easy. Something is apparently wrong. We're not going anywhere without an explanation as to the outcome of our mysterious magician slash sorcerer. Did you get him or not, and what are you going to do with him? After all, that is our department more than yours," stressed Ivy. Ivy reached over, placing her hand on Ky's arm, letting her know she had this before Ky could react.

Ky had little patience in these situations, especially after what she had so painfully endured for them. It was disrespectful to her and degrading. Ivy knew all too well Ky's tolerance level. During Ivy's divorce, Ky pleaded for permission to feed her ex-husband to the hellhounds or at least dump him in a pig farm after scaring him to death. When Ivy said no, Ky went behind her back and showed him what could happen if he ever came near Ivy again. After the divorce became final, without saying a word, he quickly left town.

"I guess I owe you that much," replied Chief Tate. "First, you should know there is no magician. Never was near as we can tell. Through the information we got out of Delaney, we were able to verify everything he said. He was being set up, and they probably would have gotten away with it, but we had our surveillance keeping tabs on him since he was our prime suspect. As it turns out, the woman he was seeing isn't who she claims, and right now, we don't know her true identity. What we think is she was using the werewolves to murder and pit them against one another. She apparently convinced all of them she could give them strength and power. For what purpose? We have no idea. Thanks to Dr. Coletrain's findings, the power she promised was nothing more than steroids for the scam. The alias she used is a woman who died six months ago and really was a nurse. Monahan had been informed before you left for your mission and had made a few inquiries to his office. The report came in about an hour ago. Turns out they had three other cases very similar in other states but no solid leads. Unfortunately for us, she's disappeared."

"What do you mean disappeared?" asked Ivy.

"I sent a team to the address that Delaney gave us. The house was empty and cleaned very well. No fingerprints, nothing. Even the coffee cup they found in the sink had been washed. Although one of the officers did step on an eyeball in the yard. It's the only thing we have to tie her in at this point."

"Another eyeball? That sounds odd, don't you think?" Dr. Coletrain commented.

"We've already established the first one was planted, and the woman who called it in fits the description of the one we're looking for other than the hair. I'm guessing multiple wigs, maybe? The second we have no explanation for. It was found in long grass, not easily seen. We are searching the property for any other possible pieces of evidence. We will run DNA tests to see if either matches one of the bodies now in our possession. So you can see why this is now an official homicide and not one of the supernatural."

"What about the robe I saw in Delaney's office? It was like the ones that were worn by those guys in the clearing that jumped our men?" asked Riley.

"Turns out it was a gift from her. Delaney is a 'Dungeons and Dragons' buff and uses it for role-playing."

"How are you going to explain any of this to the public?" Ky asked.

"I've got that covered," replied Riley. "What happened at the barn never happened. Between the local tribe and our new friends in the pack, the entire incident has been cleaned up. The story we'll release states there was one lone wolf, and it was put down immediately. Our sex-traffic story is an ongoing investigation and cannot be commented on at this time. Hopefully, the story will die in time. If not, we'll connect it to one we have pending. It's not like we don't have enough of them across the country. We can pin it to a number of them."

"Ladies, I want to thank you again on behalf of everyone involved for your help. I'm sure you want to get back home. Dr. Coletrain, I presume you can stay a couple more days as we sort this out?" Chief Tate inquired, turning as she nodded.

"Then we're done here," stated Ivy, standing up to leave. "I'm ready to get the hell out of Dodge."

"I don't recommend Ky leaving until tomorrow. I'd like to do another examination of her before letting her drive so far. After all, she did pass out. Don't you agree, Ivy?" Dr. Coletrain asked.

Ivy looked at Ky. "I do agree. Wolfe and I will take Charlie to Jess. After all, he didn't get to spend any time with her, and we both know how he gets. One more night isn't going to hurt."

"Well, if you're all going to gang up on me, I guess I'll stay." Ky winked at Lee with a grin.

Chapter 40

Ky opened the door to her room to see Charlie rolling around on the bed, still damp from his bath. Wolfe was just coming out of the shower with nothing but a towel around him.

Ky turned to Ivy. "My room is filled with wet animals." She laughed.

"Where's Athena?" asked Ivy.

"She had to go after giving him and herself a bath. They went swimming," Wolfe replied.

Ivy pushed Ky toward the bed. "Say your goodbyes. Wolfe, honey, you want to get dressed? We're going home, and Charlie's coming with us."

"We're leaving Ky behind? What happened at the station?" Wolfe asked, puzzled.

"I'll explain on the way. In the meantime"—she grabbed a towel and threw it at Ky—"I'm not riding all the way home smelling wet dog."

Ky sat next to Charlie and began drying him off. "I'll see you tomorrow night, big guy. You be good for Aunt Jess, okay?"

"Speak of the devil," Ivy said as her phone rang. "Hey, Jess, your ears ringing? We were just talking about you?"

"A little." Jessie laughed. "I was calling for a couple of reasons. First, to find out what the hell was going on. I haven't heard from you. Second, have either of you bothered to check your website? There's a message from someone that was there in Rockford asking you to find them."

"Yeah, we saw that. We thought it was from Reese."

"It definitely wasn't. It looks like it got sent before finishing and then sent again. Whoever it is needs your help, heard about you two from Reese's page, and knew you were there tied up on something else. It's a woman who wants to meet you here."

"She say why?"

"No, only that she'll be safe for the moment and will wait here till you get back. She used the distraction of your situation to get away."

"That explains why Reese didn't know what we were talking about. With everything happening, I forgot to bring it up again. Wolfe and I are coming back now. I'm bringing Charlie to you. Ky's going to stay for another day. I'll tell you all about it when we get there. Should be about eight hours."

"I'll have dinner ready when you get here. And coffee, of course," Jess snickered.

Ivy hung up, relaying the new information to Ky while Wolfe loaded the truck. Charlie laid his head in Ky's lap, content falling asleep.

"Make sure you call me when you get there," Ky said.

"You better be calling me tomorrow before you leave, so I know how you're doing. Come on, Charlie. Time to hit the road."

Charlie opened his eyes, but he didn't move. Ky leaned down kissing his nose. In return, he swiped her nose with his tongue. He lay there until Wolfe came to the door and said one word, "Dog." Charlie slowly stood up and stretched, licking Ky's face one more time before following them out.

*****

Ky woke after sleeping on and off for almost fourteen hours. The pain in her head had eased enough to let her know it was still there but not enough to keep her down. Ivy's home remedies always got her back on her feet quick. Now she was hungry. The room seemed too quiet and a bit lonely now that Charlie was gone. Ky turned on the TV to have noise while she showered. Local channels were all buzzing about an upcoming news briefing concerning the death of two law enforcement officers and recent events around the Lake Park area.

Ky rummaged through her bag, pulling out clean clothes, when she saw a piece of paper sticking out from under her door. The front was an advertisement for a memorial benefit being held at Redemptions late that afternoon in honor of Jameson. All proceeds were going to the kids program that had been his pet project, sponsored by the city in conjunction with the parks and recreation department. On the back was a handwritten note. "See you there?" signed Damon. Ky smiled to herself, laying the note beside her bag, thinking, *Maybe*, as she went for her shower.

*****

Dr. Coletrain sat across from Lee in the morgue discussing how to word their report and the death certificate when Ky arrived. She picked a chair close by to sit and listen. The room itself had been cleaned out of all evidence appearing as if they had never been there. Ky wondered if the bodies were still in their chambers or if the cremations were all done.

"They're all gone," said Dr. Coletrain as if reading Ky's mind. "It's the first thing we did once your plan was put into action. Now let's take a look at you."

"My headache is tolerable. The swelling is down but still a little tender. Past that, I'm fine," Ky said to her.

"What about your ribs and back?" she asked, continuing her exam.

"Sore. Bruised. The usual. Nothing I can't handle. How much longer are you two going to stay?"

"We're leaving in the morning, and you?"

"I think I'll stick around long enough to go to the benefit show this afternoon. I saw that the band everyone keeps talking about is playing." Ky really wanted to find out more about the man she encountered in the forest, the one that called her Arbitra. She had no idea where to find him or start. She couldn't ask anyone. All she could hope for was him being a local and hope she might spot him at the benefit as well.

"What about you two?"

"We might. I couldn't book our flight till tomorrow. Won't that put the sun in your eyes on the way home? You wouldn't get there till after dark."

"I don't mind. It's less traffic, and I have a good stereo system in my car."

"You appear to be healing well. You're good to go, so long as you aren't planning on fighting for a few more days." Dr. Coletrain grinned. "Shall we go see the guys? I'm sure they would like to see you before you leave. Make sure we're all on the same page, not missing any details."

"I was thinking that too."

*****

With the car packed and ready to go and the energy tea Jess gave her on ice, Ky chose a parking spot that was easy to get in and out of. She wasn't planning on staying after the first set, only long enough to pay her respects and maybe video the band for Reese. Still a bit stiff and sore after the twisted few days she'd had, Ky was looking forward to going home but felt she needed to say thank you and goodbye to Athena and Damon. Always prepared for anything, she adjusted the knives inside her knee-high boots. Her senses, on the other hand, went to high alert the moment she entered the bar. Nothing was ever what it seemed in her adventurous life. Wonderful, she thought, feeling the presence of werewolves, vampires, and multiple-level magic as she walked across the room. Vibrations of energy were a low threat compared to the high excitement of the crowd. Ky chose a seat at the corner of the bar, a perfect position to see the entire room. She wondered if it was more than the fire code would allow as full as it was.

"What's your pleasure?" the bartender asked.

She looked up at the coldest blue eyes she'd ever seen. Golden-blond hair fell to his shoulders framing his face like a portrait of a Greek god. A good-looking man in his mid to late twenties of milk-chocolate skin with a nice physique under a white tight-fitting tank top. *Trouble* was the only word that came to mind. A chill ran up her spine when another bartender came up and whispered some thing in his ear. Her senses said feline instead of canine. Jaguar or cheetah maybe? A bit unusual to have so many species in one room without it being a brawl or a bloodbath.

"Yeah, low-level vampires and were-animals. Had to be tonight," she said to herself.

"Excuse me?" said the girl sitting next to her.

"Oh, nothing. Just thinking out loud," she replied, turning toward the voice. Like a tidal wave, she felt the consumption of lust. "Shit! What kind of bar is this?" she whispered under the noise. The scent of wolf smothered her. Drowning in a vampire com-pulsion of hormone chaos, she slipped from her stool to the floor. "No fucking way!" she hissed, pulling herself up. "No one dominates me! Back off or die." She drew her sword as she stood. All eyes within hearing distance were on her. "Not in the mood," she growled, backing away from the bar.

"Sorry," the she wolf said, throwing her hands in the air. "A full moon can be a little overwhelming for all of us."

"Bad day, huh?" asked a vamp bartender.

"What makes you say that?" she snapped, putting her sword under her trench.

"You're obviously on edge," came a low, masculine voice behind her. Feeling a gentle hand on her shoulder, she spun to find Danny standing behind her. After drawing a deep breath, Ky released the hilt of her sword.

"Thanks for coming," he said.

"I felt it was only right. I'm sorry it went down the way it did."

"Me too, but they knew the odds. I think that's why they had Riley and me positioned with you. They seemed awfully confident when it came to you for some reason." He smiled.

"I appreciate that. I take it you two got all the loose ends tied up in your reports. What are you planning to do now?"

"Actually, the chief has me taking the detective test. He wants me to take Phil's place since I'm familiar and comfortable with everything he's been dealing with alone. I feel honored. Jameson meant a lot to me. Filling his shoes won't be easy, but now I can take some of the pressure off Tate that Jameson couldn't."

"Is this a private party, or can anyone join?" asked Riley, bending his head down between them.

"How can I turn down the company of two handsome men?" Ky laughed.

"Then please allow us to escort you to the festivities outside."

"Outside?" Ky asked, looking around.

The bar itself had to be at least fifty feet long down one side with a stage and dance floor at the opposite end. That area alone was the size of a full-service, small-town grocery store. It was at least a half block wide, a block long, and appeared to be packed to capacity.

"This is bigger than the building will handle," replied Danny. "Wait till you see where the real parties are held."

Though the guys were feeding Ky's ego, she felt humble knowing the burden of their loss. Making their way to the back door went easy with Danny leading the way. Most of the crowd knew him, clearing a path as they gave condolences. Danny wasn't kidding. The outside area was impressive. Two volleyball courts lined a metal building, the size of a football field with several large garage-like doors along both sides, all open. Ceiling fans were equally spaced on each side with double-pane glass tubes under each one. The place was overflowing with people. It looked like the entire town had shown up for the occasion. She heard, in small towns like this, everyone knew everyone, this being the proof.

"What's with the tubes?" Ky asked.

"Those are imitation fireplaces to heat the room in cold weather," replied Danny.

"Interesting concept."

"This is amazing," observed Riley.

"Best little secret in the Midwest."

"Why secret?"

"Its clientele is rough—shall we say, except on special occasions like this. That's when it's neutral ground for the public, so to speak. The owner has strict rules, and they handle their own problems. We rarely get called out here."

"Glad to see you three made it," a female voice behind them chimed with excitement.

Athena reached out, hugging Ky first, smiling ear to ear, bubbling with happiness. "Come with me. We have front-row seats reserved for you."

"I'm not staying long," apologized Ky. "I'm headed home soon."

"Not too soon, I hope," whispered Damon in her ear, making Ky jump.

"What's with you guys? You pop up from nowhere and disappear just as fast."

"Who doesn't like a mystery?" Athena laughed. "Damon, we're out of time. Let's hit it."

"What are you guys up to now?" Ky asked.

"Got to go to work." Damon grinned, leaving before she could ask any more questions.

As they started to make their way through the crowd, Chief Tate took the stage, tapping the microphone to get everyone's attention. Silence fell as the crowd listened to his brief speech thanking all for coming, their donations, and support. The sound of instruments could be softly heard when he announced, "Please welcome, the Road Rats!"

The oversized black curtains began to rise with the full sound of rock music filling the air. To their surprise was Damon with everyone on stage except Athena. With a quick look around, Ky found her off the side of the stage running lights and sound. The crowd went crazy, dancing and cheering. Some were even singing along.

"I'll be damned," yelled Riley over the excited fans.

"Why didn't you tell us?" Ky yelled at Danny.

"I didn't know." Danny shrugged. "I've heard their music. I own several CDs, but I've never seen them live or their picture on anything."

Wait till Ivy hears this, Ky thought, shaking her head.

*****

The woman stretched while running her fingers through her ruby-red hair as it gently caressed the top of her shoulders. It felt good to be home again and not in a wig. She missed the sweet aroma of the giant magnolia trees at her family's South Carolina estate. She sat at the table smiling, admiring the plate filled with all her favorite food. Her fork pierced the juicy tender slab of tongue, charred nicely on the outside. Holding it in place, the razor-sharp knife cut it nice and thin. Stabbing one end of the slice with her fork, she laid her head back and closed her eyes, laying the thin slice on her tongue hanging out over her lips, begging. A slight shiver of pleasure ran through her body as she relished the texture and taste. It felt as if it melted in her mouth when its warm, bloody juices ran down the back of her throat.

Two white ovals on a smaller separate plate glistened under the candlelight. She picked one up with a toothpick. Raising it to her lips, she slowly sucked it into her mouth like a grape. Her tongue played with it for a moment, rolling it around before squashing it against the roof of her mouth. A cold gelatin-like goo gushed out, tantalizing her senses even higher. Savoring its sweet taste for a moment before swallowing, she moaned softly.

"Mmmm, blue eyes, my favorite."

Charlie's Song

I got a moose dog
And his name is Charlie Brown
You can tell when he's happy
Cuz his tail goes round and round
When he wants to play
He will knock you to the ground
He's a big moose dog
When I brought him home
I could put him in my lap
Now he takes the whole bed
When I want to take a nap
I want a big dog
But I got two and a half
He's my big moose dog

About the Author

LJ (aka Linda Jo) resides in Omaha, Nebraska, with her husband and two Labrador mix rescue dogs. She loves spending time with her children and grandchildren. As a child, her family relocated often, but she found solace in reading.

She was drawn to mystery thanks to Agatha Christie and Ellery Queen novels. Her dream of becoming a writer came from discovering the works of Edgar Allen Poe and Arthur Conan Doyle's Sherlock Holmes series. She picked up her interest in everything paranormal from her maternal grandmother, who always said, "See things with more than just your eyes." LJ spent years occasionally writing poetry. She gives credit to the pandemic for the time to write her first novel.

www.ingramcontent.com/pod-product-compliance
Lightning Source LLC
Chambersburg PA
CBHW020758310726
48969CB00002B/590